The
Runaway
Princess

Other Avon Books by
Christina Dodd

THAT SCANDALOUS EVENING
A WELL FAVORED GENTLEMAN
A WELL PLEASURED LADY

CHRISTINA DODD

The Runaway Princess

AVON BOOKS  NEW YORK

AVON BOOKS, INC.
1350 Avenue of the Americas
New York, New York 10019

Published by arrangement with the author

ISBN: 0-7394-0094-0
www.avonbooks.com/romance

Printed in the U.S.A.

One

The Pyrenees, 1816

"Who could she possibly be?"

Ignoring such vulgar speculation as beneath her, Miss Evangeline Scoffield posed at the door of the dining room and, with icy dignity, waited for the maître d'hôtel.

Bowing, he twitched his mustache as he asked in French, "Your usual table, Mademoiselle?"

The flurry of whispers started in a dozen languages.

"Probably a wealthy widow . . ."

"Perhaps from one of the noble families of Europe. Napoleon displaced so many, you know . . ."

Evangeline knew that none of the travelers who had flocked to this spa—not the Spanish lord, not the Prussian general, and certainly not the over-loud Englishwoman—could imagine the truth.

"Thank you, Henri," Evangeline answered in his own language, blessing him with a wistful smile. "You are too good."

Henri's eyes glistened with pleasure. "I live only to serve you."

With a recently acquired, and to her, quite surprising, sense of drama, she replied, "To serve me could prove dangerous."

"For you, I laugh at danger."

"Believe me, I am not someone to whom you should make such an avowal."

The whispers continued.

"The servants hint she is a princess . . ."

"All alone, poor thing, without even a maid . . ."

Closing his eyes, he pressed his hand on his chest over his heart. "Such beauty as yours is a reward in itself."

Beauty? No one had ever called her a beauty before, but in this magical place, anything was possible. "Take this." She slipped some coins into his hands. "I have suffered such travails in my life, I cannot allow genuine kindness such as yours to go unmarked."

His eyes snapped open, and he pocketed the gold immediately. "For a smile from you, I would walk barefoot over the rocky ground, fight a dozen men, wrestle a ferocious bear, face the devil himself—"

"Enough." More than enough. He tried to speak, but she handed him another coin and his mouth snapped shut. She nodded, not like a misplaced princess but like a sensible Englishwoman. "I will be seated now."

This resort had once been a private château near the Spanish border, the summer home of a wealthy duke. When Napoleon's defeat had impoverished its owner, he had been forced to find a way to maintain his home. Taking advantage of the thermal springs nearby, he now catered to the nobles' desire to combine travel and healing. Two fireplaces blazed in the room where Evangeline now stood, cherubs smiled from marble arches, and broad windows overlooked the verdant valley below.

Château Fortuné was now one of the crown jewels of the grand tour, and Evangeline reveled in being one of its shining facets. Albeit temporarily. Her emerald silk skirt created a satisfying rustle as she threaded her way past the white linen–draped tables, and without appearing to, she observed the heads that swiveled her way.

"She's very nicely . . . formed. Do you suppose she had something to do with that scandal in Saxe-Coburn?"

"Stodgy Saxe-Coburn? Don't be ridiculous. She has the looks of an exotic."

Curiosity about this mystery woman ran rampant in the dining room, and Evangeline lifted her exotic chin and fixed an inscrutable smile on her lips. A smile she had practiced in the mirror.

None of the people here could possibly guess the truth.

With a flourish, Henri pulled out her chair. She seated herself with murmured thanks and placed her drawstring clutch on the table near the Limoges salt cellar. She pulled up her Brussels lace stole and draped it around her shoulders.

"Mademoiselle is chilly?" Henri asked. "In the mountains, it is cold at night, even in the summer. It would be warmer by the fire."

"Mademoiselle prefers to have a view of your imposing mountains," she said.

Henri shrugged in Gallic resignation. Then, in rapid succession, the waiters poured her a glass of fragrant, ruby wine and laid the snowy napkin in her lap, while

Henri announced her choice of soups and entrées. The mere recitation made her close her eyes in anticipated ecstasy. She loved good food. She loved eating in such an exquisite setting. She loved Henri's fawning approbation as she placed her order.

When she finished, the four men bowed and backed away from the table. They were kind, even beyond the kindness she bought with her generous gratuities.

Was it perhaps because they felt sorry for her?

That truth stabbed at her. Abruptly, she turned her head away from the other diners and tried to stare at the moonlit peaks. Instead, she saw only reflections in the window. Even now, as the fervor her appearance had created faded, the wayfarers lost interest in her. They returned to conversations with their spouses, their children, their lovers. Everyone here had someone else. Only she remained alone.

She had imagined that would change in the six days she had been here, but her very person discouraged familiarity. Her lingering good sense kept her apart— and alone in the Pyrenees, she'd found, was much the same as alone in England.

The reflections in the window wavered with the sudden glaze of tears in her eyes.

Alone, without a home, without a family . . .

Henri's voice spoke beside her. "We have the bread, still warm from the oven." A yeasty scent accompanied the basket of golden, crusty rolls. "We have the *soupe de poisson*." The scent of oregano and trout in a tomato-based broth appeared under her nose. "And we top off your glass with wine. You need to drink more wine, Mademoiselle, to warm your blood and bring roses to your cheeks."

Blinking the tears away, she looked up at Henri's shrewd face.

His comprehensive gaze took in her sadness. Jerking his head toward the far end of the chamber, he whispered, "You have an admirer."

She tried to crane her neck to see, but Henri said, "No, do not look!"

Settling back into her seat, she unbuttoned her elbow-length gloves and laid them in her lap. "You jest."

With the sigh of a wronged puppy, he said, "Not I! Wait until I leave, then glance around the room, and you will see him. Near the fire, facing you." Leaning closer, Henri murmured, "The virile one asked to be placed where he could watch you."

Evangeline's heart gave one huge thump, then resumed its usual smooth beat. Henri was wrong, of course, or exaggerating. Through the years men showed themselves remarkably able to resist her charms, even when those charms were dressed up with silks and lace. She suspected it had something to do with her expression, which she had been told was severe. "Thank you, Henri," she said in a dismissive voice, and ignored him as he backed away.

She was not going to glance toward the fire. She wouldn't put it past Henri to have bribed some man to show interest in her, and she was quite certain Henri's definition of virile did not coincide with hers.

Tearing a roll into halves, she buttered it and took her first, heavenly bite. She adored France. She adored the language. She adored the architecture. She adored every dish that had been set before her. But most of all, she adored their bread.

Firm, white, with a tough texture wrapped in a savory case, it fed the gourmet soul she didn't even know she owned. Almost embarrassed by the sensual pleasure she found in a simple loaf, she hastily opened her eyes and looked across the room—and saw him.

He was virile, and he *was* watching her.

She looked away so fast that the tendons in her neck cracked.

He was *staring* at her. In their moment of regard, she observed interest, speculation, and an intense . . . well, it looked like . . . but it couldn't be.

Possessiveness.

The sound of a shower on her silk skirt distracted her, and looking down at her hand, she realized she had squeezed the piece of bread until the crunchy golden crust had flaked away and fallen into her lap. Carefully, she placed the mangled roll on its designated plate. She brushed at her skirt. She gazed at the table in front of her. Steam rose from the soup, carrying the scents of warmth and security.

Controlling the tremor in her fingers, she grasped her spoon. Dipping it into the broth, she lifted it to her mouth. Good sense returned even as she swallowed.

Her spinster mind, egged on by Henri's melodramatic speculation, had exaggerated the depth of the stranger's regard. The stranger watched her, yes. Smoke circled around his head from the lit cheroot between his fingers. But no doubt he watched her with the same inquisitiveness—oh, call it by its true name, nosiness!—as did the other travelers bent on satisfying their hunger for scandal.

Taking another spoonful of the soup, she sighed as

the flavor of oregano pursued the fish and roasted garlic. Yes, soup. Heavenly, yet ordinary.

But despite the protection of the stole across her shoulders, despite the warmth of the dish before her, a chill chased up her spine.

Imagination, she told herself. Leona had always said she had too much imagination, and sometimes Evangeline thought the wicked old woman had encouraged it. Nevertheless, she experienced the urge to look up, and as Henri whisked the soup bowl away and replaced it with a plate of lamb, she did so.

The stranger stared directly into her eyes, and he lifted his glass in salute.

Her lungs ceased to function. Her heart leapt, and she gawked like a rabbit mesmerized by a snake.

His ebony lashes framed blue eyes; she could see that even from across the room. But not sky blue, or cornflower blue. Burning blue, blazing with a passion for . . . for what?

For her, if his wolfish smile was any indication.

In Toulouse, she had presented money to a boy who had smiled like that, because she'd thought him starving. She had given him more when it looked as if he would attack and take from her everything she hadn't freely yielded. She wasn't a brave woman; she never had been, and that boy, and now this man, made her nervous.

But for all his hungry display of teeth, the stranger did not seem to be starving. His tailored black frock coat fit so tightly as to be a second skin. It outlined shoulders broad as those of a peasant who worked the fields. And indeed, in some aspects he resembled a peasant. His hands were big, so big they swallowed the wine goblet he held.

He lifted the goblet to her again. His rapacious smile expanded, and she found herself on her feet.

She had to leave this place. Now. Tonight.

No, first thing tomorrow morning. This was a farce. She didn't know why she thought she could cozen everyone. Cozen herself. Normally, she was sensible, and a long history of daydreaming was no excuse for such recklessness.

"Mademoiselle?"

She turned her petrified gaze on Henri.

"Is the lamb not to your taste?"

"Yes. No. I don't know." She clutched the tails of her stole in sweaty palms and reached for her ice goddess aura. "I'm retiring to my suite."

An expression of what appeared to be acute gastrointestinal distress contorted Henri's features. "I will fix it. Whatever is wrong, I will fix it. The lamb is too spicy, isn't it? I warned that fool of a cook—"

She stepped forward.

He stumbled back. "You cannot go without eating. You never go without eating . . ."

His wail sounded in her ears as she hurried through the crowded tables toward the door. Eat? She couldn't eat. A strange man had *looked* at her. Looked with an intent she'd seen directed only at others. Nothing in her life had prepared her for this kind of . . . interaction.

Wistful dreaming, she now realized, had in no way prepared her for reality.

The buzz of conversation grew around her as the tourists noticed her retreat. Curious faces stared. Her cheeks flamed with chagrin. She was hurrying like a woman forced, through desperate circumstances, to earn a living. She had hoped never to hurry like that again.

Something jerked her stole, holding it so tightly that she was whipped around to confront . . . no one. The trailing lace had snagged on the finial of a chair. She freed it with a yank that popped the delicate threads. She continued her race to the entrance, past the bowing waiters. She reached the portal and continued, ignoring Henri's wail. Past the comfortable sitting chamber, past the curving stairway, along the dark, empty hallway to the double doors at the end. With trembling fingers, she pulled the key from her pocket. She could scarcely fit the key in the lock. Then it fit, and she turned it. The door opened, she stepped inside, and closed herself in.

She leaned against the door, her heart pounding.

Had the stranger chased her? Was he even now striding toward her bedchamber, that peculiar combination of determination and disdain on his face?

She would lock the door. She would save herself from that man.

Pressing her ear to the polished wood, she strained to hear footsteps, but the thick walnut muffled any sound. Was he standing out there, preparing to knock?

She couldn't bear the suspense, and, taking a deep breath, she whipped open the door.

The corridor was empty. No one was there. No one had followed her.

Feeling prodigiously silly, she closed herself in once more and fit the key to the lock. The tumblers inside rattled with a satisfying sound, and she relaxed for the first time since she'd seen that awful man.

She had misread his attention. She had no experi-

ence with men, so how could she know if he was interested in a mild flirtation or a torrid affair?
Removing her stole, she tossed it on the bed. Or
worse, if he was interested in asking where she had
bought the stole so he could buy one for his wife.

Her cheeks burned as she thought of how he must
have chuckled when she had fled the dining room.
Her stomach rumbled as she thought of the savory
lamb she had left steaming on the table. The food at
this resort had fed an appetite long dulled by soggy
Cornish pasties and overcooked brussels sprouts.
Now, for that reason, and for others, she regretted her
flight from the dining room.

She groped for her handbag. It did not hang on her
arm. In her witless haste, she'd left it in the dining
chamber, and, like everything else she wore, it was
expensive. She couldn't abandon it or even one of the
belongings she'd bought and treasured with all the
sybaritism of her starved soul. No, she would have to
get the purse back.

Whatever made her think she could pull off this
deception?

Ruefully, she looked around the bedchamber lit by
the soft flame of beeswax candles. She had been
placed in what had formerly been the master's suite,
and it was beautiful. Deep-grained walnut paneled
the walls. The scent of roses perfumed the air. The
enormous, comfortable bed was hung with brocade
velvet curtains. A matching burgundy velvet counterpane covered the mattress. The frame rested on a dais
that every night made her feel like a princess as she
drifted off to sleep.

She loved this room, but no amount of pretending

could make it hers. It was time she admitted the truth. She was a fraud—and a thief.

Kneeling beside the bed, she groped at the ropes that supported the mattress until she found the carpetbag. She felt the lump it created in the mattress every night as she drifted off to sleep, and she exalted in it, for this carpetbag contained the key to her independence.

Gripping the handles, she wiggled the bag free and dragged it forth. Opening it, she removed the bound sheaves of pound notes, laid them out on the carpet, and counted them.

Three thousand pounds. In less than a month, she had spent half of her ill-gotten inheritance.

Covering her face with her hand, she fought the hard, cold truth, and lost. She knew she had to go back. Back to dreary England, with its fogs and its long winters, before Leona's legacy had been entirely wasted chasing a dream of adventure and romance.

There remained enough money to open a bookshop in the farthest distant corner from East Little Teignmouth. She probably knew more about books than any woman in all of Britain, and she could make a success of it. Yet . . . yet . . . she lifted her head and stared drearily at the sculpted wall. Was she going to live and die after such a brief and bitter taste of pleasure?

The knock made her jump, and she stared at the door with dismay.

"Mademoiselle, it is Henri."

The maître d's mellow tones only slightly eased her consternation.

"I have your handbag."

"Yes." Urgently, she picked up the wadded bills

and stuffed them in the carpetbag. "Just a minute." She shoved it under the bed. Standing, she smoothed her skirt and resumed her dignity, then walked to the door. Some lingering caution made her say, "Henri?"

"You also dropped your gloves," he said.

"Thank you." She opened the door. "You are the best—"

But it wasn't Henri whose shoulders blocked the light from the corridor. It was the man from the dining room, who offered her bag and her gloves on his outstretched hands. It was the man from the dining room whose cobalt eyes glowed with triumph and who gave a mocking bow. "Your Royal Highness," he said in Baminian, "how long did you think you could escape me?"

Two

Fear took a stranglehold on Evangeline's throat.
Who was this man? How did he know she spoke
Baminian? And why, oh God, why had she left the
safety of England?

She tried to slam the door, but a huge, booted foot
stuck in the threshold. The stranger grunted as the
heavy wood struck his knee, but when she leaned
with all her weight, he pushed inexorably inward.

"Henri!" she cried. It had been Henri's voice she'd
heard; where was he?

"No, princess. None of that." Again the stranger
spoke in Baminian. "There'll be no rescue from those
quarters." He had the door completely open now.

She craned her neck to scan the corridor behind him
and saw the maître d'hôtel's form sandwiched between two other men, feet pedaling the air as they
lifted him off the ground.

The stranger took in her wide-eyed bewilderment,
then crushed her hopes and illusions with one pithy
phrase. "I bribed him. If you listen closely, you can
hear the jingle in his pocket."

"What happened to wrestling bears for me?" she cried after Henri.

Henri tried to turn, but the men beside him would not allow it, and before she could scream again, the stranger stepped inside, crowding her backward, exuding a large, dark, angry, bearlike aura.

She had no experience with any of those qualities, but she knew she didn't appreciate them. The panic that had driven her to her bedchamber swept her up, and she darted around him. His hand shot out and grasped her wrist, swinging her around, and she barely stopped before she smacked the door frame. She glanced at him; the large, dark, and angry had grown to mammoth proportions.

But she hadn't studied ancient Chinese texts for nothing. If she could just gain control of her fear, think, and *remember* . . . she took a breath. She assessed the situation. He stood at a right angle to her, his arm outstretched, the joint of his elbow vulnerable and fair game.

Yet even though he was bigger, stronger, and willing to use his strength against her, she found herself unable to ruthlessly do the same. At least, not without a warning. "Get your hand off of me," she said in French, and with a fair imitation of calm.

"No, princess." He sounded very sure of himself, and as his grip tightened, her delicate glove escaped from his other hand.

Evangeline followed its descent with wide eyes. It landed on the toe of his black boot, an incongruous decoration on that serviceable leather. Then, slowly, her gaze traveled up his long legs, clad in black trousers. Up his torso, with its black jacket over a snowy white shirt. To his face.

No kindness softened the carved features. No flaw gave humanity to his godlike looks. He appeared to be an element of nature: inhuman, dangerous, harsh. Perhaps even . . . insane?

She had to do this.

Grabbing his wrist, she twisted. His fingers involuntarily opened, and she continued twisting until she stood next to him, his arm tucked, pale side up, beneath hers.

Dumbfounded, she stared at the sight of her smaller, paler hand in command of his. The Chinese were right. The hamation maneuver worked. It really worked!

"They didn't teach you *that* in your convent school," he said. "Tell me where—"

Jolted from her incredulity by his imperious tones, she slammed his elbow against her arm, hoping to force the joint backward.

His other hand shoved her forehead, knocking her off-balance. His knee was underneath her as she fell, and she landed on the floor, still clinging to his wrist. Seizing her under the armpit, he dragged her back and in, slamming the door behind him.

Letting go as quickly as she could, she stumbled to her feet.

His scowl permeated his voice, now deeper. His fists pressed against his waist, and her other glove rested beneath his careless boot. "I'd like to know where you've been to learn all that. If you hadn't hesitated . . ."

If she hadn't hesitated, she'd be free.

But she didn't say so. This man was, after all, mad, and Henri corrupt, and she was a paltry orphan whose disappearance and possible murder would never be noticed . . . but the next time she used one of those Oriental holds, and it worked, she couldn't pause to be astonished afterward. She had to follow up her advantage.

When she remained still, the stranger relaxed slightly and looked her over as if he were a banker who'd been forced to foreclose on a hovel and found his new possession quite unprepossessing.

Fine. So she wasn't a beauty. The London dressmaker had clucked in disapproval at her coltish arms and legs, and the London hairdresser had cut her long brown hair, complaining of a distressing lack of curl. Her odd-colored eyes were faintly slanted, a heritage that would always be a mystery, and her chin tended to jut aggressively.

Only her skin had passed her personal test of nobility. Her pale complexion had seldom seen the sun during her years with Leona. But no sooner had she stepped foot out of that shadowy library and into the daylight than she'd developed a faint flush of color. Not one of her bonnets had provided enough protection, and she would not—would *not*—stay indoors and miss her grand adventure.

So she might not be an enchantress, but she also wasn't this stranger's property, so he had no call to sneer like that. "Who are you?" she asked, this time in English.

His mouth, firm, full-lipped, and surrounded by a faint black beard, twisted in disgust. "You're playing a game." He spoke English, too, only slightly accented.

"No . . ." Well, yes. The game of staying alive.

"You'll come back with me, whether you like it or not."

"Back?" Where?

More importantly, did that mean she would get to leave her room, walk with him to the main door, and scream for help? "How soon can we go?"

Something about her haste seemed to alert him. His eyes narrowed, and his long black lashes tangled together at the corners.

Not fair.

"Princess. You do realize the importance of your participation in this ceremony."

Humor him. "Of course."

"The foolish letter you sent could never be accepted. You know that."

"It couldn't?"

"Santa Leopolda forgive you!" He stepped forward until he stood too close, and she smelled the faint scent of tobacco. He'd smoked his cheroot before he'd come after her, a predator too sure of his prey. "Would you deny our people their prosperity? The fate of two kingdoms rests on the fulfillment of the prophecy."

He *towered* over her, and she had little experience with towering men. Actually, she had little experience with men at all. None had bothered to visit an eccentric, female scholar like Leona. And Leona spoke of men as they seemed in her youth. Perhaps it was a somewhat idealized notion. According to Leona, the men she had known were primitive, given to sweeping a woman away for the excitement of her mind and the pleasure of her body.

Well, Evangeline's instincts shouted Run! and she was ready to try another one of the Chinese moves when something the stranger had said stopped her.

"The prophecy? You mean the prophecy of Baminia and Serephina?"

If anything, he grew more imposing. "You dare to jest with me?" His hands half lifted, as if he would wring her neck, then he swung away and strode rapidly to the other side of the room, halting by the delicate writing desk.

She started to inch toward the door, but without glancing at her he said, "If you move, I will have to give in to my baser instincts."

He didn't say what those instincts were; he didn't have to. Her imagination galloped on like a runaway horse.

She stopped.

"I told your regents not to send you abroad," he said in Baminian. "You should have been kept in Serephina, safe from shallow outsiders."

She replied in English. "I think there's been a mistake. I am not who you think I am. That is, if who I surmise you think I am is really . . ."

He looked at her, and her voice trailed off.

"You dare deny you are Princess Ethelinda of Serephina?"

If the truth weren't so pathetic, she could almost laugh. "I'm not any of the things Henri or the guests say I am. I'm only Miss Evangeline Scoffield of East Little Teignmouth, Cornwall."

Her declaration made no dent in his imperious stance, and he dismissed her claim without consideration. "What nonsense."

She began to feel a little calmer, and, deliberately casual, she leaned down and picked up her lacy stole and long glove. "How long has it been since you've seen your princess?"

"I last saw *you* on the occasion of your tenth birthday, on the day you departed to be schooled in Spain."

"That's it, then." She laughed a little, relieved to have the misunderstanding cleared up. "You haven't seen her for . . . how many years?"

"Twelve."

"There must be some superficial resemblance between us, and I'm flattered you think I'm a princess, but actually I'm a"—her laughter dried up—"nobody."

"I see. What an embarrassing mistake." He didn't challenge her, or laugh maniacally, or show any other signs of lunacy, but neither did he bow himself out the door. Instead, he lifted the top of her new secretary and rifled through the assortment of pens. "Could you perhaps clear up a few mysteries?"

"I suppose I could." What was he looking for?

"How did a nobody like Evangeline Scoffield of East Little Teignmouth, Cornwall, happen to arrive in a spa in the Pyrenees with enough lucre to support herself like—dare I say it—a princess?"

Her jaw dropped in unrefined shock. He didn't believe her. The man still thought her a princess of Serephina. "I'm telling the truth!"

"Did I say you weren't?" he asked smoothly. "I was just curious about the source of your wealth, which seems to have impressed our little Henri. Or if not Henri, at least his well-lined pocket." The stranger picked up the ornate penknife and rolled it between his fingers with a peculiar smile.

Evangeline's original distrust returned full force. She'd bought the secretary at a carriage stop on the way to the resort. An old woman had had a stand there, where she sold a variety of unique items, and the wooden box had caught Evangeline's attention. Picking it up, she had run her fingers along the Moorish-looking carvings, and the shrewd merchant had at once seen Evangeline's desire. The old woman had opened the box, taken out the pens, the nubs, the pen tips, the penknife, and displayed them in the sunshine. She had allowed Evangeline to fondle the rich paper, all the while regaling her with an absurd story of the secretary's noble, ancient, and bloody background. Evangeline hadn't believed any of it, of course, but within a few moments, money and secretary had changed hands.

Now this madman held the knife, and Evangeline feared his intentions.

She started to inch toward the door once more, but the stranger's head whipped around and pinned her under his fierce stare.

She halted. With a false smile, she strolled in the other direction. Toward the casement window. "Actually, the money was an inheritance."

"From one of your relatives?" He was still watching her. "Your grandfather, most likely."

She skirted around the big bed, tossing her stole and glove on the counterpane, keeping keen eyes on the stranger. "Well, no."

"Your father? Your mother?"

Remembering the rampant speculation in the dining room, and knowing her own lack of skill at fabrication, she triumphantly produced, "My husband!" Then, to hide her guilty face, she looked out of the glass. Every day since she had arrived, she had admired the view from her bedchamber. It looked out over the garden, and beyond. Now, bathed in moonlight, the lofty mountains rose in a circle of cliff behind the former castle, protecting it from the worst of winter's winds. If only the former fortress weren't set so high. She could only hope that when she opened the window and climbed out, she didn't break a limb in her fall.

"Ah. You are a widow."

"Um-hm." A man walked along one of the garden's winding paths. He stopped and looked up at her, his face shadowed by his hat, and she lifted her hand. With little, desperate motions, she waved at him. Maybe he would help her where the treacherous Henri would not.

"How tragic," the stranger mused. "Yet you wear no wedding ring."

The man outside ducked off the path, and she realized no help was forthcoming. In a flurry of motion, she swung open the sash and thrust her foot out. She heard the thunder of footsteps behind her, and the stranger's cry of, "No, you don't!"

She had no time to get out gracefully, so she simply leaned forward and allowed her weight to take her.

Three

Just as gravity caught her, hands yanked her back.
Evangeline screamed, loud and shrill, as the stranger
dragged her inside. Her skirts tangled around her
legs. Her rump thumped hard on the floor, and the
impact knocked the breath out of her.

The big man slammed the window shut on her last
cry. Silence, ominous silence, fell.

She looked up to find him towering above her.
Towering. Again. She scooted back, but he grasped
her arm and wrenched her to her feet. She swung her
fist at his chest; he caught both her wrists and clasped
them in the loose bracelets of his fingers.

She hated this. The helplessness, the futility, the
fear. "Who *are* you?" she demanded.

He ignored her question and her attempt to escape
as if both were unworthy of his notice. Holding her
left hand up to the light, he said, "Henri said, and he
was right, that he did not believe you had ever been
wed, for no sign of a wedding ring existed."

Her toes curled in her silk slippers, but what good
would it do to kick him? She'd do no more than hurt

herself against his boot. "What kind of sign?" Her voice was breathless, tight; she hated hearing the proof of her anxiety.

"A marked paleness. An indent in the skin." He shook her hand until her fist loosened. "Any proof that gold encircled your finger and marked you as some man's wife."

"I wasn't married long."

"I would imagine not. No experienced woman would have fled the dining room in such flurry." He leaned over her, and she tilted her head back, watching him until her neck ached from the angle. "Not just because I looked at her."

She didn't know how to answer that. The more she scrutinized this man, the more she suspected he was right. Women didn't run away when he looked at them; they ran toward. He had a certain animal appeal, a disciplined touch, and he smelled like warm leather and fresh air.

And he hadn't killed her—yet. "How much did you bribe Henri?"

"Enough to find out what I wanted." He looked down at her hand clasped in his; his grip loosened, and he sounded amused when he said, "He likes you, you know."

Maybe the stranger wasn't planning on killing her. In fact, now that she considered him, he didn't look like a murderer. No, he looked more like one of the men Leona had told her about. Strong, manly, impatient with a maiden's protestations. Maybe he was planning a simple ravishment, in which case she would be well advised to submit.

After all, she was returning to England, and she

ought to have *something* to remember. "Henri likes me?"

"Yes. It took more than simple profit to ensure his cooperation."

"What else?"

"My bodyguards threatened to thrash him."

She snatched her hands from the stranger's grasp. What had she been thinking? That because a man held her, he wished to make love to her? She needed to find out what this crazed barbarian wanted before she found herself lying at the bottom of that cliff outside.

If only she hadn't trapped herself between the wall behind, the bed before, and *him*.

"The only thing that's keeping Henri from getting help is Rafaello and Victor and their large and able fists."

Her gaze fixed on the stranger's hands. He didn't have them coiled into fists. In fact, his fingers seemed remarkably relaxed. His fingernails were clean, well-trimmed, and broad. Dark hair sprinkled the tan skin, and a tracery of veins and chords lifted the flesh. Large hands; desirable hands, if what Leona had told her was true. She blushed at the path her mind had wandered, then paled as she realized that this man could crush her as easily as he could crush a louse. His reference to Henri's fear increased her own, and she said, "I understand. You're intimidating me."

"A princess of Serephina is not intimidated by anyone," he said haughtily.

"Then that proves I'm not the princess."

He ignored her. "I only told you because you looked so lost when Henri deserted you."

Lost. Pathetic. Yes, that was she. "I am not a princess."

"Then you're a whore."

Scandalized, she gaped at him.

"A very expensive whore." His face grew cold. "What other kind of woman comes to a spa alone, without a chaperone, without even a maid?"

The kind of woman who never had a maid, and who didn't want someone snooping into her background.

"And as a whore, you are available for my pleasure." The broad hands she admired clasped her by the elbows, and he pulled her close, curving his body over hers like a wolf protecting its mate. His head lowered toward hers, and she ducked.

"No," he whispered, pressing her against the glass and tilting her face toward his with his fingers under her chin.

Belatedly, she remembered her Chinese techniques. She tried to smash his nose with her forehead. But he, apparently, had not forgotten her early maneuver, and gripped her jaw firmly.

"I have money to pay you whatever you want," he said. "A whore is in no position to refuse money."

"I am, too!" she cried.

"But you're not in the position to have all the tourists informed of your profession."

She stiffened at the thought of her carefully cultivated mystique dissolving, at the people who resided here looking at her with contempt.

He chuckled, soft and deep, the sound of his laughter grating as painfully as a shredder across her knuckles. "They're already talking about you, little girl. Wondering about your background. If not for Henri and his steadfast support, the gentlemen would already be knocking at your door. Didn't you think of that?"

She hadn't, and she wished he hadn't told her.

He angled his head, and his mouth touched hers, a light salutation.

She almost choked. A kiss. Her first kiss, delivered by an angry maniac who imagined her first a princess, then a prostitute.

"Relax," he whispered.

His breath played across her face, fanning the sensation of intimacy. The protruding windowsill cut into her lower thighs. The cold of the window seeped through the thin silk of her gown and petticoat. She shivered, and he gathered her closer, sliding his hand across her back, kneading the chill away.

"I can keep you warm." His voice was smooth, hypnotic. "A woman of your experience needs a man to keep her warm."

Wedging her arms between them, against his chest, she said, "I'm not—"

His lips pressed more firmly to hers, cutting her protests. His eyes were closed, those ridiculous lashes shadows on his cheeks, and he looked serious, as if this kiss required his concentration.

Concentration. That was what she required to remain calm. He was kissing her, true, but whatever he expected from her, she did not have to give. She didn't know what it was, for one thing. She didn't want to arouse the beast, for another. Leona had said kissing, when done right, could overcome a man with baser needs. Leona had said—

"Close your eyes." He lifted his head and stared, holding her, all of her body crowded against all of his, by the strength of one arm. The other hand still held her chin, but moved to stroke her cheek. "Such eyes," he whispered. "So reproachful. So revealing. They ravish my soul."

"Are you being funny?" she asked suspiciously.

His nostrils flared with disapproval. "You are not at all polished."

"You're forcing yourself on me, and complaining of *my* manners?"

"A most exasperating woman." He sounded sanctimonious, and he looked bedeviled. She expected him to thrust her away, but instead he smoothed his lips over her eyelids until they closed. "Now keep them closed." And he kissed her once more.

Apparently annoyance did not dim his ardor; indeed it seemed to have the opposite effect. This time his lips were warmer, more insistent. His body heated hers like a stove.

Lovers. She had seen lovers kissing among the alpine flowers on one of her walks, and surprise had made her stare in vulgar fascination. Their mouths had been open to each other, they'd strained with some obvious fervor, and desolation had sent her hurrying in the other direction. At that moment, she had feared she would never know such familiarity.

Now she was here, in the arms of a violent madman despoiler murderer, and she was inclined to continue. That sinful something unloosed on the day she left her former life now whispered, *What harm in knowing?*

She puckered her lips and relaxed into his arms.

And his tongue touched her mouth.

With the edge of her hand, she shoved him hard, right on the Adam's apple. "Yuck!"

He dropped her and grabbed his throat.

Sidling away from him, she demanded, "What did you do that for?"

"What?" he asked hoarsely. He coughed slightly, then repeated, "Do what? I was just kissing you."

She wiped the back of her hand across her mouth in the most offended manner she could devise. "You licked me."

She had hoped to insult him. Instead, hand on his throat, he stared down at her. The brilliant cobalt of his eyes faded to a thoughtful shade of slate. "One would think you have not made your fortune by prostitution."

"I am not a whore. I told you, I'm Evangeline Scoffield, an Englishwoman. I inherited money from the ..." She stared up at his domineering features in despair. She didn't want to tell him about her silly fantasies. Especially not now. When he laughed at her, the humiliation would wither her, and all her memories of this time would be tainted.

Only, nothing but the whole truth would do. Otherwise, how would she save herself, as a proper Englishwoman should do?

"I'm listening." He folded his arms across his chest.

Obviously, passion had not overcome him. Probably, he'd never lost his discipline, for she wasn't a creature of irresistibility. She sagged with private, contraband disappointment. This week had proved that. She was only—"Evangeline Scoffield. I'm an orphan bought from a foundling school. I worked for a lady who ... died."

"What kind of work did you do?"

"Leona had this incredible library"—incredibly musty—"and she wanted a ... well, I suppose you could call it an inquiry aide."

"A dull occupation for one so vibrant as you."

"Oh, no!" She shifted away from his searching

gaze. "At least, not at first. I was eleven when I went to her, and hungry for knowledge, not to mention skinny and pathetic." Smiling, she invited him to picture the child she had been, but he stood stoically. "She taught me Greek, Latin, French, Spanish, Slavic, and an obscure dialect called Baminian."

"You speak it like a native," he commented.

"Yes, well, Leona was a skilled linguist!" Was she getting through to him? She couldn't tell. "I can translate Mandarin Chinese and German. I know how to make fireworks, how to break a horse, how to ride a camel."

Or rather, she knew how to do those things *in theory*. She had no practical experience. She and Leona had gone nowhere, done nothing but read and learn. Letters and drawings had come from distant scholars, and Evangeline had rubbed the ornate ink strokes with her fingertips and wished she could go to those places. Her adolescence had slipped by, frittered away on dreams of freedom and travel.

But she didn't think it would be wise to admit that to this cynic. "I could even dissect a human body," she said triumphantly.

"I will make sure I keep all knives away from you while you're around me."

In any other man, Evangeline might have thought that was humor. In this man, she considered it a warning.

She ought to refuse to explain herself any further. After all, he was waiting without a visible flicker of interest for her to finish. Hastily, she continued, "My knowledge was limited only by Leona's interests, and Leona was interested in everything. And I was grateful to be there."

"In East Big Mouthie, Cornwall."

"East Little Teignmouth, and yes, I was grateful. Anything was better than the alternatives."

"What alternatives were those?"

"Governess, starvation, or, your favorite, prostitution," she said in a clipped tone. She wasn't getting through to him. It was as if he could comprehend none of the languages she spoke. Perhaps if she spoke in a really low baritone . . . "She wanted me to have her money, so when she . . . died . . . I, um, inherited it."

The proportions of his face thinned with disapproval.

"I bought these trappings and came here playing a role because I couldn't bear to expire without ever having tasted the wonders of the world," she concluded rapidly.

"You call that the truth?" His nose, a craggy edifice, grew pinched, and his lips compressed. "I had hoped you would see your error. Did not the good sisters teach it is a sin to lie—Your Royal Highness?"

Had he been hoaxing her with his accusations of prostitution? Looking at him now, all dignified censure, she thought he had. He'd been testing her, trying her out like a rider with a new horse.

If he were indeed mad, then he played his delusion with a cool logic she might admire . . . if only she were not the object of that delusion. "I'm not the princess, and I'm not lying!" *Or not much.* "I've got a copy of the will in my bag. It's a good will, it really, really is. Perfectly legal. If you'll just let me get it . . ."

He caught her as she tried to step around him and into the open area of the room. "Let me tell you what

I think. I think you are the spoiled daughter of the House of Chartrier."

She would have protested again, but he held up his hand. "I listened to you," he reminded.

"But you don't *believe* me. You haven't seen this princess in twelve years, but you think you know her."

"The evidence points to your true identity. You have been attending the convent school near Viella, just across the Spanish border. You recognized me in the dining room and retreated to your room to make up a plan—an inadequate fabrication which you were ill-equipped to tell."

"I didn't feel the need to explain myself to a madman." She asked suspiciously, "And why do you want this princess so badly?"

"I don't feel the need to explain the obvious." He mocked her with her own words. "You know you panicked when you saw me holding the penknife I sent you as a present for your fifteenth birthday." He nodded toward the desk where the contents of her secretary were scattered willy-nilly.

"I panicked because I thought you were going to stab me."

He smiled, a slight lift of the lips. "Only a fool would hurt you."

She hated this. He sounded so sensible, so . . . so . . . uncrazed. If he kept talking, he could almost convince her she *was* Ethelinda of Serephina.

But even if she assumed he was sane, there was still the nagging question of his identity. Choosing her words carefully, she asked, "If I were truly the princess, and I recognized you in the dining room, why would I flee in alarm?"

"I weary of your foolish questions," he said disdainfully.

"Humor me."

"You would flee"—he said repressively—"because you know I am Danior. Danior of the House of Leon."

With a sinking sensation, she realized she was familiar with the name. "Danior of Baminia?"

He nodded. "Your betrothed."

Four

Evangeline backed toward the corner of the chamber. "But you can't be a prince. You can't!"

Danior's heavy, dark eyebrows rose. "Why not?"

"Because you're too . . . too . . ." *Big. Broad. Muscular.*

She'd seen pictures of princes in her books. Lots of them. Princes wore capes lined with robin's egg blue silk that they threw carelessly over one shoulder. They wore velvet caps trimmed with soft feathers. They trod so lightly that the ground was grateful to hold their weight. They were slender, graceful—and charming.

A prince did not wear unremitting black and white, like any gentleman of fashion. He did not have thighs as thick and sturdy as Roman columns and arms like a Roman centurion. He certainly did not stomp like a giant staking out his territory, so that the floors groaned and the crockery rattled.

The crockery *was* rattling as Danior moved toward her, obviously not charmed, his mouth compressed into a thin line. "Why not?" he rapped out.

"You have no neck," she blurted, pressing up against the nightstand beside the bed.

He reached up and touched the knot of his plain white cravat. "Of course I have a neck. How else would I swallow?" As if he realized what he'd said, he tossed his hand out in disgust. "You're talking nonsense, and *I'm* defending myself." He glared down at her. "It has been twelve years since I've seen you, yes, but I was fourteen on the day I bid you good-bye, and I think I have not changed significantly since then. If my looks displease you, I am sorry, but that is no reason to try to evade your duties. As time goes on, I am sure we will grow accustomed to each other's appearance."

She had two choices. She could either go back to her "he's insane" theory, or she could accede that this peasant-built man was Danior of Baminia. She feared the latter was the truth, and she sighed as another of her lifelong fantasies, that of the elegant prince, writhed in a short and painful death. "So you think I look different?"

"Of course you look different. You were a child, totally unformed and undeveloped." His gaze swept her quickly from head to toe, then returned to linger on her generous bosom, displayed as attractively as possible by the cut of the gown. "Although I never expected you to grow so . . . tall."

Tall? She could have sworn he hadn't been going to comment on her height, and fascination definitely sparked in Danior's eyes. Behind her, she fumbled with the handle on the water jug. "Why not?"

"Hm?"

Yes. That was interest, compounded by that possessive gleam she'd seen in the dining room. Her alarm returned and doubled. "Why didn't you expect me to grow so tall?"

"Oh." He looked her in the face. "You were such a short little thing. Don't you remember how our people chuckled when we stood together?"

She had to be firm. She had to be. "No, because I wasn't there. I'm not your princess."

He stared at her as if deep in thought, then nodded once, rigidly. "And obviously, I'm not your prince."

Her heart lifted for one brief moment before he continued.

"I forget that you are young, and wish perhaps that your life had not been arranged from the moment of your birth. So I will give you romance." Danior sank to his knees before her and took her free hand. "Princess Ethelinda, will you honor our betrothal and after the ceremony of Revealing, marry me in the Cathedral at Plaisance?"

Evangeline stared at the top of his bowed, yet not humble, head, and she realized she'd never been in such trouble in her life. Not when she'd been a hungry waif. Not when she'd been put to work at the orphanage. Not even two months ago when she'd slipped away from East Little Teignmouth in the deep of night.

Danior said, "Together, we can reunite our two kingdoms and create prosperity for our nations."

She was in trouble because she wanted him to be Danior of Baminia. She wanted to be Ethelinda of Serephina. And more than anything in the world, she wanted to believe she had a home to go to, where people looked to her with hope and affection and considered her the fulfillment of a prophecy.

She swallowed. Her grip on the pitcher loosened,

and her hand reached around to hover above his head, almost touching the thick black sweep of hair.

With one word, she could change her life. She wouldn't have to go back to England and start a bookstore in loneliness and obscurity. She remembered every tale Leona had told about the Two Kingdoms. Perched on the spine of the Pyrenees, Baminia and Serephinia had once upon a time been united. A foolish quarrel had split them, and although never had there been actual combat across their shared border, the peoples cordially despised each other. According to the prophecy of Santa Leopolda, Prince Danior and Princess Ethelinda were fated to bring their countries together again, but for some reason—Evangeline looked at Danior and thought she knew why—the real princess had written a letter denouncing her heritage.

And here, conveniently, stood Evangeline, who spoke the Baminian language and knew their customs and history. She could fool everyone into thinking she was the princess, and no one would ever know the truth.

She stood on the brink of the greatest adventure of her life. The adventure she'd always dreamed of.

She opened her mouth to say, "Yes, I will marry you."

Instead, what came out was, "I am Evangeline Scoffield of Cornwall. I'm a commoner, an orphan, and I'm going to go back to England and open a bookstore."

The substance of adventure, when compared to the dream, contained just a little too much gritty reality for plain Evangeline Scoffield.

Yet adventure clutched her by the hand, and its

name was Danior. His grip tightened, and deliberately, he lifted his head and looked into her eyes.

Determination. The man vibrated with determination. "I will marry you," he said, "if I have to cross all of Hell's rivers to do it."

"Might be necessary." Behind her, she groped for the ceramic handle, and she heaved the pitcher in a wide circle. Water sloshed as she tried to crack Danior in the head, but he buried his face in her ribs. When the weight of the swinging pitcher threw her off balance, he caught her midsection under his shoulder and stood with her.

With grim satisfaction, he said, "You are a very predictable woman, Ethelinda." And he tossed her on the bed.

The pitcher clattered to the floor as she brought her hands up, but nothing could hold off the full weight of his descent. It was like having a log fall on her, and despite what he said, there was nothing noticeably noble about this log.

"I said I would wed you."

She tried to adjust so she could get her hands out from beneath him.

Effectively, he moved to crush her deeper into the feather mattress. "I want you to remember, this isn't my chosen method of courtship."

"I didn't think you were courting me . . . her. I thought you were telling." She squirmed. "I can't breathe."

He didn't reply. He just moved against her, securing her with his weight and his hands. And she really *couldn't* breathe.

It was like before. Like at the orphanage, when she had stood up to the headmistress and her cohorts.

Charitable women, they called themselves, who ran a "school." Hags, Evangeline had said; bullies who slapped the younger girls if they wet the bed or cried out with a nightmare.

That was where she had learned that courage would be punished, and dreams never came true. How had she forgotten that lesson?

It was dark beneath him, and the feather mattress extended around the sides of her. She was suffocating, and she gasped and strained, shaking with fear. "Danior. Please."

Abruptly she was released. She lay gasping, sucking in the air that had seemed too thin, and staring at Danior's scowl. He hovered as if waiting for a trick, and when she didn't move, he said, "Interesting. Did they lock you in the closet in that school you attended?"

"Sometimes." Realizing he wasn't going to attack again, she sighed and relaxed.

His fingers slid along the jut of her jaw, lifting it to its former defiant position. "We didn't pay them to do that."

"*You* didn't pay them at all."

Pulling his hand back, he stretched out on his side, and watched her in an attitude of vigilance. "I can scarcely believe you dare to look at me through those eyes and insist you are English."

The mattress dipped in his direction, and she struggled not to roll into him. "I *am* English."

"You speak English very well, it is true. And you behave too much like an independent woman for your own good. But"—he brushed a feather of hair off her cheek—"you have Serephinian eyes."

Jolted, she tried to sit up, fighting the well-aired

mattress, which wished to envelop her. Bracing herself on her elbows, she watched him vigilantly as she replied, "They're odd, yes. But what do you mean, Serephinian eyes?"

"Slanted eyes, the color of mahogany. Eyes inherited from the first queen of Serephina. The queen who was conquered by a Moor, and who in turn conquered him."

"Indeed?"

A whisper of memory tugged at her mind. The sight of an old woman with flame-blue eyes looking down at her eleven-year-old face. Taking her chin and lifting it. Turning it from side to side in austere analysis. Saying to one of the hags in charge, "I'll take her."

Danior did much the same, stroking her chin with his thumb, scrutinizing her features. "The queen and the Moor left a combined legacy of legendary beauty and ruthlessness in my country—and in yours."

Defensively, she drew her knees up to her chest. "Who am I supposed to be? The legendary beauty, or the ruthless conqueror?"

His heavy, dark brows snapped together. "I do not think, Ethelinda, this is the time for levity."

She hadn't been trying to be funny. She had been trying to protect herself from mockery. And from that testy, proprietary manner with which he handled her. "I suppose it's not out of the realm of possibility that my parents were from Serephina."

Picking up her carelessly thrown stole, he ran it through his fingers.

The sight of the fragile lace in his broad hand gave her an odd sensation, almost as if he were threatening her. "I don't remember my parents."

His fingers paused. "I know."

"It's not so bad being an orphan, once one gets used to it." Fighting the drag his weight created, she moved back toward the headboard. "It taught me to be self-sufficient." They were in her bedchamber, this self-proclaimed prince and a counterfeit princess, and they were alone. He had wrestled her onto the mattress. When she had demanded release, he had done so, true, but he had also first made a rather oblique comment. What was it? *This isn't my chosen method of courtship.*

"You don't know me well," she said, "and certainly you have no reason to be concerned about a mere stranger." She glanced at him from beneath her lashes. He wrapped her stole around his neck and flung the end over one shoulder in an extravagant gesture.

He should have appeared effeminate. Instead, the lace contrasted with his black jacket. The fringe trickled down his broad back. Incongruous decoration on a stolid statue of a man. "But you needn't worry that I'll be unable to care for myself."

She scooted toward the edge of the bed and lowered one foot toward the floor. "I am quite practical. This adventure was only a temporary aberration in the even tenor of my life."

Her toes had just touched hardwood when his hand grasped her other ankle. "Much as I admire your attempt to divert me from my purpose by reminding me of the tragedies which have ruled your life and your rather touching attempt at bravado, I find myself unmoved—*Princess.*"

He emphasized the title with what Evangeline considered unnecessary vigor. "You also seem to be skeptical about our need for you in Serephina and in Baminia."

"But you see, you've made a mistake." She tugged at her ankle.

"I am the crown prince of Baminia, and I do not make mistakes." His fingers pressed deeper, compressing the bones. Sitting up, he continued speaking relentlessly, confident as only a man who had never made a mistake could be. "As prince, I frequently mingle with my people, and I would never mistake a commoner for nobility. So luckily for you, I am well aware of not only my own duty, but of yours, and I possess the means to enforce your obedience."

His eyes burned like the flame in the hottest part of the fire, and she could almost see the air between them waver in the heat. Compelled by the kind of appalled curiosity that made onlookers crane to view a carriage wreck, she asked, "What means are those?"

"I have the strength. I have the determination." Taking her hand, he pressed it between his legs. "And I have this."

Ignorant as she was of anything but instruction from a book, it took her a moment to realize what the shape beneath his trousers indicated.

When she did, she made a noise not unlike that of a chicken producing its first egg. She could have incapacitated him; she knew how in some rational part of her mind. But reason fled before the proof that, yes, Evangeline Scoffield could make a man lustful.

And also, that Evangeline Scoffield did not have the slightest idea what to do with that man once she had done so.

Placing his hand on her shoulder, he tipped her back toward the pillows and stated his goal. "Once I have compromised you, Your Highness, you will have no choice but to do your duty, and that is to return with me to the city of Plaisance in time for the Revealing—and our wedding—and unite our countries as the prophecy foretold. There, in the Palace of the Two Kingdoms, you will bear the royal child which I have placed in your womb, and we will live with the contentment of knowing we have done our duty."

A pang of pity for the true princess rippled through her. Then as he bent over her, a pang of panic for her own plight made her shudder. "You'd do this in cold blood?"

Something shifted in his blue eyes. "Cold?" he said. "I promise you'll not complain of a chill."

A sudden, sharp conviction that he was laughing at her made her tug away. He caught at her and they rolled, wrestling briefly. Finding herself pinned against the headboard, her wrists pressed against the carving, she glared balefully as his head lowered to hers.

"Relax," he murmured as his lips touched hers. "This is the best part of our duty. You'll see."

Silken whispers of enticement, his lips drifted over her face. They stroked the eyes he claimed to recognize, paid reverence to the high cheekbones that had so set her apart, and, as gently as a butterfly descending on a flower, they settled on her mouth.

Seduction, she reminded herself. Cold-blooded seduction for a very practical purpose.

But Danior had spoken the truth. There was nothing cold about this. She could almost smell the singe of their connecting flesh.

Then the sound of shattering glass jerked his head

up. Evangeline caught a glimpse of a round, black, shiny missile flying through the air. It bounced off the bed. With a metallic thud, it landed on the floor.

"What? . . ." she tried to say, but Danior hurtled off the bed and dragged her behind him in one motion.

She stumbled off the dais and fell to one knee.

He tugged her to her feet. "Run," he said. "A bomb. It's a bomb!"

Five

"*A bomb?*" *Evangeline said stupidly. Then,* "*A bomb!*"

Dropping to her knees, she twisted her arm.

Danior lost his grip on her.

But as she scrambled back toward the bed, he roared, "Where do you think you're going?"

"My money." She lunged under the mattress. "I have to get my money!"

Her fingertips had just touched the precious bag when he seized her from behind by her sash.

"Damn you, woman."

She screamed and fought, but he hoisted her over his shoulder.

"You're not dying on me, too."

He sprinted from the room. His shoulder bones battered her ribs, while she cried out and stretched toward the open doorway where her money, her precious money, remained.

They had almost reached the main hall when the flash of the explosion blinded her. The blast made her ears ring. The concussion of air sent Danior stumbling forward.

When Evangeline opened her eyes, she saw flames shooting from the doorway of her luxurious bedchamber.

Danior swung around and faced the conflagration. A shudder swept him. "Just like before," he muttered.

Pandemonium sounded from the dining room. Gentlemen and ladies, some holding napkins, some dabbing their mouths, crowded the doorway. They gaped at Danior and Evangeline, then at the inferno down the corridor.

Evangeline pressed her hand to her chest. "It really was a bomb." A bomb. In her bedchamber. And she'd lost everything. "My money. My future."

"Be quiet," Danior snapped.

He didn't understand. He'd never been hungry. She grabbed the waist of his trousers and jerked as hard as she could, and she hoped those manly parts he was so proud of trekked clear up his spine.

"Damn!" Danior slammed her down on her feet—feet that tried to run, but got nowhere. "Try that again and I'll . . ." He took a long breath and let it out slowly. "We'll be lucky if we escape to have a future, you and I. Don't you understand? They've found us."

She didn't understand. Why should she? The cosmic threat that he saw so clearly meant nothing to her. She only understood that when this matter of the princess was cleared up, Evangeline Scoffield would go back to England and face the poverty she had feared her whole life. Scrubbing at her wet cheeks with her fists, she whimpered, "My bookstore. It's gone."

Danior bared his teeth, but before he could shake her, a ripple surged through the guests. Ladies squealed as two darkly clad men charged through, knocking all aside with no deference to gender or age.

Danior waved to them, and like wraiths they closed around Evangeline. With a glance, each summed her up. Despite her tear-stained cheeks and wild eyes, they apparently found her of noble aspect, for they bowed their heads in one short, jerky nod. Then they turned to Danior, and the remote homage they had paid her became a very personal devotion. These men were Rafaello and Victor, she supposed, the ubiquitous bodyguards, and they clearly adored their master.

"The bastards'll be waiting outside," one said. He wore subdued, elegant clothing, but he tugged at his cravat and hunched his shoulders. Although he spoke fluent French, his lips barely moved, as if the act of articulation was arduous.

"They're waiting for us to run out." The other man was refined from the graceful sweep of his short cloak to the even trim of his fingertips, and he spoke easily, with the polished delivery of an aristocrat.

Yet whatever their differences, the three men communicated with the ease of those who had been together for years.

Their master spoke. "Take care of it, Rafaello."

The aristocrat turned to the throng spilling out of the dining room. With a perfect, upper-class English accent, he called, "I say, I think that was a bomb. Do you suppose more will come flying through the dining room windows?"

As a diversion, it worked well. Well-clad people shrieked as they streamed into the large sitting chamber.

The maître d'hôtel bounded out on their heels, and Evangeline screamed, "Henri! Help me!"

Danior's big hand covered her mouth, cutting her off, but Henri barely glanced her way. Instead he stared at the flames that ate at the château, and shrieked at the servants, "Get buckets! Pans! Anything! Start a line from the kitchen well, or we'll be out in the snow this winter!"

"Don't look for help from him," Danior murmured to Evangeline. "His livelihood is going up in smoke. And Your Highness—it's your fault."

He took his hand away, and when she kept quiet, he let go of her. But it didn't matter. She was incoherent. Her fault? How was this her fault?

Futilely Evangeline hunted for a handkerchief. The madness around her was sweeping her up. The shouting and increasing hysteria made her wonder if she would make it back to England at all. Or if others might agree with Danior and somehow deduce that this catastrophe was her fault. After all, the world had run mad.

She sniffed and dabbed at her nose with the back of her hand.

"Women." Danior stuck a clean square of linen in her hand.

As if she weren't going to cry after all this! She wiped her eyes, then hiccuped and pressed the material to her mouth, wishing desperately she could blow.

"It'll be safer outside," Rafaello shouted, his voice aimed above the hubbub. He made shooing gestures, and although a few rational voices raised objections, the hysterical herd advanced toward the exterior door.

Victor tossed a cloak over Danior's shoulders. When Danior turned up the collar, he covered the white of his shirt and cravat, and his somber figure became positively grim. Then the men joined the flow of refugees, carrying Evangeline in their midst. When she tried to wiggle away, Danior simply grasped her arm and hustled her along.

These men with their conservative clothing and their obvious tension stifled her. Worse, the two bodyguards looked remarkably like Danior in their height and coloring, and she had no doubt they were of like temperament.

She was surrounded by bullies.

Even in a crowd, their stature should have made them stand out, but as they cleared the threshold to the outside, they bent their knees to make themselves shorter and to blend in with the crowd.

The throng scattered along the verandah and out into the garden, encouraged by comments from Rafaello, their harrying guard dog. "It'll be safer away from the building," he called. And, "This is all Napoleon's fault. I imagine his Frenchies are trying to liberate him."

"Why would anyone toss a bomb *here* to free Napoleon?" Evangeline asked logically.

Her unwanted companions ignored both her comments and her dramatic sniffling, staying with the crowd until they reached the deepest shadows. Then they broke away, hastening toward the stables. At some prearranged signal, Rafaello and Victor picked up speed, leaving Evangeline with Danior.

Danior tugged her into the shadows of a tree and held her there, unseen by the stable boys who ran past them, lugging washtubs full of water.

"Help!" she yelled. "I need—"

"Be quiet!" Rudely, he pulled her close and shoved

her face into his chest, holding her by the back of her neck as a tomcat did with a field mouse, then he moved them farther from the path, farther from human activity.

It didn't matter. She could shout all she liked. She could struggle. No one paid attention. No one cared about one woman's kidnapping. Not when the château was burning.

The shouts of the toiling servants almost drowned out Evangeline's subdued lament. "Who did this thing?"

She wasn't still crying, not really, but the slow leak of moisture from her eyes must have wet his shirt, for he answered, "It was the revolutionaries."

Her mind blanked. Revolutionaries? What did he mean, revolutionaries?

Yet Danior seemed to think she knew what he was talking about. "That's why we've got to go, and quietly, too."

"The revolutionaries." She tasted the word, not liking its flavor.

"Damn their souls." He vibrated with outrage.

"But I thought Serephina and Baminia were safe."

"They are safe. We have to get there."

For some reason, she had not even considered visiting the two countries, although she knew they weren't far.

For good reason, it seemed.

"Look." He turned her so she faced the rocky heights. "Serephina is just over that line of cliffs."

A chill ran up her spine. "So close."

"Yes, but the cliffs run for miles from east to west, and we have to go around. The horses are good, trained in the mountains, and with luck we can cross the border in two days."

"Only two days." To escape him and go back where the world was sane.

His hand rotated slowly, soothing the muscles on her rigid neck. "Despite my best efforts, Dominic's band has grown active again."

"Again."

"Yes. And you remember what happened last time."

"I do?" She searched her mind. Leona had never mentioned any problems.

"It was a time of great sorrow for all of us."

She wasn't sure, but she thought he dropped a kiss on the top of her head.

"Dominic's gang wants the end of the monarchy, and they'll get it any way they can—by our deaths, if necessary." He turned her back into his arms. "That's why we must convey you back to Plaisance and fulfill the prophecy."

She detected something in his voice; chagrin, perhaps, that he hadn't been able to control the situation by himself.

Speaking into the soft linen, she asked, "Is that why you said this bomb was my fault?"

"I spoke without thinking. It is not right for me to blame you. But surely you understand now that your letter was unacceptable."

"The letter." He'd mentioned the letter before. "Just what did the princess say in that letter?"

Obviously irritated, he answered, "You know very well what you said."

"But I am not Princess Ethelinda."

With a great deal of satisfaction, he retorted, "As far as Dominic is concerned, you are."

Six

With both hands, Evangeline muffled her gasp of horror. Danior was right. Revolutionaries, men who considered bombs an art form, now thought she was a princess. "Because of you—Your *Highness*," she said. As she struggled free, she made his title an insult. Looking up at his face, she saw the stark contrasts of hollowed eyes and brows and flesh made pale by the rising half-moon. For the first time since the bomb exploded, she forgot about her money. "*You* led these revolutionaries to me. They've been following *you*."

"Yes. Incredible as it seems, somehow they discovered our tracks."

The damnable man was right. It didn't matter whether she was Princess Ethelinda or not. If revolutionaries had indeed found them—and she had no reason to believe Danior was lying about this—then she, Evangeline Scoffield, was in danger. And this madman prince was her only savior.

Her only current savior, she corrected herself. She'd always saved herself before, and she would find a way out of this dilemma, too. She'd use him to help her flee this place. When they were well away and had lost the revolutionaries, then she'd escape back to England, and face the consequences.

Resolved to resume control of her life, she asked, "Where are Rafaello and Victor?"

"They've gone to the stable to get our horses."

Scanning the area, she caught a glimpse of movement along the path. "There they are," she started to say.

Danior's hand covered her mouth in a swift, silencing gesture. His voice spoke softly in her ear. "Quiet."

She could see them now, two strangers. Dressed in black, they walked just off the edge of the path. The light of the burning château showed her nothing of their features, for they wore black scarves. She could see only their intense, narrowed eyes, which darted back and forth as they scanned the shadows. A woman ran along the trail, panicked by the fire. They caught her, and Evangeline saw the flash of a blade as they held it under her chin. She cried out in fear. They slapped her and shoved her away, and she fled, whimpering. She wasn't who they sought.

Evangeline was.

The pistols they held gleamed in the light of the flames.

Pistols. Oh, God. She'd read about the harm a pistol could do. The damage to the muscle and bone of a limb, making amputation necessary. Or to a vital organ, with the result being . . . death. Her heart gave one hard, appalled thump, then accelerated to a nauseating speed. She stared straight ahead, afraid to move, and barely breathed as they passed.

At last Danior said, "They're gone."

Red dots swam before her eyes, and her knees gave way.

Danior caught her as she slid down. "Don't worry, little Ethelinda. I won't let them get you."

"I'm not Ethelinda," she said faintly.

"Of course not, Serephinian eyes," he mocked.

"I told you I was an orphan." She took great breaths of cool air. "I don't know who my parents were. But perhaps they came from these mountains." Perhaps they had fled the revolution Danior spoke of. She might even be noble. A countess, or a duchess.

He stiffened. "We are royal."

"I am common," she retorted.

"If that were the truth, it would be a tragedy, for a commoner and a prince may not marry." His voice grew as rich and strong as Turkish coffee. "And I have every intention of wedding you."

British society was divided by class, but Evangeline didn't like such pomposity there, and she found she cared for it even less coming from this already over-bearing prince. "And what dreadful thing would happen if a prince married a commoner?"

"It is not proper, as you very well know. Fish mate with fish, birds mate with birds. If those who are royal by divine right mix their blood with the lower classes, it is against the natural order."

"Your people must love you," she said sarcastically.

He answered simply and with great certainty. "They do."

And why did she care, anyway? If the people of Baminia and Serephina wanted to be ruled by a stuffed shirt, it didn't matter to Evangeline. She would escape this mess somehow. "What if this Dominic has the real princess and you're wasting your time with me?"

"If Dominic captured the princess, he'd be announcing it from the tops of the cliffs. He knows I'd come after her . . . you. He has dreams of holding a tribunal, as the peasants did in France, and trying us for the crime of being royal, as if killing a crown prince would lift him from the foulness in which he revels."

He was a snob about the common people, but he hated the revolutionaries, and with no ordinary hate. Some instinct prompted her to ask, "Are the princess's parents still alive?"

"*The princess's* parents died in the rebellion of ninety-six, as did mine, and you know this very well."

In seventeen ninety-six, she had been four. "There was an actual rebellion?"

"Of short-lived duration, but a dreadful tragedy nevertheless."

Suspicion crowded her mind once more. This story couldn't be true. Nothing fit. "If your parents were killed, why haven't you been crowned king?" she asked suspiciously. "You should have been crowned as soon as you reached your majority."

"I can't be crowned king until I marry you, Princess Ethelinda." His baritone whisper vibrated with frustration. "That is the part of the prophecy to which I am bound, and that is why I must have you, so stop playing the part of an ignorant observer."

How could Leona have failed to mention this vital part in the history of Serephina and Baminia? And what other things had she failed to mention?

"I don't like this," she muttered.

"Neither do I." He scanned the area. "Victor and Rafaello—they've been gone too long."

She, too, looked around, trying to convince Danior, and herself, that she was no weakling, no feminine sniffler who had to be protected. She had to be strong, bold, crafty. She'd had to be to survive the orphanage.

Then she ruined the effect by shivering.

"You're cold," he said, although she would have sworn he paid her no heed.

"I will survive." She'd been colder, she comforted herself. Of course, not for a long time. And a body got used to heat on a regular basis. But she would toughen up.

"Good, because there they are." Gripping her arm, he pushed her ahead of him. Then he slowed. "But they haven't got the horses."

The bodyguards sprinted up to them, and Victor panted as he spoke. "Horses ... chased away. Stable ... a trap."

Danior didn't seem surprised, or even at a loss for a plan. "We'll walk."

"Walk?" Evangeline wiggled her toes inside her thin-soled evening slippers. "Where?"

"Where I lead." Danior firmly guided her with the flat of his hand in her back.

Victor and Rafaello led the way, skimming swiftly and silently toward the cliffs. Evangeline followed them, and Danior strode behind her, his hand ever ready to catch her should she fall—or should she try to escape.

He didn't need to worry. Escape, at least right now, wasn't part of her plan.

As the shouts of the guests and the faltering flames of the spa faded, darkness closed in around her. She found herself aware of the stillness of the night, and aware of her companions. The silence, the pale moon, and the ever-increasing darkness heightened the evening's chill. They reached the shadow of the cliffs and there turned to pick a path along the base among the stones that had fallen from above. Ahead of her, Rafaello and Victor moved so smoothly, so fluidly, that they might have been wolves rejoining their pack. She knew they were there, yet she could scarcely see them. Behind her, Danior was equally invisible. The gravel beneath her feet crunched, and she knew Danior must be walking the same path, but although she strained, she could hear nothing. This trek was eerie and horrible, cold and exhausting. She shivered occasionally, then constantly, the cooling air breaching the thin silk of her gown with ease. Not even her exertion kept her warm. Each breath hurt her lungs, and although she tried, she couldn't control her harsh breathing.

The further they walked, the more brambles sliced at her legs, the more loose gravel covered the path, and the more painful each step became. She began to complain under her breath, then to whimper very, very discreetly. Finally, she stubbed her toe on a jagged stone. "Ouch!"

"What's wrong?" Danior sounded distinctly annoyed.

"These shoes are not for trekking across uncharted territory filled with rocks and bugs." She slapped at a lingering mosquito. She had been walking for over an hour to who knew where with total strangers as companions and revolutionaries behind them, and she thought she'd been very brave. Surely Danior could acknowledge that.

Instead he snapped his fingers, and, silently, Victor and Rafaello moved to her side. She stopped and stared as they bent, crossed their hands, and clasped them behind her—and waited.

A chair. They were making her a chair. If she had any doubt about their sincere belief she was their princess, this act of servitude dissolved it completely. They willingly offered themselves as a sedan for her comfort, over rugged terrain in the middle of the night.

"Hurry," Danior the boor said tersely. "We must arrive by dawn."

"Where are we going?" she demanded again.

He answered her this time. "To the convent."

A convent. Sanctuary.

Placing her hands on the bodyguards' shoulders, she seated and steadied herself. They lifted her, and for one brief moment, memory stirred in the depths of her mind.

Of sitting between two people as they held her in a seat made of their hands, the scent of their fear palpable, their breathing labored as they hurried up and down mountain paths similar to these. And she, too young to understand their haste, yet gripped by the need for silence and an unchildlike dread of some thing that hid in the darkness just beyond sight.

Then the party started forward almost at a trot, Danior in front, the other three behind, and the memory sank into the abyss from which it had come.

"Your Royal Highness, you're cold," Rafaello murmured.

"No." The night air flowed past her, but she gathered warmth from the men.

"You shivered."

"A ghost walked over my grave," she answered.

Danior turned on them and said ferociously, and far too loudly for her taste, "There's going to be an army of revolutionaries trampling over your graves, and very soon, if you don't lower your voices."

He was glaring. She didn't even have to see him to know it. When he was satisfied he had sufficiently cowed them, he moved on. Softly she assured Rafaello, "It's nothing."

He placed his mouth close to her ear. "If you wish, you may take my cloak."

Now this was what a real prince should be like! Evangeline thought triumphantly. Then the triumph faded. He wasn't the prince, he was the bodyguard. She wasn't the princess, she was an impostor.

"Sh," Victor warned.

Toady, Evangeline thought. But Rafaello seemed thoughtful, almost human despite his resemblance to Danior and that odd dedication he displayed. "I'm warm enough," she whispered.

Danior's head half-turned, and she ducked. She shouldn't care what he thought, but in her room back there he had somehow intimidated her. Probably, she thought grumpily, it was that barbaric fanfare about placing a babe in her womb and thus forcing the marriage. He didn't frighten her; oh, no. She had seen what had happened to poor little Joan Billby when she'd gotten caught with a bun in her oven. Her mistress had thrown her out, and if Leona hadn't taken pity on her, Joan and the baby would have been forced into the poorhouse.

Yes, that was it. Evangeline was frightened of being left alone, pregnant, and in despair, when Danior discovered she wasn't the real princess. She was *not* afraid of that extraordinary possessiveness he displayed, or the brief taste of smoky passion.

The path slithered along the foot of the cliff, rising and falling. The bodyguards labored, walking sideways with her weight between them. They were in magnificent condition, but with each upward grade they breathed a little harder. Yet they were making good time, and probably they would soon be at the convent.

At the convent. Could she appeal to the holy sisters for sanctuary?

She watched the broad, dark shoulders that traveled the trail before them.

Or would Danior make up some tale about her being mad and in need of confinement? She'd be put in a cage and put on exhibit for hoards of sniggering travelers who would say, "I knew she was a nobody." Or she'd be manacled to a stone wall and forced to take cold water baths until she lost her mind and fancied she was the princess. She'd admit it then, and be treated like royalty all her days.

Or be killed by Dominic.

And she'd have to marry Danior.

She looked ahead at the silent, darker shadow among the shadows.

She was imagining things. Danior really thought she was the princess, and he wouldn't let anyone mistreat her. No, more likely he'd make up some story that she was already his wife so he could keep her in his bed.

Her mouth dried, and she tried to swallow. Her imagination had allowed the skinny, frightened, defiant orphan to make up stories when no hope remained. Her imagination had whisked her from

Leona's house in East Little Teignmouth, Cornwall, to China and the Canary Islands and Turkey. Her imagination had been a blessing.

Now, her ability to fantasize placed her between the sheets with Danior, and trapped her between anticipation and fear.

In her quietest voice, she asked the bodyguards, "What would you gentlemen do if you knew I wasn't the real princess?"

To her surprise, Victor answered. "I'd drop you right here in the middle of the path and let the revolutionaries pick you up."

Victor, she discovered, had no sense of humor at all.

Danior whirled around again. "Santa Leopolda's bones!" Plucking her out of her living chair, he said, "If they can't keep you quiet, I can."

Seven

Danior didn't, as Evangeline feared, throw her over his shoulder again. This time he held her against his chest—and he was warm. Not like the faded warmth she'd received from the other men, but really warm, like the blacksmith's forge back in East Little Teignmouth, Cornwall.

"If we get caught," she muttered, "it'll be because of your shouting, Your Highness."

"I was not shouting."

Of course he wasn't, it was only that his voice didn't go below a rumble, much like a subterranean volcano. "Almost."

He put her on her feet so fast that she thought *he* was going to leave her for Dominic. Instead, he removed his cloak, turned his back, and squatted on his haunches. "Climb on," he said quietly.

She, too, kept her voice to a murmur. "Wh... what?"

"Climb on my back."

She glanced around, half expecting to see Victor and Rafaello ready to make her obey. They'd faded into the darkness. "Why?"

"I need my hands free."

What he said made sense, but . . . she looked down at her evening gown. The fine silk skirt was gathered beneath her bosom, with cotton petticoats beneath. "What about my . . . limbs?"

"What about them?"

His obtuse ignorance fed her stubbornness. "They'll be exposed."

"It won't be the first time I've seen your legs, nor carried you this way. Remember how, when you were a child, you used me as your horsie?"

"No." She wanted to stomp her foot, but that would hurt the blisters that had formed. "No!"

"We don't have time for these games. Dominic can't be far behind. Get on, girl!" Then Danior corrected himself through clenched teeth. "Highness."

She couldn't prevail. She either had to walk in her thin shoes and ruin her feet and with them her chances of ever escaping from this madness—or she had to get on his back. But she remembered something from her years of research. A tip from a sixteenth-century Italian mediator. *When your enemy is backed into a corner, that is the time to negotiate.* "Evangeline," she said.

"What?"

"My name is Evangeline. If you'll call me that, then I'll get on your back."

"I don't believe this." His tone made it clear he'd been driven to the limit.

"Dominic can't be far behind," she reminded him.

His teeth gleamed, his breath rasped, his hands twisted, and she realized he was mangling his own cloak rather than her neck. For one moment, she wondered if he would attack. Then, in a goaded voice, he said, "Get on my back . . . Evangeline."

She'd won. Oh, God, she'd won a skirmish with Danior! She wanted to jump, to yell, to dance. But the mere fact he'd surrendered—a novel experience for him, she was sure—told her the danger did indeed nip at their heels.

This adventure was a little too real for comfort.

He turned his back again, and she leaned into him, wrapped her arms around his neck. Shaking out his cloak, he gathered it around them and fastened it loosely at his throat, effectively tying them together. To keep her warm, she knew, and probably to conceal her light-colored gown beneath the enveloping black. But it gave her a claustrophobic sensation, and when he rose she just dangled there by her arms.

That detestable name rumbled through his chest. "Ethelinda?"

He obviously knew how to negotiate, too. "Oh, as you demand." She wrapped her legs around his waist, and he started down the slope after his body-guards.

Not since the orphanage when the girls huddled together for warmth had she experienced such famil-iarity—and this was not the same sensation at all. Her arms rested on his shoulders, her head was at the level of his. She could smell the scent of his hair. Her bosom pressed against his back. She experienced his every breath, and found herself pacing her breathing to his. The base of her torso, a place that had tingled when he'd kissed her, rested against his spine, and the movement of his body gave her an odd thrill, much like the scientific experiment she'd once done for Leona. Electricity, Leona had called it, and it had knocked Evangeline off her feet.

She supposed he'd done the same.

She hugged her legs to his waist tightly, for if they slipped—

His head turned. "What is that noise?"

She stiffened, listening behind them for the crunch of boots or the clatter of hooves.

"You're grumbling." His lips barely moved, yet she heard his words, or felt them perhaps.

"I am not." Then she realized what he meant, and admitted, "It's my stomach."

"You should have eaten your dinner."

With her mouth close to his ear, she could retort, and the sound did not travel. "For once, you are right."

They passed Victor and Rafaello, and the bodyguards waved them on.

Danior dug in the pocket of his waistcoat. "Here." He pressed something into her hand.

Cautiously, she freed her hand from the folds of his cloak and looked. She held a white package—something wrapped in a handkerchief. She opened it, and realized she held a firm, crusty roll.

"Henri insisted I take it for you. He said you'd be hungry."

"The traitor."

"You don't have to eat it."

"Ha." Bracing her elbows on Danior's shoulders, she lifted the bread to her nose. She inhaled the yeasty smell, then said, "I spent most of my early years hungry. I don't scorn food from any source."

He laughed, low and rich. "You weren't hungry.

You were chubby. But at least I know why you grew so tall."

She wanted to argue with him. She wanted to eat. And eating, she knew, would provide her with a great deal more satisfaction than banging her head against the immovable wall that was Danior. She nibbled the end of the roll, and sighed as the first bite slid down her throat and comforted her stomach.

"It's good that you're not chubby now," Danior said. "This trek would be difficult."

She paused in her gustatory quest. "It must be difficult, anyway."

"Nonsense. I'm strong."

Leona had told Evangeline about this, too. Men, she had said, were notoriously proud and stubborn, never admitting to weakness, and a wise woman always catered to that pride.

"Nobody's that strong," said Evangeline, unwise woman.

"I am."

He sounded confident, and in fact he moved along the path without pause. The long muscles in his back stretched and contracted as he walked, and she could feel his stomach muscles flexing against her calves like a living illustration of William Harvey's *Studies of Anatomy*.

Too intimate. Much too intimate. Hastily, she asked, "Would you like a bite?"

"*I* ate *my* dinner."

Briefly she considered crooking her arm under his chin and choking him. Unfortunately, that would only work if he had a neck, and he didn't. So she ate the sour bread in a brooding silence, which affected him not at all, then she brushed the crumbs off his shoulder.

The trail dipped down into a woods. Nearby a stream trickled over stones, and at the sound, her already dry mouth parched.

But she suspected he would take a request for a halt badly. Craftily she asked, "Aren't you getting tired of carrying me?"

"No."

She'd forgotten. A man never admits weakness. "Perhaps we need to stop and allow your bodyguards to catch up."

"They've gone different ways to throw Dominic off our track."

She didn't want to say it, but she had to. "I'm thirsty."

He halted in mid-stride. "How can you be thirsty?"

"The bread was dry."

"The bread was dry," he repeated. "I should have stopped and buttered it. And toasted it before the roaring fire *created* by the *bomb*."

The man had an incredible and uncalled for capacity for sarcasm. "No, Your Highness, but a glass of wine wouldn't have come amiss," she said tartly. "Let me down by the brook and I'll get a drink."

He sighed like the blacksmith's bellows, but he changed directions and followed the sound to the creek bank, releasing the fastening of the cloak as he walked. The ease of her victory surprised her, and she wondered at it, but when he swept off the cloak, she hopped off his back, glad to get away from the brooding disapproval, if only for a moment.

The chill of a mountain night struck her through her gown, and she shivered. The stream ran almost at her feet, catching bits of moonlight as it filtered through the trees. The damp air smelled of moss and pine, and Evangeline took a grateful breath before kneeling at the edge of the water.

He towered over her. "How will you drink?"

"I'll form a bowl with my hands."

"That sounds easier than it is."

"I've done it before," she said haughtily. Tapping the shallow depths, she found a spot lined with rocks where she hoped the water ran clear. Cupping her hands, she brought them to her mouth in one efficient swoop. She slurped undaintily, but she didn't care.

"Where did you learn that?" he asked.

She turned her head and looked up at him, a dark shadow in a land of shadows. "In Cornwall on a bracing walk through the countryside."

He snorted and moved down the bank, and she continued drinking until her thirst was quenched. As she dabbed at the water she'd splashed on herself, she heard similar slurping sounds from downstream.

Danior had been thirsty, too.

Damn the man, he'd been thirsty, and he hadn't wanted to admit it. If it hadn't been for her insistence, he would have gone forever without stopping until he'd dropped from dehydration.

Had Leona said anything about this masculine aspect? Something about how men created a great and boundless exasperation?

"I'm going upstream a little further," she announced softly.

The slurping noises stopped. "Why?"

She had known he was going to ask that. "I have other needs." She enunciated her words carefully, the way she would when teaching a small, intractable boy.

"Ah. That's fine, but don't go too far." He slurped again. The man was drinking like a long-unwatered horse. "And don't think you can escape me."

"I am hardly likely to try in an unfamiliar wood in the middle of the night." No, not here, but when they reached the convent. The bread and water put heart back into her, and she made plans. In a place full of women where Danior was alien, surely she would be able to get help. Don an inconspicuous habit. Or even just climb out a window. It could be done. She would do it.

When she returned, she climbed on his back with less reluctance. She was tired, ready for this pitiable escapade to end, and that wouldn't happen until they reached the convent.

The convent. It had begun to assume the aspect of heaven.

"Ethelinda." He corrected himself before she could. "Evangeline. Look."

Muzzily, she noted that her cheek rested on the top of his shoulder, that he'd hooked his arms under her bare knees to keep her in place, that her right heel rested in a place no self-respecting heel would ever visit.

She'd been asleep, and probably been snoring in his ear. Or worse, drooling on his jacket. She was never at her best during slumber.

"Look," he whispered.

She pried open her eyes. Streaks of dawn light banded the light blue sky like ribbons on an Easter package. Lifting her head, she realized they'd left the cliff sometime in the night and stood just inside the shadow of the forest. Just ahead and across an alpine meadow, Mother Earth gave birth to a split and rocky crag. Behind it the sun was rising, and the rugged stone that lifted itself to the heavens was topped by the spires and walls of a medieval structure. "What is it?" she asked.

"The convent of Santa Leopolda—and our destination."

She blinked against the light and stared again at the forbidding gray walls perched on the sheer rock spike. This was a Gothic fortress, built to withstand attack and accessible only on a narrow, precipitous path carved into the very rocks that gave it existence. The trail wound its way to a narrow door—the only entrance to Santa Leopolda.

The only exit from Santa Leopolda.

Dear God. She could never escape. Never in this lifetime.

Eight

Evangeline stiffened on his back as she gazed up at the convent silhouetted against the sky, and Danior experienced a surge of satisfaction. In the short time since he'd plucked her from Château Fortuné, he'd formed a favorable opinion of her intelligence, and he knew Evangeline must see the impossibility of escape from this place.

Evangeline. A foolish name for a foolish girl, and Danior could scarcely believe that the princess—his little princess Ethelinda—had forced him to accede to her wishes and call her by that ridiculous moniker.

But his princess had changed. She had grown tall, with an aura of dignity that bespoke her noble heritage. She had acquired a lively tongue, a defiant attitude, and some rather unusual skills. And she had grown wily.

So he would call her Evangeline. It was, after all, a common name in Serephina, and it could not be an accident that she had picked one of the many family names given at her christening. If she preferred Evangeline, that was fine, and he was willing to call her that as long as she behaved herself.

Which, from what he had seen of her, was unlikely.

When Rafaello had brought him the rumor of a wealthy mystery woman at Château Fortuné, he had gone to the resort expecting to retrieve little Ethelinda without incident. He'd planned to scold her, to humor her, and to have her humbly agree she was being unreasonable in denying her destiny. Instead he'd seen across the crowded dining room an Amazon: fullbreasted, round-hipped, wary-eyed.

He'd lifted his glass to her, aware of several things. That he'd been too long without a woman. That beneath his fashionable, restrained clothing lurked a barbarian and a descendent of barbarians. And that this woman, with her sherry brown eyes and fluttering eyelashes, was his. Totally, completely his.

His body had surged in anticipation. Stupid, really, when he'd known he had to wed the girl and be stuck with her for the rest of his life, but there it was, an inexplicable excitement.

Miss Evangeline Scoffield of East Little Teignmouth, indeed.

Some might say he should have patience with her prevarications, reading them as the panicked fluttering of a woman innocent of the ways of men.

He said she should be used to the thought of wedding him—they'd been betrothed since the day she was born. And any forbearance he might have felt was washed away by his rampaging determination to be king.

He would be king. King of Serephina and Baminia, united after a thousand years of acrimony. And this little princess and her loss of nerve would not stop him.

That was why he had brought her to the convent

of Santa Leopolda. The towering precipice would protect them from attack, yes. It would also assure him
that Ethelinda—no, Evangeline—remained in his cus-
tody, and her dowry, the country of Serephina, would
be his.

"Let me down," she said. "You need to rest."

"I will. When we're up there." With a jerk of his
head, he indicated the convent above.

"You are a stubborn man," she exclaimed, as vexed
as he had heard her.

"That is a wise thing to remember," he answered,
gratified. At the same time he examined the open
space around the base of the convent cliffs. Trees had
been stripped away to provide a defense against marauders, and when they left the forest, they would be
exposed. If he could get them through this one peril,
they would be safe—until they once more left on their
journey to Plaisance.

But he had learned to confront one danger at a time.

He scrutinized the tree line. He listened to the care-
free calls of the birds. He looked for unusual shadows
among the boulders at the base of the cliff. It was safe.
As safe as possible. "Hang on," he muttered.

Realizing his intention, she struggled. "No. Let me
run!"

"Where?" he asked grimly. Gripping her, he sped
away from the protection of the trees and toward the
narrow path that led to the entrance to the convent.

Evangeline clung, her legs and arms wrapped
around him tightly, riding him like a horse, lessening
the impact of his step. His breath came hard, his arms
and back ached, but he did what he had to do. It was
a lesson he'd learned well.

A future king always did what he had to do.

Gaining the lowest reaches of the path, he continued more cautiously. The rebels might be hiding behind one of the stony bends.

"You can't carry me up that path. It's too steep!" Evangeline protested.

"Sh." As he reached the first bend, he turned and surveyed the meadow. No one raced after them. Above them, he could hear nothing, and on the ground he saw only one set of footprints. Victor's.

They were safe—for the moment. Moving on at a slower rate, he tried to regain his breath and answer Evangeline's most recent protest. "Of course . . . I will carry you. Your shoes . . . have not grown . . . new soles."

"I'll walk carefully, but listen to you! Your lungs are working like bellows and your arms are trembling from my weight."

Carefully he regulated his breath and adjusted her weight to a more comfortable position. "I'm fine."

He wasn't, not really. The sleepless night and strain of carrying her had taken its toll. But it irked him that she should think him such a milksop that he couldn't complete the journey.

More than that, he took an odd pleasure in carrying her on his back.

His own doggedness didn't even make sense. Trudging along as she weighed him down was a constant, meticulous torture—but not because of muscle strain and fatigue. Oh, no. It was that she was open to him in some eccentric, reversed imitation of lovemaking, her arms around his neck, her legs around his hips. Her breasts pressed into his back, the nipples hardening with each chill, then softening as she warmed, like a woman brought to desire, then satisfied. Her spread legs left the feminine softness between them unguarded.

He might have thought it was only him who noticed. He might have thought himself a pervert of the first water. But she couldn't hide her discomfort, or that her own vulnerability embarrassed her.

He had known, because at first she'd tried to hold herself away. That aroused him, and he'd wanted to tell her he knew of a woman's curves, and how all women were made.

A lie, of course. He knew how *other* women were built. Somehow, his body had convinced him that Evangeline was different. Unique.

When she gave up the struggle and relaxed against him, he had been satisfied—and tormented. She trusted him to carry her to sanctuary.

Well and good.

She rested oblivious on his back.

He was not some tame bear trained to cart her to safety. He was a wolf, and he wanted nothing so much as to eat her whole.

Only the lack of time and the possibility of ambush saved her from becoming a meal for a hungry man.

That, and his eternal vigil over himself and his baser urges. To take advantage of this woman in such crude circumstances and without control seemed like something his father would do.

His father. Danior clenched his fists. If it weren't for his father and the revolution he had incited, all would be well in his kingdom. Danior could have tracked Evangeline and fetched her back to Plaisance without furtiveness, with the honor she deserved. If she had the chance to see her lands, to realize what this union meant to the people, she wouldn't struggle against her fate. She would embrace it.

They had reached the halfway point in the path when she tried again. "Just let me walk from here."

"You'll try to escape." She wouldn't, he knew. She no doubt recognized the futility of such a gesture.

"I'm not stupid."

"You haven't proved that to me yet, Your Highness."

"You are *so* cranky."

So he was. This chivalrous constraint made him cranky. Hell, it had made him furious. Didn't she know who he was? Not a prince, nor a gentleman, but a warrior who had stalked the enemy, who had fought and killed to keep his country free. A warrior who held his woman, limp and quiescent, on his back. His hands supported her by the round globes of her buttocks, and right now, all he could think about was sliding his grip in a little. If he did, he would reach the slit in her pantaloons. He could touch her moistness . . .

"You're sweating," she complained.

She refused to comprehend the danger she courted. In fact, if he had to pick out one complaint from the ever-lengthening list of What was Wrong with the Princess, it would be that she heedlessly raced to embrace danger. Hitting him, defying him, running from him, enticing him, lying to him . . . she even claimed to be an orphan with no breeding or background. Only another royal could comprehend how he would hate to lower the majesty of the Leon family line by breeding with a commoner.

Everything she did she aimed at him. At him, and at evading the destiny that bound them together.

She would never escape him, on that he was determined.

They reached the end of the path. The door to the convent loomed before them, and he knew he could put her down at last. But he didn't want to seem too eager. And in fact, while he wanted to rest, he hated to allow her to place even the slightest distance between them.

Maneuvering her so she could reach the rope dangling against the solid rock wall, he gasped, "Ring the bell."

Nine

"Not until you put me down." Evangeline *couldn't* believe how stubborn this man was, but it was time he learned she was stubborn, too. "I am not going into a convent clinging like a barnacle to your back."

She felt his spine stiffen. His body communicated his absolute disbelief right through to hers, and his hands flexed on her knees. As far as she could tell, no one had ever told *this* man no.

About time someone did.

Reaching around his throat, she loosened the fastenings of his cloak and dropped it. He let go of her legs, and if she hadn't caught herself, she would have dropped, too. Her feet should be tended, it appeared, but he didn't care about the condition of her backside. She couldn't walk to Serephina on her backside.

Carefully she climbed down, moving away from the warmth of him, from the faintly musky scent of a healthy, active man. Then she realized she carried it with her. The intimacy of their journey had marked her with his aroma, and deliberately she sought to create a distance between them, to place formality where familiarity had been. "Thank you for carrying me, Your Highness. You must be tired."

This time he agreed in as sarcastic a tone as he could manage. "Yes."

"But I thank you nonetheless." With a flourish, she rang the bell.

With awesome patience, he picked up his flowing black cloak and draped it over his arm.

Ignoring him, she looked at the country spread out around them like a map. Off in the distance in every direction rose mountains upon mountains, each taller than the next, snow-covered and forbidding. She observed the line of cliffs they'd followed from the château until, not too far away, the escarpment plunged into the surrounding forest. And right around the convent, the alpine meadow was nothing more than a cleared area, a place where the surrounding forest had been shaved away in a circle.

"Napoleon's armies marched through these mountains on their way to conquer Spain."

Evangeline looked at Danior. He, too, gazed across the countryside, his black brows drawn into a fierce frown.

"For a time, he succeeded there, but he never conquered *us*."

Such a thought had never occurred to her. Baminia and Serephina perched together on the spine of the Pyrenees between France and Spain. Of course Napoleon must have coveted them. "Did you fight Nappie?"

His blue gaze burned her with contempt. "Of course I fought him. Why do you think I left you at that school for so long? According to the prophecy, we cannot be wed until Revealing, but you would have lived in your castles, toured your country, been surrounded by your servants and my advisors. You would have learned your royal duties and I would have supervised the final stages of your training."

"Oh, the poor girl," Evangeline exclaimed from the heart. "You would have crushed her like a bug."

"I would have treated her—you!—with all the respect due a queen of Bamphina."

For a moment, confusion held her in its grasp. "Wha . . . Bamphina?"

"When the crystal case is opened and we reunite the two lands, we shall rename our one new country. That will help end the strife forever."

"Bamphina?" Now she understood. A combination of Baminia and Serephina. Irritation prickled her skin. "That's a stupid name. Sereminia sounds better."

"Don't be ridiculous."

She took a breath to fight him, then realized she *was* being ridiculous. She wasn't Ethelinda of Serephina. It didn't matter to her what they called their piddling country.

He watched her expectantly, waiting for her to object. She folded her lips firmly, and she could have sworn he sagged with disappointment.

Damn the man. Did he enjoy their confrontations?

Ringing the bell again, he said, "I wish they would hurry. You'll be safe inside."

Safe? Oh, yes, they'd be safe. Evangeline looked up at the convent. It rose straight from the door, gray stone piled on gray stone in endless, monotonous repetition. On this front side there were no windows, no way for an intruder to enter except through the short, narrow door bound in iron. As if any self-respecting intruder would try to make it up that circuitous trail. The path alone was an ample deterrent to an army. If she was going to escape from this place, it would have to be with help from the nuns.

Leona had always said Evangeline could talk her way into next week. This was her chance to prove it.

The iron hinges creaked as an elderly nun opened the narrow door. A white wimple surrounded her broad, wrinkled face, and she smiled as she offered the traditional Baminian greeting. "My home is your home. My life is your life. Come in and take comfort."

Leona had drilled her on Baminian manners, and Evangeline stammered, "Blessings be on your house."

"Not the princess, eh?" Danior muttered as he placed his hand on the top of her head and pressed and pushed at the same time, guiding her through the low, narrow passage as firmly as if he knew she'd been thinking of escape. "We are pilgrims seeking shelter," he said, and ducked to enter.

"Much like the other Baminian pilgrim we welcomed earlier." The nun sounded amused.

"Is he well?"

"Very healthy," the nun answered.

Danior relaxed infinitesimally, and Evangeline realized he worried about his bodyguards.

He pulled the door shut with a thump that echoed through the dark and stony reaches of the lower floor.

The abrupt cessation of morning's light, the sense of being trapped and enclosed made her chest feel tight, her lungs struggle for air.

Apparently Danior noticed, for he said roughly, "It's a large chamber. Your eyes will adjust."

Squinting, Evangeline realized Danior was right. While this entry boasted no windows, other doors opened off it, and feeble morning light came from them. The convent's stone well rose from the center of the worn board floor. The kitchen, too, was down here, for from that lighted opening came the buzz of conversation and the scent of baking cherry pies.

Evangeline's mouth started watering.

In her soothing voice, the nun said, "I am Soeur Constanza. You may hang your cloak on the hook. Then follow me and we will find your friend." She turned and led the way into a stairwell.

Once again Danior laid his hand on the small of Evangeline's back and pushed her in front of him, and when she looked up the five stories of stone steps spiraling into one of the towers, she found herself glad he walked behind her. Arrow slits allowed in the only light. There was no handrail, no concession to the frailty of human balance, and the steps, worn by generations of holy women, tilted every which way. This old castle was hard and cold, a remnant of the Dark Ages.

Danior, Evangeline thought sourly, would have been right at home in the Dark Ages.

Speaking just in her ear, he said, "Remember, the nuns don't know we are the prince and princess, and the less who realize the truth, the better."

She stopped and jerked her head around to stare at him. "I'm not telling them I'm a princess. I don't lie to nuns!"

He grunted and pushed her, and she followed the sweep of Soeur Constanza's black habit up the stairs.

On the first landing, the nun opened the door and led them into a community dining room filled with long, polished tables and benches, and occupied only by one man.

Victor stood, and for fully a minute Evangeline thought it was out of respect for a lady. Then reality caught up with her, and she realized his homage honored his prince—and his princess.

"You're hungry and weary," Soeur Constanza said. "I will bring breakfast."

"Very good." Danior's black brows twitched as if he were amused. "Breakfast will be much welcomed by my *cranky* companion."

The Dark Ages? No, Danior would be at home during the reign of the barbarians. "Visigoth," Evangeline snapped.

"Careful. You'll hurt my feelings." Danior swaggered toward his man.

She dragged wearily to the table. She'd slept perhaps an hour in the last twenty-four, and that on his back. She was so tired she thought she heard singing, choirs of heavenly angels. Slumping onto the bench Danior pulled out for her, she leaned her elbows on the long, polished wood table. Yes, she heard singing . . .

"The sisters are at Mass," Victor was saying.

Not heavenly choirs, then. Nuns singing the praises of God.

"No word from Rafaello?" Danior pressed down on Victor's shoulder.

Sinking back onto the bench, Victor assured him, "Rafaello'll be fine. He's got cat's eyes, that one. He can see in the dark."

"Yes . . ." Danior sounded thoughtful as he seated himself. "What about you? Did they pick up your trail? Were you followed?"

Victor grinned, a smirking display of white teeth. "Until I lost them."

"What about the nuns?"

"Most of them haven't seen me, and Soeur Constanza says no one has visited the shrine in weeks."

"What shrine?" Evangeline asked.

Danior fixed her with all the brooding intensity of his gaze. "Don't play the fool. I'm in no mood."

She straightened up and brooded right back at him. "By which I can assume the *princess* would have known about the shrine?"

Staring at her as if she had grown a second head, Victor asked, "Is Her Royal Highness pretending to be someone else?"

"I am *not* pretending."

Victor laughed out loud. "Serephinians are all liars."

"Mind your manners," Danior warned.

Victor nodded to her, a quick, insincere bow of apology.

"She says she's Evangeline Scoffield of East Little Teignmouth, Cornwall," Danior said, proving he had been paying at least a little attention to what she said. "That's in England," he added for the sake of his goggle-eyed bodyguard.

"Cornwall? Why would anyone even want to pretend to be from *there*?" Victor imbued the word with a skeptical aversion.

Evangeline's hackles rose. "East Little Teignmouth is a pleasant village." Not always, with its narrow streets that funneled the ocean winds, the long winters filled with the crash of waves, and the narrow-minded lawyer who clutched her money close to his chest and mouthed on about the seven-year waiting period. But *this* man had no right to scorn East Little Teignmouth.

"You should be ashamed," Danior said, and she cast Victor a triumphant glance. He sobered immediately, but Danior was looking at her. "You deny your heritage. You deny your parents."

She should once again proclaim her identity, but he was so intense, and she was so tired. "Serephina and Baminia seem to have trouble with revolutionaries."

"They wouldn't, except for"—Danior hesitated, his mouth a grim line—"well, your father, at least, was a good man."

Obviously, Leona *hadn't* told her everything about the region's history. "What do you mean by that?"

"He means the only good Serephinian is a dead Serephinian," Victor said with stinging distaste, "especially when it comes to women, and your family in particular. Your Highness."

"I'll not tell you again, Victor." Danior slashed the air with his hand. "Mind your manners. Repeating old sayings can do nothing but harm, and doesn't change the prophecies. Now here comes Soeur Constanza with our breakfast. Evangeline"—he caught her gaze—"no more deliberately artless questions."

Evangeline's mouth dropped open.

"And don't appeal for help. I will silence you." Scorn laced his implacable warning.

"Deliberately artless?" She sat up straight. "Do you think you can just insult me without a qualm? My lineage may not be as exalted as yours, but you have no cause to scorn me."

"Indeed not, Evangeline." Danior accepted a bowl from Soeur Constanza. "We both have our familial embarrassments." He placed it in front of her.

His admission made her want to probe deeper, but

as she took a breath, she smelled barley and—she sniffed—yes, cinnamon.

Danior handed her a spoon, then he poured thick, rich cream over the steaming cereal. Wordless with bliss, she lifted a spoonful to her mouth. Closing her eyes, she savored the first taste. The nutty flavor of the barley promised satisfaction, and she perceived just a hint of . . . she opened her eyes. "Is that roasted apple?" she asked Soeur Constanza as the nun removed Victor's bowl.

Soeur Constanza nodded. "You have a discerning palate."

Victor, a barbarian in his own right, snorted.

A bell sounded below, and Soeur Constanza started toward the stairwell at a trot.

When the nun was out of earshot, Danior leaned intently toward Evangeline. "If you go back to the Two Kingdoms to reign as my queen, you'll eat whatever you wish."

Evangeline paused, the filled spoon halfway to her mouth. Visions of roast pork, crusty and crackling, of fresh oranges, peeled for her delectation, of piping hot cups of tea laced with real white sugar beckoned and swayed with demonic temptation.

She exorcised the tempting fantasies, and answered calmly, "Then I'd be fat, and I wager you would not like me like that." She took her bite.

To her surprise, his gaze dropped from her eyes to her lips, then to her bosom. "I wager I would."

She choked on the barley. Danior stood and, grasping her arms, lifted them over her head. "Say something."

"Pig," she gasped—and found her airway unclogged and her heart thudding in her chest. Danior seemed to have an exorbitant appreciation of her bosom.

At the clatter of boots on the stairway, he looked around, and when Rafaello appeared in the arched doorway, he walked toward him with every evidence of pleasure. "Good man." He grasped Rafaello's hand and shook it warmly. "Did you have any trouble?"

"There were a few more rebels than I cared for," Rafaello admitted. "But I handled them."

"Did they follow you here?"

Rafaello frowned. "Never!"

"I didn't doubt you," Danior said. "Sit down and eat. The good sister will bring you food to break your fast."

The men sat together, a cluster of virility. Soeur Constanza brought Rafaello a wooden bowl, Danior took up his silver spoon, and as they ate they spoke in lowered voices, leaving her in virtual isolation to finish her barley. She did so efficiently, scraping the bowl clean.

Soeur Constanza must have been watching, for as they all finished, she whisked the simple bowls away. "If you gentlemen would come with me, I will show you to the guest quarters."

"What about . . . Miss Scoffield?" Danior grinned at her, clearly convinced he had found a use for her alias.

He thought he was so diverting.

"The ladies stay among us, separate from the gentlemen. Miss Scoffield will be given a chamber suitable for a pilgrim."

"Do you have one with a lock?" Danior asked.

Evangeline shot to her feet. "You're a madman!"

Even the serene Soeur Constanza looked shocked. "A lock?"

"She'll try to escape if she's not locked in."

Soeur Constanza looked from one to the other. "I . . . we don't have locks. We're a convent!"

"You must have one somewhere." Danior sounded revoltingly rational. "This was a castle once. There must be a dungeon."

"Long filled in." Soeur Constanza quivered with indignation.

"He's mad," Evangeline said to her.

Danior ignored both Soeur Constanza's consternation and Evangeline's aside. "A storage room?"

"It's on the level below with the kitchen, and filled with garden tools and broken furniture. You can't ask a gentlewoman to stay there."

He had that flinty look Evangeline had seen him wear in her bedchamber the night before. "I'm not *asking* her to."

The autocrat was back, and she was so very, very tired. Did they have to resume their struggle *now*?

"This is most irregular, sir, and quite impossible." Soeur Constanza fluttered like a plump pigeon facing a wolf. "I'm afraid I'll have to report this to the Reverend Mother herself."

"You do that. In the meantime, I'll take Miss Scofield down to the storage room."

Ten

Evangeline tried to sidestep him, but he caught her arm. Mostly by accident, she trod on the top of his foot.

He seemed to suspect she deliberately provoked him, for the veins on his forehead stood out, he opened his mouth to shout—then with a look at Soeur Constanza, he shut it. In English, he said, "I'll not forget this." He marched Evangeline toward the stairwell.

"What are you going to do, Your Highness?" she taunted. "Starve me? Abduct me? Lock me in a storage room?"

He turned his head. He looked down at her and smiled.

Her breath caught in her throat, and blood rushed to places it had no business being. Whatever he was thinking, it wasn't torture.

"Maybe we should get married here and now," he said.

Picking up her feet, she kept pace and rapidly recited, "According to legend, the prince and princess must be married on the day of Revealing."

His smile deepened. "I wonder how would Miss Evangeline Scoffield of East Little Teignmouth, England, know such an obscure myth?"

She scowled at him. "Study. Long hours of study."

The stairs seemed steeper going down than going up, and once at the bottom they had several doors to choose from.

"Not the kitchen," Danior murmured, "although you would be happiest there. Here, I think." He walked her toward the door in the deepest shadow of the entry hall, and, sure enough, light leaked through a keyhole.

"There's no key," she pointed out triumphantly.

"So I see." He smiled again, that smile that meant he would enjoy taking a bite out of her. "Well, if it can't be found, you'll have to sleep with me."

"I will not!" Except she hadn't got her way about much since she'd met him, and she wouldn't wager a single shilling on winning this—not even if any of her shillings had survived the fire.

He ignored her spurt of defiance with the contempt it deserved, turned the latch, and pushed the door open. A window spilled sunshine into the good-sized room, filled with a conglomerate of tools, broken furniture, and dust. Lots of dust. He had found his storage room filled with everything a convent could need or had ever needed.

He examined the chamber critically. "Yes. This will do."

It *would* do. The dust she could handle. A closet she could not. Breathing a sigh of relief, she sagged against the wall.

Walking to the window, he put his hands on the high sill and looked out, then looked back at her. "It's a sheer drop, with jagged rocks at the bottom. Tsk,'' he said with spurious sympathy. ''There's no escape that way.''

Automatically sarcastic, she said, ''Maybe I can fly.''

''No. I've clipped your wings.''

His certainty jarred and infuriated her. Clipped her wings, had he? He couldn't even begin to know of what she was capable—and she wasn't going to tell him.

''You'll need a bed,'' he decided.

''Please, I don't want to inconvenience anyone. Let me sleep on the cold bare floor.''

''Or the table,'' he pointed out amiably. ''It's long enough. I could shove this coil of rope and those gardening tools off, and you could sleep there.''

''You are such a swine.''

He took her by the arms and swung her around.

She clenched her teeth. ''Have you decided to take vengeance?''

''For what? Because of what you think? What a woman thinks is the most insignificant part of her. No, I only care what you do, and I direct your actions now.''

He steered her stiff, protesting figure into the center of the floor, then hooked a short stool with his foot and dragged it from under the table. ''Sit.'' Allowing her no choice, he pressed her down.

Driven to protest by a last, weary remnant of defiance, she said, ''It's dirty.''

''The dress is beyond redemption. Now sit still.''

She looked down at her lap, at the beautiful, stained skirt, and stroked it lightly with her fingertip. She was—had had to be—a thrifty soul. She could turn the fabric and find enough unmarred material to make a shawl. Or . . . a handkerchief.

He left the room and didn't see her swift rush of tears, and she controlled them promptly. Not for anything would she show him weakness now. Instead, she propped her elbow on her knee and sank her chin into her cupped palm to contemplate escape. But only because she felt she had to. Without help, there was no way out of this convent, and besides, where would she go? She was in the middle of nowhere.

From out in the entryway, she heard a splash from the well, then the rattle of chain and the creak of the windlass as Danior brought up the laden bucket. Returning, he blocked the doorway and contemplated her, the bucket dripping in dark splotches on the wooden floor. Then he walked toward her with the intent and purpose she'd come to recognize.

She was a hedge that needed shaping. He was the shears.

He put down the bucket and knelt before her, eye-level, and she stared at him with as much menace as she could contrive. He whipped off the cravat that hung limply around his neck. He dipped it in the water, wrung it out, cupped her head in his hand and washed her face with speed and efficiency.

When she emerged, sputtering and damp, she gave voice to a sudden, horrifying suspicion. "You have children!"

He rinsed the limp cravat in the bucket. "Why do you say that?"

"Because you scrub like a parent!"

"We have a number of orphans in Baminia." He wrung out the cravat again.

She flinched back.

Taking her hand, he cleansed it thoroughly. "I occasionally serve in the orphanage."

She had to know without a doubt. "So you're not a parent?"

"I have had only a few liaisons, and with those I took much care. I have fathered no children. You will not have to bring up my bastards." He watched her with too much comprehension. "I am not my father. Is that what you wanted to know, Evangeline?"

Yes, although not because she disliked the thought of raising a strange child. Rather, it was a sudden, unnamed distaste at the thought of Danior's closeness to the mother of that child.

He smoothed the cool water up her arm, and his ministrations felt almost good.

So she rushed to divert his attention. "Why do you work in the orphanage?"

"Because I, too, am an orphan and know that occasional attention can make the difference between a king and a . . . revolutionary."

She examined him from several angles. He appeared to be serious. "I'll bet they hate to see you coming if you wash faces like that."

"Only the little ones, and they forgive me quickly enough when I carry them on my back."

As he had done her. Of course he had to deliberately remind her of that, and inadvertently remind her of how very grateful she would have been if someone, an adult of any kind, had taken even a passing interest in her when she lived at the orphanage.

She imagined the scrawny children with their odd-colored eyes riding on his back, and thought how they must adore him. If she weren't careful, the scrawny orphan she had been would come to adore him, too. "You treat me like a child."

"You almost nodded off in your barley. You're not capable of taking care of yourself."

A sputter of laughter escaped her. "I've been taking care of myself for more years than I can remember."

"Of course you have." He washed her other hand, then lifted it and placed it on his mouth. "Your Highness."

His lips formed the two words, his breath touched her fingers, and each syllable felt like a kiss pressed to her palm. She snatched her hand away, but his face remained level with hers. Weariness ringed his eyes with dark, yet still he challenged her. And although she desperately fought, she slid toward the warm, deep blue comfort of his gaze.

"Mother Leopolda says it is permissible to lock Miss Scoffield into the storage chamber." Soeur Constanza's voice broke the bond and conveyed disapproval, all at the same time.

Evangeline sprang back and bumped her head against the table.

Danior whipped his head around and glared through narrowed eyes.

Rubbing the sore spot on her skull, Evangeline contemplated her luck. If Soeur Constanza and her companion had been a mere minute later, she might have committed herself to Danior's madness. But much as Danior might wish to, he couldn't command Soeur Constanza to leave them alone.

Torn between satisfaction and relief, Evangeline said, "You can't bully a nun."

He looked back at her, his gaze lethal, which she took as an agreeable sign that she'd annoyed him.

And of course, he couldn't let her savor her trivial victory for long. "You have the key, Soeur Constanza?"

The elderly nun lifted the heavy iron key dangling from an equally large and forbidding ring.

"We'll lock her in, then." He rose, took the key, and tried to slip it into his waistcoat pocket. The key could be wedged in; the ring could not.

Evangeline grinned. How lovely to see him frustrated about this, at least.

Soeur Constanza gestured at the young nun who stood behind her, eyes fixed downward in an excess of meekness. "We've brought food for Miss Scoffield in case she grows hungry during her incarceration."

Evangeline's grin faded. "Incarceration?" Nothing about this was really funny. They were going to lock her in.

"We also have a pallet for her which must be brought down," Soeur Constanza said. "Perhaps, sir, since you are the one who has made this unusual request, you could trouble yourself to carry it?"

"It's the least I can do." With a threatening frown at Evangeline, he followed Soeur Constanza.

Evangeline breathed a sigh of relief as he left.

"He *is* overpowering." The young nun seemed to read Evangeline's mind as she carried the tray into the room and placed it on a clear spot on the table. "He breathes all the air in a chamber."

"Yes. Yes, that's exactly it!"

The girl appeared to be sallow, but perhaps that was the effect of the unrelenting black robe and the long gray scarf over her head. Tufts of hair stuck out at her forehead, giving her a fey appearance, yet now that Danior had left she seemed sure of herself.

"Not that I'm in awe of him." Evangeline struggled to her feet. "Only he saps at my resolve, and he offers these nuggets of temptation . . . but you don't know about that."

"I'm a nun, not a saint." The nun lifted her gaze to Evangeline's.

Serephinian eyes. The memory of Danior's words jumped out at Evangeline. Serephinian eyes, just like her own.

Suspicion sharpened Evangeline's voice. "Who are you?"

"I'm Marie Theresia, a postulant here at the convent." She tucked her hands into her sleeves, looking totally at home with her impending vows of poverty and chastity. "Who are *you*?"

Evangeline's brief rush of conjecture died. The girl was almost a nun. "I'm Evangeline Scoffield of—" Exhaustion struck her hard. She'd been saying this for so long. No one believed her. Right now, she almost didn't believe herself. Sinking down again, she put her head on her knees. "I'm nobody."

"Nonsense." Marie Theresia pressed her palm to Evangeline's shoulder. "We are all somebody in God's eyes."

"No, we're not." Evangeline's breath puffed back into her face, and her skirt muffled her declaration. "Most of us are ardent nobodies, living forever in the shadow of a somebody because it's easy."

"But not you." Marie Theresia sounded as if she could read Evangeline's soul.

"No, not me. I recklessly struck out to become a somebody." Evangeline confessed her greatest sin. "All my life I prayed to be somebody."

"There's no shame in that."

"Yes, but I see now I should have been more specific."

Marie Theresia chuckled warmly. "Your companion seems to want you to be who you are."

Evangeline lifted her head. "Not who I am. Who he *thinks* I am."

Marie Theresia knelt before her, her round cheeks glowing. "God has brought you here, and *I* want you to be who you really are. Your companion will, too, someday."

"No, he won't. When he realizes who I really am and what he's done..." Evangeline cringed as she imagined the resulting outburst. Catching the little nun's hand, she begged, "Sister, would you help me get away?"

Marie Theresia tugged. "Away?"

"Yes. That man is half-crazy and half—" *Aroused.* "Well, he's half-crazy. He kidnapped me!"

"He did it for your own good." Those Serephinian eyes shone with admiration.

For that beast! Evangeline sat all the way up. "How do you know that?"

"This convent houses a few Frenchwomen, a few Spanish women, but most of us are Serephinian or Baminian." Marie Theresia clasped her hands together before her, and smiled a joyful smile. "We know who he is, and we know who you are."

Evangeline's mouth worked, but she had no words to say.

"Santa Leopolda's prophecy is coming true. With your help, our countries will be reunited at last."

"But I'm not the princess!"

Marie Theresia paid no attention. "It's destiny."

"But it's not *my* destiny."

"Everyone has a destiny. My destiny is to dedicate myself to God and renounce all worldly pleasures." For just a moment, a divine light shone from the young postulant's face. "Your destiny is to unite the Two Kingdoms, and you haven't much time to get back to Plaisance before Revealing. You have only three days."

"Three days?" Evangeline was horrified. "It can't be in three days!"

"I am not wrong about this. The Two Kingdoms have waited one thousand years for this particular celebration."

"Three days to Plaisance. Three days to marriage?" *To intimacy?* "Why didn't he tell me that?"

"I suppose he thought you knew. Besides, what difference would it make? With the revolutionaries after you, you have no choice but to go with the crown prince."

The defiant orphan answered. "I make my own choices." Especially now that she knew. Three days! Three days to escape Danior. She was in worse trouble than she had realized.

As Marie Theresia watched the proceedings, she walked to the window and tried to peer out. It was too high. She grabbed the edge of the long table. It weighed too much. Rapidly she removed the tools, the heavy coil of rope, the bag of rags. She peeked under the napkin that draped the tray and saw a small loaf of bread, a hunk of cheese, and wine. With the care engendered by an always hollow belly, she placed the tray on the floor against the wall.

She still couldn't budge the wretched slab of stout oak, and Evangeline glared at Marie Theresia. "Help me."

"As you wish." She went to the other end, and together they dragged the table to the window.

Evangeline climbed on it. Now she could see—and wished she couldn't. She looked out the back of the convent, and it was miles to the ground. Straight to the ground with hardly a bump or an outcrop in the entire, breath-stopping, stomach-tightening, sheer and terrifying drop.

Eleven

Evangeline sagged against the wide stone sill. She had a better chance of fashioning wings and flying like Icarus than climbing to freedom.

From behind her, Danior asked cheerfully, "Going to jump?"

She *did* jump, smacking the top of her head. She turned, and her gaze went right to him, just inside the doorway. There he stood, bulging with obnoxious strength, holding a cot with as little strain as he had carried her. The muscles in his neck corded as he balanced the wooden frame, but he was neither out of breath nor out of energy.

Damn him. The more exhausted she got, the more animated he seemed to be. It wasn't fair, and when she had slept about twenty-four hours straight, she would do something to turn the tables.

Behind him, Soeur Constanza held a mattress and bedclothes folded in her arms, and she stared as if Evangeline were making a fool of herself, perched up on the table.

And perhaps she was, but *she* refused to recognize

it. "No jumping today," she answered, and climbed off the table with as much gentility as she could manage.

Danior maneuvered the pallet against the wall. "There," he said, dusting his hands. "Miss Scoffield will be comfortable." He smiled at Marie Theresia, exerting a charm he hadn't bothered to exhibit for Evangeline.

The postulant didn't move. Instead, she watched him as if he were some alien creature from a world beyond her own. As Danior stared back, his smile disappeared and his brow knit.

At a sharp command from Soeur Constanza, Marie Theresia woke from her contemplation and hurried to help make the bed.

"Why was she staring at me?" he muttered.

"Because you're an ugly brute."

"No, that's not it," he answered without an ounce of concern. "The poor thing probably hasn't seen a real man for so long she's fascinated by me."

Evangeline sputtered with a laugh. "Do you even know the meaning of modesty?"

"What?" He spread his big hands in bewilderment. "Did I say something wrong?"

Unable to stop herself, Evangeline laughed again. "I guess that answered my question."

He gave an exasperated snort and pointed to the short stool again. "Soeur Constanza says they'll find you some boots for our walk tonight. I'll trace your feet for the size. Sit down."

"Don't you ever ask?" Evangeline inquired resentfully.

"That would get me nothing but a refusal." He

stepped toward her, and she sat down promptly. "No, it takes a firm hand to deal with you."

That statement brought both nuns' heads around, and they studied him as he knelt before Evangeline with a long, charred stick and a board to trace on.

His shoulders twitched, and he lowered his voice. "They're watching me again, aren't they?"

"They probably don't see a *real* man for weeks on end," she mocked quietly, "and when they do I doubt if it's as spoiled a man as you."

He slipped off her tattered slipper and placed her foot on the board with rather more vigor than the simple task required. "I am not spoiled. I am sober, hardworking, rational, and intelligent."

"Large, overweening, arrogant, and too sure of yourself."

He thought about that as he outlined her toes. "Yes," he decided. "All of those things. But not spoiled."

He ran the stick along her arch to her heel. Her breath caught. Her toes curled. Quickly, she relaxed the tiny, betraying movement.

With considerably less force, he removed her second shoe and placed it on the board. "I do not drink to excess, nor fight unless cornered, nor debauch innocents." A lock of black hair thawed the severity of his brow as he looked up at her, his position servile, his manner assured. "I am, in short, the husband of your dreams."

How he irritated her! Did he never think of anything but his goal? Did he have to turn every conversation into a crusade? "You're anything but short," she snapped.

Precisely, he outlined her other foot.

Without volition, her toes curled again. Immediately she moved to distract him. "They know you're the prince. That's why they watch you."

His hand tightened on her ankle. "They do not!"

"They think I'm the princess."

"You are." His grip eased. Sliding a glance over his shoulder, he found the nuns tucking up the last of the covers.

Evangeline could almost see his mind working, turning the knowledge to his advantage.

Standing, he handed the board to Soeur Constanza. "You're Serephinian."

"Yes, sir."

He glanced at the younger woman. "Both of you are. I can tell by your eyes. I know you understand how important it is that we get to Plaisance before Revealing. I treasure your assistance with the shelter, with the food, and with my dear princess's boots. Her every need is important to me, even though she, like all shy brides, balks at the wedding night."

Evangeline lurched to her feet. "I do not!"

The holy women twittered.

His smile sat ill on his rugged features. "Of course not, my love. That's why I have asked for a lock for your door—to contain your love for me."

"I never agreed to a wedding *day*, much less a wedding *night*."

"It's not necessary for a princess to agree. She knows her duty." The smile was gone, the sword of resolution unsheathed. "Now if these sisters will leave us, I would wash your dainty feet."

Her dainty feet were as gigantic as the rest of her, and she hated him for the mockery as well as for this relentless, ongoing single-mindedness.

The nuns scurried from the room. With the sign of blessing and a quick dip into a curtsy, Soeur Constanza pulled the door shut, leaving an echoing silence behind her.

Evangeline broke the silence, of course, broke it as quickly as she could. "I never expected them to leave us alone."

"Nor I." Danior managed to instill a fair amount of consternation in his tone as he dug through the piles of crockery. "Soeur Constanza has no romance if she thinks I would take you for the first time in a storage chamber."

The world tilted on its axis again, and Evangeline grabbed the edge of the table. Why did he have to say things like that, so casually, as if their alliance was assured? As if it had been foretold and was inevitable? "I'm not the princess," she whispered.

He stepped close to her, holding a cracked basin in one hand. "If I thought that were true"—he skimmed his thumb across her lower lip—"I still would not let you go."

Alarmed at the spark in his eyes, she moved backward and knocked the stool across the floor. The clatter embarrassed her.

He didn't notice. "Evangeline." He followed her, his voice was warm, savory, like plum pudding at Christmas. "You want to kiss me."

"I do not!" *She did, too.* During the night's long journey, she'd panicked about the danger, she'd moaned about her feet, she'd wished for more food, she'd wanted to wring Danior's neck, yet always, always the memory of his kiss had flavored her every thought. "Kissing you is the last thing I ought to do." She blinked. "*Want* to do."

One side of his mouth kicked up; half a grin, half amused at her denial. The other half . . . ah, that line of determination. He wanted her. That's what that expression meant.

And he thought he had every right to. He saw no reason for restraint.

His cobalt eyes blazed with the kind of fire she could warm herself by, if she dared. "I'm not the prin—"

He lifted the basin. She stumbled back one more step. The edge of the table struck her against the thighs. He reached past her and placed the basin on the table, and in one smooth transition wrapped his arms around her waist and swung her around.

Now their positions were reversed. He rested against the table, trapped by the length of her body resting against his. Only she didn't make the mistake of imagining he felt trapped. Quite the opposite. With his legs spread and his bottom resting on the tabletop, he had evened the difference in their heights. He'd tipped her off-balance, sprawled against him, breast to chest.

He'd managed to match their loins together in a most explicit manner.

He had no discretion at all. Of course, a man in his obvious state of arousal could not be discreet. But he could, perhaps, be a little more subtle.

She tried to get footing, scrabbled to move her hips away. He leaned back, slid one hand down to her flank and pressed her even more firmly against him. The other hand moved up under the fall of hair on her neck. He tugged gently, turning her fevered face up to his.

"Don't be embarrassed."

God knew he wasn't.

He went on, "I've been in this condition since I saw you enter that dining room at Château Fortuné. All heads turned to look at you, and you ignored them so disdainfully, just like the princess you deny you are."

Chills skimmed along the surface of her skin, racing from nerve to nerve and igniting response where she should be indifferent. "I was acting." Her hands curled against his shoulders; she tried to get her elbows beneath her to lever herself away.

He moved his hand around to the front of her neck, lifting her chin, examining her pulse, checking her flight. Reminding her he knew how to block any move she might make. "You *act* like a princess."

She'd seen him in candlelight, in moonlight, in darkness. Now she saw him in daylight, and the play of sun and shadow brought definition to his face, sculpting the craggy nose, the jutting brow, the dark growth of beard on his square jaw. Not handsome. Oh, no. Not princely or graceful, but an earthy man who desired her and saw no reason to dissemble.

"Evangeline." He whispered her name, holding her still as he brought his head forward. "Evangeline."

Her eyes widened, transfixed by the half-smile that lingered on his wide mouth.

And when he laid his lips against hers, she found that her faint, slack-jawed surprise allowed him to share her breath. Her eyes slid shut, weighed by tiredness, by resignation . . . by wonder.

Slowly, as if he were testing her, his tongue entered her mouth. The intimacy still shocked her, yet she liked the sample of him, rich with the mingled flavors of comforting barley and sweet apples.

She relaxed against him.

"Content to let me lead?" he asked against her mouth.

"Just this once." The brush of their lips resonated along unexplored nerve endings.

He clamped her closer, holding her in place. "I'll guide you true, Evangeline." Smoothing the hair away from her ear, he pressed her head onto his shoulder. "Comfortable?" He didn't wait for the answer. His lips persuaded hers again, opening her wider, relieving any lingering qualms with pleasure conscientiously applied.

And she liked it. She truly did. But it seemed very circumscribed, ardor that followed a formula. First, a press of the lips. Then a dab of tongue. Then a little more tongue. Then his broad hand sweeping down her neck to her breast . . .

She took a hard breath as he cupped her. Her eyes opened, and she looked into—his eyes.

They weren't closed. He watched each one of her fleeting joys with the satisfaction of a man who knew he'd performed well.

Oh, he did want her, she knew. His body didn't lie. But he wasn't driven by passion. He had himself under stern control, a prince seducing his princess into submission.

The *ass*.

The slab of body beneath her flinched, and he jerked his head back from hers. "Evangeline, your claws. You're digging into me."

"So I am." One by one, she removed her fingernails from the flesh above his collarbones. Then, driven by instincts newborn and squalling to be utilized, she tugged his shirt open and reached beneath it, to the abused skin, and massaged each wound with the flat of her hand. "I was overcome." She spread his shirt wider still, baring a ruffle of dark hair across the breastbone. She paused, fascinated and surprised, then pushed on to her goal. She'd marked his skin with five little crescents, and with an incoherent murmur of contrition, she laid her mouth on them in a leisurely kiss compounded in equal parts of moisture, breath, and reprisal.

Every muscle in his body went rigid, and from the corners of her eyes she checked his expression. His blue eyes flamed, his nostrils flared, his lips parted across teeth clenched against a surge of emotion. Then his hips lifted beneath her, and she knew that emotion to be passion.

This time, he wasn't in control.

Twelve

With both hands holding Evangeline's bottom, Dan-
ior lifted her, spread her legs around his hips, and
sealed them together.

She'd overwhelmed his restraint, all right. She'd
overwhelmed it too well.

Her skirt remained between them only because her
weight rested on it. Her feet lay on the table, her
hands clutched his shoulders. The position utterly
lacked dignity, and she didn't care. All she cared
about was the sudden hard pressure of him between
her legs. She hadn't known she wanted him there. She
did. His hands moved along her buttocks, pressing
them together, and she rocked against him, igniting
the same flame in her that scorched him.

Rational thought burned in the conflagration, leaving Evangeline at the mercy of this sweet agony. Heat
rolled through her in waves, linked to the thrust of
his hips, the taut glitter of his gaze, the strength she
experienced beneath her hands. This was like riding
a wild horse; she didn't know how to handle him, she
didn't know what he would do next, but each buck

and lunge carried her further along some unexplored path, and she wanted the journey to go on forever. Yet she sensed it couldn't, that somewhere there existed an ending that could satisfy her.

"Please, Your Highness, please . . ."

And as if the words brought him back to sanity, he stopped. She could almost see him reining in the passion, and she wanted to pound on him and shout, No!

But she didn't. She'd just discovered a well of passion in herself she hadn't suspected; the established wariness of a lifetime didn't allow her to exhibit any more of her emotions. Not until she understood them and where they would lead her. And then—maybe never.

"Why do you call me that?" he asked. His voice had a rasp to it, as if he'd run too far or fought too hard.

Tentatively she brought her legs around to the front of him. "Call you what?"

"Your Highness." He allowed her to slide down him.

It was an excursion fraught with peril, with the friction of two bodies already overheated with a mixture of passion and frustration. She didn't dare stop; she scarcely dared go on. She clung to the conversation, inane and aimless as it was, using it as a distraction. "You are a highness. Aren't you?"

"Not to you." Her toes touched the ground, yet he held her for one last moment. "To you, I am Danior."

Yes, he was. In her mind, he was. Not a prince, not a highness. Just Danior, a man she knew too well on too short an acquaintance. When she thought about how well, she couldn't meet his gaze, couldn't contain the blush that covered her whole body.

"Do you want me to let you go?" he asked.

Now she looked at him. "Yes!"

"Then, like you, I will demand that you call me by my name."

When your enemy is backed into a corner, that is the time to negotiate. Apparently, he had read the same sixteenth-century Italian mediator as she had.

Well, of course. He was a prince, and princes had to know the fine art of parlay.

"Danior," he prompted.

She couldn't ignore the hands that still held her against him, or the fact that his arousal had not subsided. One had to know when to admit defeat. "Danior."

Without gloating—he showed more control than she did—he helped her stand on her own. She stood swaying, her knees shaking, but he kept her close with his hands on her elbows. "Look at me," he said.

She didn't want to. To meet his eyes would be distressing and somehow dangerous.

"Afraid?" he asked.

Her gaze snapped to his. "Of you? No."

"Good. I don't want you to fear me."

His chin was set, his mouth was straight, his eyebrows knit over his serious eyes. If she were given to alarm, his expression would have sent her scurrying.

"I want you to realize how it will be between us. This marriage will not be polite and bloodless like most royal marriages. Like the marriages of both our parents. You and I have a fire between us, and what we'll do will be heated and sweaty and beyond our control." He corrected himself. "Beyond your control."

She didn't care for that. "What about your control?"

He smiled, a brief, restrained curve of the lips, and straightened. "I assure you, you wouldn't like it if I lost control."

"You just did!" He had. She knew he had.

"If I had totally lost control, my dear, you would be flat on your back with your legs in the air."

The crudity was somehow more menacing for his lack of inflection, but he calmly picked her up and moved to the bed. He sat her down, and her heart gave a thud. Was he going to join her after all? It would be adventure, just as she wanted, but she now knew the danger was too great. A beast lurked within him, cloaked by a thin layer of civilization. He even admitted it.

And something lurked within her, too. A wanton? A madwoman? A woman so driven by loneliness that she responded to the first man who touched her?

She pulled her legs up to her chest, shut her eyes, and wished she were back in East Little Teignmouth, ruining her vision as she pored over an ancient, blotted manuscript in safe solitude.

Instead she heard a splash of water, and looked to see Danior filling the cracked basin from the bucket. He came back to her, sure, silent, almost kind, and set the basin on the floor. Sticking out his hand, he said, "Give me your foot."

She stared at him, then at his empty palm, without comprehension.

"Your foot, Evangeline."

She didn't understand him. Not at all.

Grasping her ankles, he straightened her legs to dangle off the edge of the mattress. As efficiently as a nursemaid, he reached to her knee, untied her garters, and stripped her hose away. If this was seduction, he didn't know how to go about it, she decided.

Dipping her foot in the water, he used a rag from the ragbag to wash the calluses and leathery soles that should have proved she was not a princess but a woman who walked where she had to. He didn't seem to see that, but shook his head over the bruises. "We'll have you boots before we start again, I promise, and some thick socks to protect this delicate skin."

Her toes curled as he stroked across her sensitive arch, and she took back her condemnation of his seductive abilities. This service could prove beguiling if she let it. "Why are you doing this?"

Placing her foot in his lap, he dried it and reached for the other. "Washing your feet?"

"Washing my feet, giving me food, carrying me on your back. Why should you be so kind to someone you think is a runaway princess?"

She thought he wasn't going to answer, he paused so long.

But when he did, she wished she hadn't asked.

"Because I want you dependent on me for everything—the air you breathe, the food you eat, the water you drink." His voice hummed with intensity, his dark brows drew together, and his eyes lured her to believe. "When you marry me, I will give you everything."

"I can't marry you. I'm not the princess." But her voice faltered.

"Your Royal Highness, it's time to drop this facade

of independence and remember who will be your strength for the years to come."

She swallowed, her independence threatened, not by him but by her own weakness. God help her, she had lost everything—her money, her clothing, her home. She didn't know what she was going to do now, and this man was offering her an easy solution. Go and be the princess, no one will ever know, and she would have someone else to depend on besides herself.

Danior must have been watching her, and seen too clearly the longing etched on her face. "That's it," he murmured. "Give in. It'll be easy, you'll see."

"Easy until the real princess shows up." Evangeline offered her up like an offering on a silver salver. "Sooner or later you need to find out where she is."

"I have her." He touched the middle of her forehead with the flat of his thumb, and she felt too clearly the calluses caused by experience and hard work. "I'll addict you to the taste of me, to my scent and touch. When I'm done with you, you'll be bound to me by the strongest fetter in my forge."

She suspected she didn't want to know, but she had to ask. "What is that?"

"Passion." Still on his knees, he leaned over her and brushed a final, intimate kiss on her lips. "You'll depend on me for passion."

Thirteen

You'll depend on me for everything, Evangeline. You'll depend on me for passion.

Evangeline woke to find herself clutching the pillow between her legs. But a sack of feathers was no substitute for Danior, and she was no substitute for his princess.

Angry, aroused and dismayed, she sat up on the cot. This had never happened before. Never. Nobody else's kisses—not that there had been many—but none of them had excited her enough to weasel their way into her dreams. She'd read about *amour*. Mrs. Ann Radcliffe wrote novels of terror and mystery, and the youthful Evangeline had been addicted to them. *A Sicilian Romance* had thrilled her to her curling toes and *The Mysteries of Udolpho* made her swoon with adolescent delight.

But this . . . this was something else. Obsession or passion or . . . Danior's fault. Yes, this was all Danior's fault! And if she didn't get away from him there would be dire consequences.

Like she'd give in and go to his bed, and he'd find

out she wasn't the princess and abandon her. Or worse, he wouldn't realize she wasn't the princess until it was too late, and all chance of uniting Serephina and Baminia would perish.

The fate of two countries rested on her ability to get herself out of this convent and far out of Danior's reach. Perhaps then when he searched, he would find the real princess.

And Evangeline knew how to escape. She closed her eyes to shut out the sight she wished to ignore.

A coil of rope. The iron ring from the key. A likely sized window, unencumbered by locks, protected by the sheer drop below it. And her own endurance and knowledge.

She was no fair flower of the nobility to be protected and cherished. She was an orphan child, and on her knees she felt the calluses she'd earned through years of scrubbing orphanage floors. Her hands were the same, callused beneath each finger. She owned many fine pairs of gloves—or had, until that blast in her room, and she could blame Danior for that, too—and she liked them for more than the genteel air they gave her. They also hid the proof of her common upbringing.

And her knowledge—all of it lurked there in the periphery of her mind.

She knew how to descend the cliff on that rope. The native Swiss did it to rescue those who strayed too far from the beaten path and fell, mostly goats, although there were a few humans—those mad Englishmen who traveled the country on their Grand Tour. Evangeline knew this because Leona had corresponded with one of the Swiss mountaineers.

Evangeline had reveled in Leona's foreign correspondence. Each letter that had come through her hands, each word she had translated had lodged in her brain, and she had been proud of her memory before. Now that proficiency was likely to get her killed.

How long had she slept? How much time did she have?

She hastened to the window and climbed on the table.

The afternoon light cast the tower's shadow across the meadow and into the trees, emphasizing its height, underscoring the need to hurry, and showing that, without a doubt, the drop was just as sheer as she remembered.

She glanced at the door. There were less dangerous ways to escape. She knew how to pick a lock, and that sharp, narrow implement used to dig weeds would easily fit in the keyhole. But if she succeeded, what would that earn her? Nothing, if Marie Theresia was telling the truth. If everyone here in the convent really thought she was the princess and the savior of their countries, then when they saw her sneaking across the entry they would block the outer door until someone could call Danior.

She looked out at the window again and caught her breath at the vista spread out so far below. Sadly, having Danior stop her from escaping seemed the ideal solution right now.

That was not acceptable.

Picking up the coil of rope and a pair of rusty pruning sheers, she chopped a length long enough to wrap around her twice. With that, she fashioned a crude seat, and tied it onto the iron ring. She wrapped the contraption around her. The seat would bear her weight as she moved down, protecting her from a fall that would leave her mangled and bloody.

"That would serve him right." She slapped the seat on the table, then dragged the remaining coil of rope to the stone column, tied it—she knew how to do that knot, too—and slipped the other end out of the window, hoping against hope the rope wouldn't reach the ground.

After all, she couldn't go then, but her conscience would be clear. She would have tried.

Whispering a prayer, she leaned out and looked.

The contemptible rope lapped at the highest boulders surrounding the base of the cliff. From there she could climb to the ground and make her escape, and her heart jolted with a mixture of fear and anticipation.

Stupid thing, anticipation, but she wasn't afraid of heights, only of falling, and if the seat worked as described, she would not fall. No, she'd have the adventure of her life.

She dragged the rope back up, all the long way back up, and placed it beside the seat and the ring. Wiping her sweaty palms on her chemise, she donned her petticoats and her green gown, trying futilely to smooth the wrinkles away. And when she saw the series of little rents created by the brambles, tears welled in her eyes.

The gown had cost her over two hundred pounds, an unbelievable sum, and to a woman in dire need of adventure worth every pence. The silk had flowed across her body like a dream, making her almost believe she was, in truth, a princess. She loved it for what it represented—wealth, freedom, and a frivo-

lous dream she dared pursue. Now the dress was ruined.

Well. She straightened her shoulders. There would
be other gowns. Valiantly she ignored the fact that she
no longer had two hundred pounds, nor two pounds,
nor even a ha'penny. Leaving here was an act of courage for more than one reason. A woman in her straits
could be sent to the workhouse.

She tied the garters that held her thin silk stockings,
then pulled on her slippers. The sole of one was almost gone, battered by last night's flight, but she
couldn't wait for the new pair of boots promised to
her. Especially since she had the strong idea Danior
would want to place them on her feet himself.

You'll depend on me for everything.

Terrifying words, for she wanted to depend on
Danior.

The day was waning. By the look of the shadows,
it was after five o'clock. Danior would be in with supper soon; she knew it like she knew her own name.
"Evangeline Scoffield of East Little Teignmouth,
Cornwall," she announced to the walls. Taking the
bread and cheese from the tray, she tied her makeshift
supper in a clean rag from the ragbag. That she fastened around her waist. Taking up the goblet, she
gulped down the wine and hoped the spirits would
dull her pounding dread.

The seat had to wrap around her waist and tie into
the ring—not a problem. And between her legs and
into the ring—a big problem. Gently she cherished the
gown's fine silk between her palms. Ruthlessly, she
found a tear in the front and with a quick jerk, ripped
the skirt up to her knees. She repeated the procedure
at the back, then trussed her petticoats all the way up

around her waist and her gown almost that high. Her calves were showing, but who would see them?

She found gardening gloves and donned them. She tied herself into the seat, the ring in front, then looped the long rope through and leaned against it. The knot at the column stretched and held. The knots of the seat stretched and held, and the length of rope slipped through the ring. She could control it with the grip of her hands. This was going to work. It had to work.

Grimly, she sat on the wide stone of the windowsill, then inched backward. She maneuvered one leg out— into nothing. Nothing was up this high except for a light breeze, laden with the smell of freedom. She gritted her teeth. Getting out the window was the worst part, she assured herself. Even if she fell she could catch herself with the grip of her hands. All this would take was a little courage.

Too bad her stock of *that* had been so depleted.

Her knee slipped off the edge and scraped across the rough stone. Then she lay on her stomach and worked her other leg free. Slowly, she slid backward until she dangled, held up only by her increasingly frail-looking arms. Pulling her feet up, she placed them flat against the outer wall, her knees bent to her chest. She would straighten her legs when she started. When she let go.

Slowly, she released one hand. The rope held more of her weight now. She hung, attached to the building by a death grip, with one arm. The moment had come, the moment when she must signify her trust in the rope, the knots she'd produced, and the Swiss mountaineer's knowledge. She looked at her hand, fingers clenched around the sill, tendons on the back raised and taut. She looked at her arm, saw the muscles bulging with the strain of holding her weight. *Just let go*, she told herself. *You'll be all right.*

And if not, the prayers over her body would be many and immediate, because she'd scream all the way down.

On that resolve, she released her hold and snatched at the loose end of rope.

She didn't fall. She hadn't fallen. She let her breath out with a whoosh.

Cautiously she straightened her legs so that her body formed an L, then she took her first tentative step down. The rope held steady. She took another, and another. The rock wall was almost smooth beneath her feet. The distance between her and the window widened, and she wasn't foolish enough to look down. Her knees trembled as she walked down the wall, but that nuisance was minor compared to her growing exhilaration. This was fun. This was adventure. *This* was what she'd dreamed of!

Tossing prudence to the wind, she pushed both her feet against the wall and gave a big bounce, just as the mountaineer had described. For a moment, it was like flying, a pure birdlike release from the autocracy of gravity.

Then her hand slipped. Her breath lurched. She grabbed hard, catching herself before she gained too much speed. Her feet struck stone and she skidded to a stop, her toes bent inside her slippers, her soles scraping along the weathered rock. She hung, trembling, and risked a glance down.

The boulders at the base of the tower were both too far and too close. From this height, they probably wouldn't kill her, but they would break every bone in her body.

Then she looked up. She was more than halfway down. Her hands burned inside her gloves, and she tried no more mountain goat leaps. Instead she descended steadily, her sense of triumph expanding with each step. She looked down occasionally now, and each time the boulders appeared closer. Closer.

They were here. She walked her legs down the wall and onto the flat surface of a rock. Her knees were shaking, she noted. Blisters throbbed on her palms, and somehow during the climb a sharp edge had sliced through one of her soles; the bottom of her foot was bleeding.

But she was down. She had made it. Her fingers shook in delayed cowardice as she worked to free herself from the knots, and she kept glancing up at the window, sure Danior would stick his head out and roar at her.

She mocked herself for giving him credit for intuition when the man didn't have an intuitive bone in his body. Yet in his determination to bring the princess back to Serephina, he had assumed almost mythical proportions to her.

The last knot gave way, and she allowed herself one quiet shout of glee. Then, using her battered hands and feet, she climbed off the boulders and jumped onto the grassy meadow that surrounded the convent. Falling to her knees, she kissed the blessedly level earth. Rising, she walked backward toward the edge of the forest, staring, amazed, at the rope dangling from the window so high above.

She was here. She was free. She had succeeded!

Turning, she ran toward the shadow of the trees.

Right into the arms of the revolutionaries.

Fourteen

Danior stared up at the rope dangling from the storeroom, down the sheer cliff and into a coil on the ground.

Rafaello stood beside him, his complexion blanched, his gaze fixed on the wicked boulders scattered at the base of the tower. "The princess is mad."

"More than mad." Danior shoved the lock of hair off his forehead. She was crazy, insane, totally feckless and without concern for her own safety.

"We could have found her at the bottom." Rafaello turned even paler. "All bloody and whimpering . . ."

"Don't think about it," Danior said. As usual, Rafaello was squeamish. Unusually, Danior found himself to be a little squeamish at the thought of *her*, lying broken and lifeless . . .

Danior used to think he understood women. In fact, he had flattered himself into believing he understood them very well. On the whole they were a simple gender, delighted by little tokens of affection and awed by a man's wisdom and attentions.

Some men disagreed with Danior. Victor told him

bluntly that women only acted amiably because he was a prince. Victor said that when women were on a manhunt, they dissembled and simpered. After a man had been bagged, he claimed, they became bold and disrespectful.

But that didn't explain Ethelinda.

She hadn't bagged him. Quite the opposite. Just to evade him, she'd run like a fawn into the most hideous danger. When had the gentle girl changed so much? He remembered her well, all smiling grace and amiable goodness, obedient and mild . . . and somehow she'd become this termagant.

This woman.

He had never been particularly enthralled with marrying a Serephinian. His country and hers had quarreled for generations, and every good Baminian knew that Serephinians were light-minded, interested only in the trivial, and given to unsteady morals. Yet the prophecy had correctly predicted both his birth and Ethelinda's, and the people of both kingdoms had taken that as a sign that the terms of Revealing would come to pass. In his youth, Danior rather relished being the one on whom all hopes were pinned. Now he was older, the responsibility weighed on him, and he was impatient to reign—over *two* kingdoms.

If only the woman Evangeline would cooperate!

At Château Fortuné, he had pursued her to her bedchamber, listened to her ineptly told tale, then tried to seduce her.

Stupidity. He'd frightened the girl with his impetuous appetite, an appetite that had taken even him by surprise.

But my God, if he could have had her, he now would have been glad for it. She wouldn't have descended that rope, risking her life and falling into rebel hands.

Instead, she would be in his arms, contented from his lovemaking, and, when he was done stroking the shell of her ear, kissing the wide sweep of her mouth, suckling on those magnificent breasts, she would be looking forward to the next lovemaking.

His frustration at his own stupidity made his blood race, and deliberately, he turned his mind away. By Santa Leopolda, she was *not* hurt. She was only captured, and that because she had been reckless and wayward. He should have suspected her plan, but . . . with his gaze, he measured the distance between the window and the ground.

No. He never should have suspected *this*.

When had Ethelinda become the kind of woman who would climb down a cliff to escape her true destiny? He rubbed a tight muscle in his neck. To escape *him*.

Damn the girl!

"Master." Victor knelt at the edge of the forest, his face bent close to the ground as he examined the footprints crushed into the young grass. "Four men were here, but come and look at this."

Vibrating with anger and fear, Danior strode to Victor's side.

"A bloody footprint. She cut herself on the rocks on the way down. As long as they make her walk, and as long as she keeps bleeding, we can follow."

Danior looked into the darkening forest. It would be evening soon. The shadows were lengthening, and the kidnappers had an hour's head start on them. But Victor was the best tracker in Baminia, and he would find Ethelinda somehow.

Then it would be up to Danior to free her.

A kerchief fluttered in the breeze, caught on a bush's branch. Below, a chunk of cheese lay smashed, and a loaf of bread was covered with ants. "She lost her dinner. She'll be hungry." A thought that unduly distressed him. For all the slenderness of her waist, Ethelinda had shown a surprising dedication to her dinner. He had thought to lure her with the promise of his chef's skill; he did not like to think of her hungry. "We need supplies."

"We'll have them." Victor straightened and pointed to a contingent of four nuns approaching from the convent.

Soeur Constanza walked in the lead, carrying a pair of boots, socks stuffed into each one. Marie Theresia assisted an old nun, hobbling and bent. And a young nun led a donkey laden with traveling bags.

Danior had admitted his identity to the good sisters, and now he was reaping the benefit. They were coming to his rescue. "We can't use the donkey," he decided. "It'll slow us down."

To his surprise, the old nun heard him and lifted her head. Her voice sounded clear across the distance, and her blue eyes pierced him. "It's not for you, young prince, but for us. We're making our pilgrimage to Plaisance."

Danior stared over Soeur Constanza's head at the old woman. "In the midst of a revolution?"

"No one can hurt me. I go with God's authority."

"You could wait."

She smiled slowly, as if his ignorance amused her. "Regardless of any danger, Your Highness, all of your subjects will be leaving their homes and making for

Plaisance. You know well that in three nights, the moon will be full."

It was true. After the night of the full moon, the day would dawn that had been prophesied a thousand years ago by Santa Leopolda herself, and Danior knew his people would crawl to Plaisance to witness the miracle. Yet the holy lady wasn't taking his advice to stay home, nor was she offering to help him, and his princess had been kidnapped.

Dominic would hold Evangeline, waiting for Danior to come after her, and when he had them they'd be tried at a sham tribunal for the crime of being royal.

Danior had to get her before Dominic reached his stronghold. "There won't be a Revealing if I don't find the princess."

"There won't be a Revealing if *we* don't get to Plaisance, either," the nun answered without a speck of deference to his position as her prince. "You'll need a blessing, my prince, before you can open the crystal case."

Something regal in her manner reduced him to the role of sulky boy in knee breeches, and he replied rather more sharply than he should. "If you are not there to bless us, I'm sure the archbishop will be glad to substitute."

"Whether *I* am there matters not a bit, and the archbishop, you'll find, will not be able to help you in your need."

He didn't understand her, and he didn't care for the way her lids drooped or the barely visible gleam of intelligence in her eyes. She knew something. The old woman knew something he didn't know, and she relished her insight and his ignorance in a manner that lifted his hackles. And every moment he spent arguing, Evangeline slipped closer to a trial and execution.

The old nun must have read his thoughts, for she demanded, "Why are you dallying with me? You should be rescuing your princess. She has been lost before; you dare not lose her again." She pointed a crooked finger at Soeur Constanza, who lifted a bulging bag from the donkey. "Soeur Constanza will give you the lady's boots, and some supplies, as many as you can carry and still move quickly."

She offered help, yet this old woman who had spent her life in the convent was telling him how to outfit his expedition, and while she was none too tactful, she was furnishing the inventory, and the bag looked like the size he would have packed.

Stiff with reluctant gratitude, he stood with his hands hanging by his side. "You're most generous."

"Take the boots," the old nun commanded. "Take them."

Soeur Constanza lifted his hands and placed the boots in them, then turned and handed the sack to the silent Victor.

"Find she who would be your queen." In a voice that allowed no doubt, the old nun said, "There'll be no other chance."

The little party moved along, and the first whisper of old wives' tales winnowed into his mind. Tales of the holy woman who had foreseen the schism of her beloved countries, taken their treasures, and uttered the prophecy that drove him in his quest today.

As Soeur Constanza moved to join the little band, Danior caught her arm. "Who is she?" he asked.

"Our mother superior."

"And?"

In the tone she had used to announce dinner, Soeur Constanza said, "A thousand years ago the saint came to live among us, and she is with us still."

"The saint," he repeated, not believing it, not daring to disbelieve.

"Of course. Our mother superior is the living incarnation of Santa Leopolda."

His paralysis allowed her to break free.

With a lift of her snub little nose, she straightened her robes and strode away.

Stunned, he watched them as they found the path to Plaisance. The mother superior—Santa Leopolda, if he believed Soeur Constanza—turned as she entered the woods, and across the distance he saw the spark and the warning in her gaze.

Recalled to his duty, he hurried in the other direction, after his lost princess.

Fifteen

For one horrified moment, Evangeline thought Dan-
ior had watched her descend from the tower and now
held her in his arms. Danior—but in a scarf that covered the lower part of his face. But this man's frigid
blue eyes crinkled as he smiled with genuine amusement, and Danior, she knew without a doubt, would
not be entertained at her escapade. Nor would he be
holding her so tightly that he bruised her.

"Your Highness." The man spoke cultured Baminian in a voice as low and warm as melted honey.
"How good of you to come out to meet us."

The rebel Dominic. She opened her mouth to
scream. Off to the side, she saw a flash of steel, and
someone jumped at her with a bare blade. "Die, princess," a man's voice rasped.

Dominic swung her away. "Not yet."

Two tall men, the other members of the party,
shoved their short, knife-wielding companion aside.
"Let's get away from here first, fool."

"Wait." As they hustled her into the forest, Evangeline dug her heels into the mixture of humus and
pine needles beneath her feet.

Dominic wrenched her arm to keep her abreast of him.

"Wait! You don't understand. I'm not the—"

Shorty attacked from the side and smacked her across the face. "Shut up."

Without a thought, Evangeline kicked him between the legs. He went down like a lead weight. For a moment she thought his companions would surely kill her, but the two tall men burst out laughing. She scarcely dared look at Dominic, but when she did she found his frigid gaze fixed on her, observing her, weighing her.

This man hated her with an intensity that shook her to the bone, and that gave her the impetus to do what she had to. Dropping to her knees, she hunched over the purple, squirming Shorty. "I'm so sorry." She wrung her hands. She clutched at his shirt. "Did I hurt you? I didn't mean to hurt you." She grappled with his belt, playing the role of the woman appalled at her own temerity and all the while thanking God for the friends she'd made at the orphanage. The ones who had picked pockets on the street.

Gasping, Shorty held his groin and glared at her.

"Is it bruised? Let me see." In an artlessly inadvertent movement, she slammed her fist against his hand.

He howled and squeezed his eyes shut.

And she lifted a weapon from his belt and slipped it into her bosom, then wrung her hands close by her chest in what she hoped looked like ladylike distress. "Please forgive me. I'm just so clumsy."

That sent the hyenas into new paroxysms of hilarity.

"Yes, interesting." Dominic lifted her to her feet, tied her hands in front of her, and yanked her on a leading rope through the brush. The two hyenas had followed, laughing more as she protested that she wasn't the princess, they had the wrong woman, and why didn't they let her go? Dominic ignored her, releasing branches to slap her face until she quieted.

After about a half hour, they heard a thrashing behind them, and Shorty puffed up behind them.

He walked with a limp now, and he carried a grudge. "Kill her."

He shoved Evangeline's shoulder, and she stumbled on the rocky ground. The cut on her heel opened again. The blood was sticky against her skin, and sand shifted into the hole in her heel.

"Kill her," he repeated. "She's useless. Look, she can't even walk."

"Please, kill me," Evangeline said. "That wouldn't be the worst thing that's happened to me lately."

Clearly unimpressed with her bravado, Dominic kept walking, dragging her along. "She's our bait for the prince, and when we have them both, we'll purge the country of royalty."

They traveled for hours. Dominic, Shorty, and the two bodyguards passed through the underbrush, their brown leather breeches and vests blending with the forest. Each one carried a primitive musket, a long knife, and enough gunpowder hung in sacks from their belts to blow up a city. Despite the weight of their arsenal, they walked without a sound.

Not Evangeline. She gasped in the thin air. Her side had a stitch. Her aching calves told her they had been ascending steadily. The trees of the forest were tall and mighty in the lower elevations, but the higher the little band went, the more the thinning trees struggled to survive. Short and withered, they showed the wear

of constant wind in their branches, and each defor-
mity was more grotesque than the next. Thoughts of
enchanted forests, of hoary evils that lived beneath
bark and limb, crowded Evangeline's mind.

Then they rose above the tree line, and towering
boulders watched like ancient giants. Sweat beaded
her brow from her exertions, yet the wind struck chill,
and she shivered convulsively. No thought of escape
entered the exhausted recesses of her mind. All she
knew was that she needed to rest.

But she couldn't because of the despot who led
them tirelessly. That despot who put her through this
torture. Dominic.

Shorty shoved her again and cackled when she fell
to her knees. "Some princess."

"Am not," Evangeline muttered. She felt as if she'd
been denying a royal heritage forever. And with the
same results.

She was ignored.

Shorty said, "Look at her, weak and whiny. She
can't keep up with us. She's accustomed to luxury.
Kill her, Dominic, and put her out of her misery."

Dominic waited while she dragged herself to her
feet again. "She's smart enough to want to get away
from Danior. That alone makes her of interest to me."

She didn't want to be of *interest* to them. She especially didn't want to be of interest to *him*.

Darkness had already come to the lower elevations,
and the sun's rays crept up toward them bringing the
promise of a cold night. They headed straight for a
barren cliff, chiseled by the winds that blew off the
snow-capped peaks, its only decoration a series of rib-
bonlike waterfalls cascading down from the glaciers.
Mammoth crags clustered at the base, then spread

across the landscape like a giant's building blocks, and dirty patches of snow huddled in their shadow. The site was ugly, detached and hard, just like the men who surrounded her.

One of the hyenas tweaked her hair. "If you're going to take her to the lair, at least cover her eyes."

"Why?" Shorty's eyes shone with fanaticism, and he moved like a weasel, his body constantly in motion. "She won't be coming out again."

The hyenas laughed, and Evangeline blinked away a rush of weak tears. Her feet hurt, her face ached where Shorty had hit her, her wrists were raw from Dominic's rope, she was desperately thirsty, and no one cared. Victor and Rafaello had treated her well because they thought she was the princess. These men treated her crudely for exactly the same reason.

"I thought Robin Hood lived in a forest," she mumbled in English.

"Robin Hood was a fool. Give money to the poor! Better he should have spent it to overthrow the king," Dominic answered in English, without looking back.

She was glad. If he'd seen her astonishment, he'd have laughed at her again, and she found his bitter amusement harder to take than blows. He spoke English, and he knew an obscure English legend. How? He was both more casual and more dangerous than the other men. He frightened her to the depths of her soul.

A bird called nearby, and Evangeline's head swiveled to catch sight of it.

Ugly bird. It was Shorty, lips pursed, wrinkled throat vibrating as he produced the most beautiful call she'd ever heard.

"I keep him for a reason." Dominic spoke to her as

if to an equal, while treating her like a despised prisoner.

Pebbles skittered down one of the towering slabs of rock, and a boy of about fifteen slid into their path. He was dirty and ragged, a scarf hung loose around his neck, but his eyes gleamed and his teeth shone sharply. "You got her."

And it wasn't a boy, Evangeline realized, but a girl.

"Did you ever doubt it?" Shorty asked.

"No," the girl said, but her worshipful gaze was fixed on Dominic.

Dominic reached out and ruffled her short hair. "Good to see you, brat."

The girl beamed.

"Now, pull up your kerchief."

"It itches." But she obeyed, dragging the rough wool over her fine features. "Anyway, she's not leaving here."

The tether must have jerked in Dominic's hand, for he said, "You didn't think we could let you go, Your Highness?"

"I'm not the princess," she said for the thousandth, millionth time.

"Then no one will care when we slit your throat, will they?" he answered smoothly.

She wished he would stop smiling. "This is the second time I've been kidnapped in two days."

"Then nothing should come as a surprise." Passing her tether to Shorty, he strode forward to the men stepping out from a crevasse in the central cluster of boulders.

They glanced at her, but their gazes returned worshipfully to Dominic. They slapped him on the shoulder, spoke in congratulatory tones, but for all their camaraderie it was clear he was the center of their universe. This man led their rebellion.

Then he presented her with a wave and a sardonic bow, and they let loose a cacophony of catcalls and huzzahs. They strolled toward her, surrounding her like a pack of prowling wolves, pinched her cheeks, her breasts, her rump, and laughed uproariously as she tried to cover herself. Her helplessness reminded her of the orphanage, but not even there had the humiliation been so great. When she slapped at their hands, they slapped back, stinging her with their amusement and making her wish she could flatten them all.

But there were too many to fight, and if she tried, they would know she should be watched. She'd already made a mistake with Shorty; she dared not make another one.

So she whimpered and whirled, trying to confront each one of the circle of faces that moment by moment grew more vicious.

Then that clear, warm, generous voice said, "Enough."

The torment halted as suddenly as it had begun.

"Bring her here."

Shorty jerked on her tether, breaking through the chafed skin on her wrists and gloating as if each drop of blood sizzled with his revenge. He shoved her forward to stand in front of Dominic.

"Now you know." Dominic looked at her, no longer smiling, his eyes blue and frozen as the glacier on the heights above. "Stay quiet and we'll judge you and perhaps give you a quick death. Try to escape, and we'll pluck your eyes out and leave you as carrion."

"But . . . why?"

"You dare ask that, between the harm the old king and your mother did? These people are my people. They have suffered, and they remember." The last gleam of sunset draped the clouds in royal purple and crimson, and lit the cruel, sharp face above the scarf. "The sins of the father, my dear . . ."

"I'm not the princess."

"You're consistent, I'll say that for you." Dominic snapped his fingers, and his people rushed to surround him. He handed her tether to the fifteen-year-old. "Here, brat. Tie her to the post and keep an eye on her. She's not as stupid as she looks."

Brat visibly drooped. "We're not going to kill her now?"

That hateful smile appeared on Dominic's face again, and he mocked, "She'll want to die with her prince."

The girl perked up. "Have we captured him, too?"

"Captured His Royal Highness the Crown Prince Danior?" His head thrown back, Dominic laughed aloud. "That is surely beyond even our feeble capacity. No, we'll let him come to us. Victor is the best tracker in the two kingdoms, and the non-princess left ample proof of her passing. Her shoe is torn and her foot is bleeding."

He knew. He knew how Evangeline had suffered, and he had been glad because it had furthered his cause.

She had thought he looked like Danior. He didn't look anything like Danior. Danior could never look so callous.

"No one's to touch her. No one's to hurt her." Dominic looked around at the men, but his contempt lashed at Evangeline. "She's not worth our spit. I want every first-shift man watching for His Royal Greatness. You're not to interfere with his progress. Every second-shift man should be resting, preparing for the capture and our tribunal. Remember, the prince is a fighter, too, trained by Napoleon just as we were. Now get to your positions. Tonight will win all."

Half the men scattered into the gathering darkness. Dominic, Shorty, and the bodyguards led the other half through the stone-lined crevice. The girl followed them, and of necessity, Evangeline followed her.

The narrow, crooked path led them around through the stones and into an open space against the cliff. A low fire burned in the middle of a rough circle formed by more stones, some stuck straight up, taller than Dominic's head. Some were scattered and toppled to lay flat and spread with blankets. A corner was formed where a particularly tall crag shouldered up against the cliff. A pole stuck out of the ground, and Brat led her there.

Impassively, she tied Evangeline's hands close to the pole and left her. With a low groan, Evangeline sank to the ground. Just sitting was the greatest pleasure she'd ever experienced. She lifted her foot and squinted at her sole, but it was too dark to see more than the dark blot where the blood had oozed out. Not that it mattered. A shudder shook her as pain, chill, and dread jerked at her tightly strung nerves.

Unless she did something, something dramatic, she was going to die.

She didn't want to die cold, thirsty, and hungry, and most especially not if it made that heartless bastard happy. And for the first time since she'd been

forced to flee the burning château, she wasn't address-
ing her wrath toward Danior.

"Build up the fire. Give the royal party an easy tar-
get." Dominic roamed the encampment, blending
with the darkness yet drawing the eye with his dy-
namic energy. He spoke to his men, laid a carelessly
kind hand on Brat's head. Everyone smiled as he
walked past; they adored him, but Evangeline leaned
against the pole and hated him with her gaze. Inevitably, he noticed. His eyes crinkled in that offensive
smile, and he strolled over and sketched a humble
bow. "Are our headquarters all you could wish?"

She ought to be polite. She ought to debase herself
in hopes of mercy. But she didn't believe he had any,
so she snapped, "Your headquarters are fine. Your
hospitality suffers."

He placed his hand over his heart. "You have
crushed me to the bone. What do you desire, Your
Highness? A truffle, perhaps? Marzipan? A carafe of
fine wine?"

"Water." Her tongue felt swollen in her mouth. "I'd
like a drink of water."

He dropped his toady's mask. "Why should we
bother?"

"It won't advance your cause if I die miserable."

His eyebrows twitched together, and he examined
her as if something didn't add up. "You're no fragile
flower." He tapped his leg with his fingers. "All right.
You can have your water."

As he turned away, she said, "And bread. And
stew."

He looked back. "Greedy."

"Hungry."

And cold. She watched as he spoke to one of the

bodyguards. He didn't get an argument, but the rebel did no more than walk close and toss her his boda bag. Her numb fingers fumbled and dropped it. Shorty lounged by the fire, and he laughed as she snatched it up and poured the thin stream of water down her throat.

She didn't really expect food, too, but when she looked up, Brat stood offering her a steaming bowl.

"There's no spoon, Your Highness." Brat gave the title the same sneering intonation as her leader had.

A chunk of bread floated atop the broth, and as Evangeline grabbed the wooden bowl she said, "I'll use the bread."

Brat looked startled, but Evangeline knew how to make do. Those worthy people who endowed English orphanages seldom saw the need to coddle the children with unnecessary implements.

The warmth of the earthenware bowl seeped into her frozen hands, and she whispered, "I would use the palm of my hand if I had to."

Tearing off a chunk of bread, she dragged it through the stew and brought up something brown and something white, and greedily consumed them. Rabbit and turnip, slightly scorched, totally unflavored, boiled in water. She had read much fancier recipes in Mrs. Buxton's personal collection of Cornish recipes in East Little Teignmouth, but Evangeline didn't really care. The plump Mrs. Buxton had never had occasion to realize how hunger added spice to a stew. Right now, Evangeline would have eaten anything.

The food put new heart in her, and she scanned the camp again. A good number of the men had bedded down, although they weren't asleep. They spoke in low tones to each other, the habit of furtiveness well established.

The fire burned too far away for her to reach, and she desperately needed to get closer. That Dominic had granted her wish for food and drink boded well for her. If she could get him to bestow a last wish for a doomed woman, perhaps she wouldn't be doomed after all.

Or perhaps she would; she planned a desperate endeavor about which she had no practical experience.

The decision came too soon. Before she had finished half the stew, she heard a bird call and saw every person in the rough enclosure pause. Dominic smiled that cruel smile and started toward the stones. "They have him."

"Wait!" Evangeline called. "Before you go—can I get closer to the fire?"

Turning, he placed his fists on his hips. "Untie you? You'll run."

"How can I? Your men are here." She gestured around her. "You said yourself I'm not as stupid as I look."

Shorty stood and took a step toward her. "Let her freeze. It'll be warm enough where she's going."

Frantic, Evangeline yelled, "I want to be warm. Let me get closer to the fire."

Dominic hesitated.

"Shut up." Shorty took another step.

Evangeline couldn't shut up. Her chance was walking away. "Come on, Dominic, don't be such a bastard."

There was a clatter, an audible gasp, and when Evangeline glanced around she saw Brat horrified, Shorty triumphant, everyone waiting.

Dominic strode back. He grabbed her by the back of her hair and half lifted her. "I take back what I said. You *are* stupid."

Pain brought tears to her eyes, and she whimpered. "And cold. Please . . ."

"Kill her," Shorty chanted. "Kill her, kill her."

Dominic opened his fist and let her fall. Drawing his dagger, he lifted it above her, and for one terrified moment Evangeline looked death in the face.

With a downward slash, he cut the rope holding her to the pole. "I'll kill her when she's served her purpose," he snarled at Shorty, and stalked out, leaving a tremulous silence. Men trailed after him, then Brat, until only Shorty and a small contingent remained.

Evangeline drew a quivering breath. She watched the humiliated Shorty out of the corner of her eye. She scooted toward the fire.

When she was close enough that the warmth struck her on the face and she could see the glowing bed of blue coals, she drew from her bosom the heavy leather pouch she'd filched from Shorty.

And threw it into the flames.

Sixteen

Grinning with obnoxious delight, Dominic slapped Danior with an open palm. The small, vicious circle of revolutionaries laughed, but Danior didn't care. Laughter meant nothing; survival was all that counted.

"I give you the respect, my prince, due your noble House of Leon." Dominic slapped him again.

Danior's hand flashed out and caught Dominic's wrist. "Where's the princess?"

Dominic looked at his captive wrist. "You're so strong, Danior." He snapped his wrist free. "But I'm stronger."

"No one's beat you tonight." Rafaello stood at Danior's right side, Victor at his left.

"It's not going to happen, either." Dominic jerked his thumb toward the crest. "She's eating stew and warming herself by the fire. I'm doing you a favor by killing you, Danior. She's a bit of a handful—"

A flash lit the night skies, and the percussion rumbled the ground beneath their feet.

As one, the pack of rebels turned uphill, their features illuminated by the grand flare. Other, smaller explosions followed.

"What the hell?" Dominic stepped away, then swung back to Danior and pointed an accusing finger. "It's that princess of yours!"

"Ethelinda?" Evangeline had been in that explosion? A high scream rent the air, piercing Danior with its anguish. "By God, if you've killed her—"

"Brat." Dominic broke into a run.

Without a thought to the mob, Danior followed on Dominic's heels, running across the dark barrenness. Behind him, he could hear men panting as they ran. Near the looming cliff, weathered rock cracked as it threatened to rupture. Dominic increased his speed. Danior kept pace. Stones defined the shadowy path they trod. Dust swirled in the air. Dominic's steady stream of cursing led him over the shattered pieces of an overturned boulder. They rounded the corner. The faint starlight allowed Danior to see nothing but a tangle of forms, inert or slowly moving within an oblong of stone. There was no fire, only a few flame-lit splinters burning randomly around the site.

Was Evangeline dead?

No, the rebels had kept her alive to try her. She had to be alive.

"Ethelinda!" he shouted. Men shoved him from behind, Dominic's men, streaming into the campsite, exclaiming and cursing. He raised his hands to his mouth and yelled through his cupped fingers. "Evangeline?"

Someone grabbed him by the arm and squeezed. "Quiet."

Her voice, hoarse, weary, and desperate-sounding. Her scent, wrapping him around, close as his cloak.

Her scent, spice and citrus and some indefinable fragrance undeniably hers. He would know it anywhere by the tug she induced on his senses.

Elation jolted him. He grabbed her, felt her fine bones beneath his hands, enveloped her in a hug. "Ethelinda." Then, without reflection, he pushed her away and shook her. "Don't you ever scare me like that again."

She coughed and struggled in his grasp. "We have to go."

Immediately he contained that peculiar euphoria, subdued that abrupt surge of fury. What was he thinking? Of course they must go.

He looked around, trying to locate Victor and Rafaello. He could recognize nothing in the darkness and confusion. It was a man shrieking in a high tone, his declaration of pain mixed with searing invective toward Evangeline. A few people moaned; more cursed and called.

Soon someone, probably Dominic, would light a torch. Danior had to get Evangeline away.

At his right side, Rafaello said softly, "We're here, master."

Danior relaxed infinitesimally. Thank God for Rafaello and his ability to see like a cat in the dark. "Does one of you have the supplies?"

"I do." Rafaello sounded completely self-satisfied.

Then someone lunged at the princess. Some black material enveloped her head. She struggled and gave a muffled shriek. Danior grabbed for her attacker, but she was set free as suddenly as she was seized.

"Her Highness had a glowing cinder in her hair," said Victor in a low voice.

"I thought I'd got them all." She sounded shaken,

more fearful than Danior had realized. "Are there any more on my back?"

Danior twisted her around. "None."

"Fire flew everywhere. I rolled in the dirt to douse it." She drew an audible, quivering breath. "Please, can we just—"

Danior hoisted her off her feet and onto the stone that blocked their path. "Stay there." He leaped over and presented his back. "Climb on."

Without a moment's hesitation, she slid her arms around his neck and hooked her legs around his waist, and they were off.

Danior almost laughed at the elegance of their escape. Everyone had run inside the camp, trying to discover what had happened, who'd been hurt, if their meager possessions had survived. He and the princess, Victor and Rafaello, raced outside without interference, and if that shout he heard as they cleared the boulders was Dominic ordering a search for them, it didn't matter. The rebels weren't in position, the darkness that had worked to their advantage now worked for Danior, and he had no intention of stopping until they were far, far away.

He had his princess; by Santa Leopolda, let no one try to take her away.

Sighting off the North Star, he started downhill toward the cover of the trees. "We'll take the direct route to Baminia. With luck, we'll cross the border by daybreak."

Victor and Rafaello trotted at his heels, working to keep up with his huge strides while maintaining the silence years of stealthy combat had taught them.

Evangeline clung to him. The high, dry air hurt his lungs, and the strain of carrying her quickly made itself known, but he never slowed until they reached the tree line.

Then he lessened his pace and paid more attention to where he put his feet. The stunted trees of the higher elevations soon gave way to the lush coniferous cover, rich with scent. He cast a learned gaze at the round of moon hovering just above the horizon. It rose earlier this night than last and in two nights would be full, but the trees would shield them from hostile eyes while the light helped him pick a trail through the forest—a forest he knew well from his time fighting the French. From this point a dozen ways led into Baminia and Serephina, and the rebels had no idea which way they would go.

Still he pressed on. Those explosions had been a gift to help them escape. He had no intention of wasting such a boon.

Yet Dominic's accusation returned to haunt Danior. *It's that princess of yours,* he'd said. But she couldn't have . . . could she?

Off in the distance, they heard a faint rumble.

"What is that?" she asked.

"A waterfall," Danior replied. "Jean Falls, one of the biggest."

"Jean Falls," she said wistfully. "It sounds beautiful."

Using the cover of its noise, Victor said, "I want to know what caused those blasts."

"Oh, I did that, I threw a sack of musket cartridges on the fire."

Evangeline spoke so matter-of-factly that it took Danior a minute to react. "A sack of musket cartridges," he repeated.

Rafaello hustled closer, creating a careless disquiet

of snapping branches and sliding pine needles. "Your Highness, where did you get a sack of cartridges?"

"And how large was it?" Victor challenged her with his tone.

"I suppose a sack is too big a word." She sounded thoughtful. "It was more of a . . . you know . . . one of those little leather bags men carry their powder in."

"A cartridge pouch," Danior clarified.

"Yes. I saw it hanging on Shorty's belt when I kicked him between the legs. When he fell, I knelt beside him. I pretended I was sorry—men always believe women must be sorry, regardless of how much they deserve the boot—and I stole it from him while I was apologizing."

Shock quivered in Rafaello's tone. "With all due respect, Your Highness, I didn't know a lady of your cultured antecedents knew how to kick a man."

"Yeah, much less where." Victor seemed considerably less horrified than his compatriot. "Restrain me from ever getting too close to *your* mule kick."

"When you think about it," she said, "it was ironic that I blew up their camp with their own gunpowder."

Danior wavered between being appalled and proud. How could he explain this sheltered girl's talent for survival? The nuns were supposed to have taught her *needlepoint*. "Do you sew?" he asked.

"Of course!" she said, insulted.

Danior wished her answer comforted him more.

"Really, we could expect nothing less than an explosion from this princess." Victor kept his voice down, but his sarcasm could not be tamed. "If she's going to climb out a convent window and down the side of a cliff to get away from you, master, I suspect a little gunpowder in the fire is all in a day's labor. She claims she's not the princess. Perhaps she's telling the truth."

"Yes!" Evangeline almost leaped off Danior's back.

"No." Danior kept a good grip on Evangeline and a tight rein on his fury, but he coldly noted Victor's opinion, and more important, that he felt secure enough to voice it. "I don't make mistakes. You, my princess, wrote a letter claiming you weren't called to be my wife and fulfill the prophecy, but you were sure 'good things would come to me.' " The thought of her missive and its naively cheerful tone, made him want to take fate by the throat and force it to do his bidding.

From the day he was born, he had been fated to be the prince to reunite Baminia and Serephina. Every day he had taken pride in his destiny. Nothing could stop him. Reunite the two countries he would, regardless of rebels, his father, the princess's mother, and the princess herself. Even fate. "When we questioned your teachers, they said you seemed troubled in your spirit before you disappeared. And so I should hope, for you left the school at Viella taking your dowry."

"But I told you how I got my money."

"Oh yes," he said caustically. "You inherited it from the old lady you worked for."

She shifted uncomfortably on his back, and he could feel her heart begin to pound in her chest. "Y . . . yes."

"Little girls who are raised in a boarding school by nuns are notoriously inept when telling lies. They stammer and generally act as guilty as a thief."

She jumped. She literally jumped, her body convulsing with remorse. "I didn't steal the money!"

"It was your dowry, to be spent preparing for the wedding, not on an adventure so dangerous it's put all our lives at stake!"

Her hands tightened on his shoulders; her thighs tightened on his hips. "*I* didn't choose this adventure, *you* chased me into it, so don't try to put the blame on *me*. And the money wasn't a dowry. I wasn't lying. Leona left it to me, only . . . only I . . . well, she didn't exactly die."

Seventeen

The only sounds in the forest were the ceaseless drumbeat of the waterfall, the march of feet, and the almost audible tension of curiosity. Evangeline shouldn't be saying such things in front of his body- guards, but the damage was done. Danior could only hope she spun such an outlandish tale that they would find it impossible to believe. And if he goaded her, most certainly she would.

With meritorious poise, Rafaello asked, "If she didn't die, how could she leave it to you?"

"She told me she was tired of the dull life in En- gland, and the next day she vanished. I searched for her, but she was very old and determined, and I fear she walked into the sea and let the current take her." Evangeline's voice shook with the telling; this was no poorly thought out tale, but one into which she poured her heart and soul. "I reported her disap- pearance to the authorities, and when they read the will I discovered she'd left me her entire fortune."

"Convenient," Danior said.

Evangeline cuffed him on the side of the head.

"Don't say that. I loved her. She saved me!"

The waterfall was getting louder, masking the sound of their voices, or Danior would never have allowed the conversation to go on. But Evangeline spun a good tale. Even *he* was interested, and so he permitted her the smack—she would say he deserved it for some brutish act or another—and allowed Rafaello's next query.

"From what did she save you?"

"The orphanage," Evangeline answered.

For the first time, Rafaello's civility toward his princess broke down. "Uh-huh. Master, let me fall behind and check for trackers."

What would have been a straightforward request a week ago now seemed weighted with calamity, and Danior didn't hesitate. "We've left them behind, so let us remain together for now."

Rafaello barely stifled his astonishment, although whether it was real Danior could not venture to guess. "As you wish."

Victor didn't believe the princess now and had never believed, yet she obviously entertained him. "Your Highness, you inherited a fortune from the old lady who saved you from the orphanage. So what was the problem?"

"Leona's solicitor, the most pompous man in East Little Teignmouth"—by Evangeline's tone it was clear she despised him—"told me the bankers would wait until the body turned up, or for a decent interval, which was seven *years*, before they could declare her dead, but once the death certificate had been passed through the courts, I'd have a considerable sum of money. Enough money to last my whole life." She paused painfully. "*If* I used it wisely."

Victor cackled. "That'll be the day when a woman can use money wisely."

"I meant to, I really did," she said. "He talked me out of it."

As they neared the base of the waterfall, a faint mist swirled in the moonlight and moss hung from the trees. "The solicitor talked you out of it?" Danior questioned.

"He pointed out that I was no longer young, that I had never been pretty, and that no one knew what my background could be."

She sounded so much like she believed the tale that Danior was moved to tighten his grip, not painfully, but in an attempt to comfort her.

Heedlessly, she charged on with her yarn. "For all anyone knew, my parents could have been murderers, and at the very least they were vagrants or gypsies. But Mr. Isherwood said if I were careful with my money, I would never have to hire myself out again, and perhaps some decent man would deign to take me as his wife."

"How kind of him," Victor said.

"He was a widower, and he rather leered at me."

Victor cackled again, but this time it sounded a little sympathetic. "Such advice would send any woman flying to the shops."

Danior cleared his throat.

"If this tale were true," Victor added hastily.

"Yes. Especially since the solicitor was quite right on all counts. I'm twenty-four, no man had ever found me irresistible, and if I waited all those years for that money, by the time I got it even Mr. Isherwood could begin to look good." She sounded impossibly earnest. "I was sorry about Leona, more sorry than I can express, but she used to urge me to follow my dreams. I couldn't leave her when she was alive, but, well . . . I took the strongbox.''

"You *stole* the strongbox?" Victor clearly relished the word. "From where?"

"Mr. Isherwood allowed me to assist in crating up Leona's possessions and to contract the men who would take the boxes to auction. The men didn't realize the contents were supposed to go to Glastonbury, not Avebury, and when I went to inquire about the strongbox, Mr. Isherwood said he had misplaced it. I don't know even now if he knows how easy it was to find his hiding place.''

"Our princess. Stealing." Rafaello sounded winded.

"It wasn't stealing," Evangeline lashed. "Everything was mine! And Mr. Isherwood had already dipped into the money. If there'd been nothing left in the end, who would have cared that I had been cheated? I'm *not* the princess.''

What a lie! Danior thought. She was good at this, and he couldn't allow her to continue unchallenged. "You are a very *imaginative* princess."

Her exasperated sigh quivered through him. "Didn't you see my dress? It's from London. So are . . . were . . . my bonnets, gloves, and luggage. I bought them all in London, then I took accommodations across the Channel, engaged guides to show me Bordeaux and Toulouse, and hired a private carriage to bring me to the spa. I enjoyed it all very much.''

"Until the bomb," Danior said.

"Until about an hour before that," she corrected. "When I saw you."

She sounded stanch, yet her head bobbled against his shoulder. She seemed to be growing heavier.

At first he thought it was because he was tiring. Now he realized her muscles were limp. As the night wore on and the excitement of their escape wore off, it appeared she at last had been driven to the limit of her endurance.

He was almost glad. At least he knew she wouldn't run off again.

"Will we see Jean Falls soon?" she whispered.

Her breath feathered his hair and slipped across his face, warm and spicy, reminding him of the kisses they had shared—and the kisses yet to come. "We won't see it at all. I came this way because—"

"Please. To come so close and not see it!" She sounded as disappointed as a child deprived of a treat.

He shouldn't humor her, he told himself. The spongy ground underneath his feet received their footsteps and sprang back up. He had planned this route for just that reason, for in the daylight, there would be no trace of their passing.

"Danior, please."

For a woman who had displayed so little in the way of feminine wiles two nights ago, she displayed a remarkable aptitude for manipulating him. And with peculiar insight, he realized he held a remarkable susceptibility to her manipulation.

With a gesture to his men to stay, he moved slowly and with deliberate caution toward the creek formed from the waterfall. He scanned the open area alongside it, but nothing moved, and so he stepped out of the shadows and into the pale luminescence of moonlight.

He felt her intake of breath. She pushed away from him, and he let her down. She stood leaning against him, her face lifted toward heaven, her lips slightly parted and moist as mist fogged the air.

Above and beyond them stretched the limestone cliff, polished and scoured, channeled with gullies that plunged down its face. Within each gully a waterfall slipped like a liquid chain of silver music. From the highest point above them dropped the greatest cascade of all. The water dropped without interruption from the highest point, constantly flowing, flying, singing tribute to the moon. At last the water crashed and splintered across the rocks in an eternal crescendo.

Danior had seen the cliff and the falls before. He'd prowled these mountains, learned to use the noises and disguises of nature. But engrossed in the business of staying alive and driving the enemy from his lands, he had failed to take the time to note the beauty. Only now, looking at the elation on Evangeline's upturned face, did he become aware of the wonder his childhood had never allowed.

And that made him weary and too well aware of the distance he'd traveled and the innocence he'd lost.

Now, at last, he permitted himself to think what the rebels might have done to his princess. Had they beaten her? Raped her? She'd been pure before; had they used her in the basest way they knew? He would kill them if they had.

He looked at her again, and this time he saw the smudges on her forehead, the dirt on her cheeks. Her hair stood up in wild profusion all around her face except in one spot; there it seemed to have been slashed close to the scalp. He touched the ends; they crinkled beneath his fingers, and he smelled the faint scent of burning.

THE RUNAWAY PRINCESS   167

He remembered now. The cinder had done this damage.

With his thumb, he tried to wipe the darkest smudge off her cheek. She flinched away from him.

A bruise. She'd been hit by something—or someone.

Fury twisted along his veins like liquid fire. He would make Dominic sorry for this. He would make him pay.

Taking care not to frighten Evangeline with his outrage, he touched her cheek again, soothing away the hurt, and with a slight wince, she let him. "Evangeline, we can't stand out here anymore," he whispered, and grasped her wrists to move her.

She gave a gasp of pain and fell against him. "Don't!" When he let go, she whispered, "They tied my wrists. The rope . . ."

He felt the stickiness of blood beneath his fingers, and looked at the wounds. Blood circled each wrist, dried and blackened in the moonlight.

He would kill Dominic. He would rip his arms out. The bastard. The pitiless bastard.

He had thought her brave and worthy to be his bride. Now a voice in his head mocked, *She is quite worthy, indeed.*

Cradling her hands in his, he asked in a tender voice, "What else did those—what else did the rebels do to you?"

"Not too much." She drew a shuddering breath. "Dominic wouldn't let them."

"Noble of him." Danior would still kill him.

"Just a slap or two, and everyone got a chance to pinch at me." Her hand went to her throat. "I didn't like it, but I wasn't . . . they didn't . . . nothing happened.''

An ignoble, niggling bit of tension inside him eased. She said she hadn't been raped. He didn't have to worry about his Baminian honor, or the fact that his firstborn might not be his.

"Danior?" She looked into his face, and not even the moonlight could hide the exhaustion that dragged her down. "Do you believe me?"

"Of course I believe you," he said gruffly, disgusted that he'd not thought to reassure her. "Princesses do not lie."

Although she did. She had lied from the first moment she'd seen him at Château Fortuné. She had lied about her past, her background, her very self. Yet he believed her about this. "Neither do I," she answered, sticking to her tale of mistaken identity with a persistence he might have admired in another. That she convinced him she always told the truth must make her a liar of the highest order.

Turning his back he squatted before her, and she slid her arms around his neck and her legs around his waist as if they'd been traveling in such a manner for years. Standing, he shifted her on his back, his hands sliding along her thighs to better support her.

She adjusted herself, trying to help him, unselfconscious about touching him, and he realized a deeper relief. She would not face their wedding night with loathing. Indeed, she liked him well enough that he could overcome any resistance she had to mating with him.

Keeping to the moss, he strode back into the forest. Rafaello and Victor stepped in behind him, and they made their way down the hill, keeping a parallel course to the creekbed. As the song of the waterfall faded, his thoughts turned more and more to his predicament.

She aroused him. She always aroused him. He hadn't expected that from a political marriage; he had sworn he would be faithful to his princess, regardless of any indifference to her face and form. Now he found himself wanting to lay her down on a bed of pine boughs and make love until the lies and pretenses and protocol between them had been burned away, leaving only two bodies, two people entwined.

Her chin jolted on his shoulder, and she whimpered.

She was exhausted. He knew it, yet as the first sharp edge of jeopardy faded, here he was, erection straining at his buttons in some asinine, callous denial of the danger they all faced. His mind coldly weighed their peril; his body complained in blithe unconcern.

His stomach clenched. If he weren't careful, he would turn into his father.

But no. Danior had sworn he would never be such a libertine, and for that reason he eternally maintained a watch over himself.

Yet if he didn't distract himself, and soon, all his restraint would be for naught. He would send Victor and Rafaello away and pounce on Evangeline. On poor, exhausted, bruised Evangeline.

Turning his head, he spoke to his men. "Damned rebels. When they jumped on me from the trees, they almost ripped my arms from my sockets."

"They cracked my head half open," Victor added enthusiastically. "And I suspect I shall bleed on and off all night."

"Oh, yeah?" Rafaello joined in. "They slammed me against a rock. I think they broke my ribs."

Danior relaxed a little of his tension. This kind of talk he understood; a comparison of wounds, a bit of boasting about who had sustained the most damage. "All in all I think they were saving us for later, like spiders who have caught too many flies."

Evangeline sucked in a breath. "I don't feel well," she choked, and her hands fell away from Danior's neck.

Eighteen

Evangeline never actually lost consciousness. She heard Danior's cry, and felt hands, Victor's or Rafaello's, grab her as she fell. They laid her out on the ground on a cloak, and the chill woke her completely. "I'm well," she said.

Danior paid no attention. "She's not well."

"She's a lady," Rafaello said. "She's too delicate for this grueling trek."

Victor snorted. "She claims she's not a lady."

She tried to sit up, but nausea lapped at her, and she sank back. "I just couldn't listen to that gruesome report."

"We were trying to distract you," Danior said in obvious irritation.

Turning her head away, she groaned.

His hands reached for her, touched her with remarkable gentleness, skimmed over her throat, her shoulders, down her arms. "You *are* hurt."

She didn't care how impersonally he was handling her, she wasn't about to let him run his fingers over her torso and points in between. "It's my foot!"

The hands stopped. "Of course." Standing, he stepped away, and spoke to the bodyguards in a low tone.

She lay on her back and looked up at the sky, trying to imagine a gown of such smooth velvet accented by a handful of twinkling silver spangles. She couldn't. She shivered weakly, her teeth clinking together.

Ever vigilant, Danior twitched the edge of the cloak over her. She fingered it. Rough wool, the scent of wood smoke and tobacco—it must have come from the camp. Rafaello or Victor had filched it.

An argument ensued, and she heard, "A cut foot!" uttered with great indignation. And, "Dominic will be watching there."

Wrapping her hands around her arms, she wished desperately to be back in England with its scuttling clouds and constant fogs. She wasn't some delicate lady, but neither was she a hardened veteran of war. Her swoon humiliated her, yet she was bruised from rough hands, her wrists burned from the rope, and her foot throbbed with such intensity that she feared a killing infection.

When she'd lived in East Little Teignmouth, she'd read the tales penned by Thomas Aquinas of religious martyrs who died for their honor or their savior, and she'd imagined how she would embrace the stake and ignore the tortures.

Now she knew she wasn't brave. For relief from her pain, she would confess any sin, betray any secret. She had lived a small life, and a small life was all she could handle. She was a coward.

"Evangeline." Kneeling beside her, Danior opened

the sack and rummaged among the contents. "I'm taking you to a village nearby."

But while *she* might comprehend she was a coward, she felt a remarkable aversion to letting Danior know. "I thought we had to go to Plaisance."

"We will. Open your mouth."

"What?"

He popped a piece of hardtack between her lips.

She should have been indignant to be fed so off-handedly, but the crunchy biscuit settled her stomach. Sitting up on one elbow, she chewed slowly and swallowed.

"Better?" Danior's voice was a rumble above her head as he tucked the cloak tightly around her, hoisted her up, and held her against his chest. "Rafaello and Victor will first lead our pursuers astray. Meanwhile, we'll get to Chute, and there bind your foot."

Her arms wrapped around his neck. "But the border . . ."

"Don't worry. We'll make it."

Rafaello moved in very close, and spoke with such elegant diction that she could almost see a prince's robin's egg blue cloak. "You mustn't fret about your wounds, Your Highness. The master has the royal touch."

"Enough, Rafaello," Danior interposed pleasantly enough, but beneath his voice flowed an undercurrent of molten steel. He shrugged the shoulder with the bag slung over it. "I put more faith in the supplies the sisters gave us."

"Of course, master," Rafaello said.

"We'll meet three days hence in Plaisance." Danior

spoke quite pleasantly, but it was clearly an order. "Go with God."

"And you, master." Rafaello melted into the forest's shadows.

Victor was different, of course. Nothing elegant about him. Instead he ruffled Evangeline's hair and in a voice that grated like fingernails on a slate, he ordered, "Watch out for him. If anything happens, I'm holding you responsible."

The man never wavered from his mistrust, and Evangeline discovered she took an odd comfort in his consistency. "You would."

"I would," he confirmed. Then he, too, faded into the darkness, leaving her alone with the prince.

Immobile, Danior strained to listen to the night sounds of the forest. The creak of the treetops in the wind, the scuttle of small creatures in the underbrush, but from the bodyguards, no sound as each man made his way into the lonely depths of the forest. They were assigned to protect their royalty, and from what Evangeline had seen, they did so ungrudgingly.

Yet it gave her an odd sensation to know another human would offer his life for hers, especially when she'd so recently faced her own cravenness.

"Danior, I'm really—"

"Sh." He stood still another minute, then, carrying her in his arms, he started toward the west. They came to the creek, and as he sought a crossing clear of trees, Evangeline thought he lingered in the moonlight.

"Someone will see us," she murmured.

"Yes," he said. "Be quiet."

They slipped into the forest on the other side, and he walked confidently west until they ran into a well-traveled path. The character of the timberland changed. The spicy pine gave way to the drier scent of cork oak.

"Where are we?" she asked.

"Sh," he said again.

He seemed driven, moving quickly, paying little attention to their surroundings. His carelessness struck an odd note with her; she'd grown used to having him constantly scouting for peril.

They crested the ridge, and she looked down on a village nestled in a mountain valley.

"Chute?" she asked quietly.

"Yes." He paused again in the open, then walked down the hill. "Be silent now," he instructed. "Say nothing."

Mystified, she nodded.

The path curved. He walked straight—into the trees.

She wanted to speak, to question him, but she knew he must be up to something. He sat her on a flat stone and stealthily crept back to the path. He squatted there, watching.

She could see his silhouette against the moonlight on the path, and she marveled at his immobility. The cloak didn't mitigate the chill or the unyielding quality of the rock. The eerie atmosphere made her restless, and she ached all over.

At last he came back to her. Without a word he knelt before her. She put her arms around his neck, and he lifted her again. She almost groaned from the pain in her aching biceps and abused joints. But he didn't complain. So neither would she.

Now again he set a pace like the one she was used to; watchful, covert, almost inaudible, yet smooth and swift. They were ascending again, for the wind carried the pine scent, and her perception of wildness increased. They were leaving civilization behind, and she and Danior were the only humans awake in this world of untamed creatures and primitive trees. She thought she saw glowing eyes peering at them from the brush, but she clung to Danior, amazed by her confidence that he would keep her safe.

Then she woke with a start to find him settling her into a mound of pine boughs and tossing the cloak over her. "Stay put," he murmured and disappeared into the darkness.

Cold and alone, she blinked painfully at the stars shining down through the branches, and she wondered if she was truly awake even yet. She could hear the burbling of water, smell a faint odor of sulfur. Mist floated past in endless wisps like London fog that had lost its way. There wasn't a waterfall, so where . . . ?

Lifting her head, she looked around. She lay on the edge of a clearing caused by a pool that arose from seemingly nowhere. Ferns draped the shoreline, steam rose from it, and as she watched, bubbles rose to the surface.

She sat up. A hot spring. Danior had brought her to a hot spring. She'd read of such things—she'd read of almost everything—but she'd never seen one.

She'd never bathed in one.

The thought gave birth to action. Huddled under the rough cloak, she stripped off her wretchedly inadequate evening slippers and her stockings. She slipped the elegant rag of a gown off her head. She untied her petticoats and wiggled out of them, and plucked at the fine linen chemise that covered her from shoulders to knees.

But no. She would retain the chemise.

Chill nipped her as she discarded the cloak across a bush. Holding onto a trunk, she stood painfully, and limped to the pebbly shore. The ground beneath her feet was pleasantly warm, for the heat of the earth huddled close to the surface, undeterred by the frigid night air. Traveling with Danior was like living the life of Marco Polo. She discovered one thing after another.

She stuck the toe of her injured foot in the water. "Hot!" She jumped back a little, then inched her toe in again, then all her toes. It *was* hot, beautifully hot, just like the luxurious bath she'd taken at Château Fortuné with servants carrying steaming buckets and a fine bar of milled French soap to wash with.

So what if she didn't have the soap?

Shivering, holding her breath, she inserted her whole foot. The laceration stung like a thousand bee stings. Every sinew clenched, and tears flooded her eyes. Gradually, the sensation eased. She inhaled the steam off the pool, and edged deeper. Her other foot, her ankles, her aching calves . . . her eyes closed, and she allowed the warmth to work its magic on her sore muscles.

She had died and gone to heaven.

She giggled when she realized how far she had fallen, that she considered a private moment in a pebble-bottomed mountain hot spring a celestial treat.

The pool was wide, with a weak current that flowed toward an outlet hidden in the shadows, yet when she reached the middle, she found it only as deep as her knees. Substantial stones jutted from its depths here and there, and she placed her palm on one of them and languidly lowered herself into the water.

She filled her cupped hands with water and washed her face. She scrubbed at her skin beneath the water. Then she slipped beneath the surface and scoured her scalp with her fingertips. Dirt and ash slipped away, and not even the uneven stubble of her burned hair could distress her now.

Coming up for a breath, she breathed deeply of the cold mountain air, and she smiled.

Amazing how a brush with death could transform the loss of a modish haircut into a triviality.

She let the current push her spine against the gentle slope of the rough-textured stone. Her head fell back, and her eyes closed as heat enveloped her. Her mind drifted with the current, free of earthly care.

"Don't you ever stay where you are put?" he said from directly above her.

Opening her eyes, she smiled on Danior—until she took in his dishabille. He wasn't wearing a shirt or trousers. His only garment was a tight white pair of underdrawers that made her thankful for the darkness, although the night's illumination made it possible to view the muscles in his shoulders and arms. "Huh?"

The moon, almost round, sailed directly above them. His head was bent and his face shadowed, but she thought he surveyed her thoroughly. Seemingly satisfied to find her unharmed, he stirred the contents of a small bowl with his finger. "No harm done."

"Good of you to approve." She wanted to wave her hand airily, but found it too much trouble to lift her arm. Yet through the layers of relaxation, she felt the stirring of wonder and a distant unease.

It seemed a little late to wonder what he must have thought upon returning and seeing her gown and petticoat strewn about. Did he consider it an invitation? Did he think she wished to become intimate with him?

And did Evangeline care?

Leona had warned her about men like this. Why hadn't she warned her about her own wanting, need, softness?

As he strode toward the shore, she noted his broad shoulders. He could push a plow all day—or carry a woman all night.

He made his way into a small cluster of stones from which steam rose in unsteady puffs. Kneeling, he placed the bowl inside, then picked up a small clay crock—where did he get that?—and waded back to her. His legs cleaved the water, his arms swung freely; maybe he wasn't a peasant, or a prince, but Poseidon rising to claim his bride.

The thought fed that tingle of uneasiness.

"Here." He thrust the crock toward her. "Drink this."

Visions of a mysterious drug slipped through her mind. "What is it?"

"Fresh water from a cold spring. Drink."

Thrusting it into her hands, he turned and left her feeling foolish.

But still she sniffed the crock before she drank. It smelled like dirt, but the contents were water, and she tipped it up and swallowed.

She'd been thirsty and hadn't even realized it. How did he know?

He moved about on the shore, arranging a pine bough bed, lining a fire pit, washing some rags in the water—they looked like her clothes—and tossing them over a bush. Rummaging in the bag he'd carried, he extracted several somethings, then once more he strode purposefully into the water.

Nervously she sat up a little straighter, then wished she hadn't. She didn't like the way he stared at her, focused not on her eyes but on her shoulders. The wet chemise clung to them, the cold air brought gooseflesh to her skin, and she wished, not for the first time, that Danior was a normal-sized man. This excess of breadth and height seemed an extravagant array of muscle and bone, especially when she was seated down so low, and the way he stared at her seemed to be some kind of earthy, wordless form of communication. Worse, she thought she comprehended. "What are you going to do?" she whispered.

A prince like the one in her dreams would kneel beside her and say, "I have come to profess my undying love and devotion."

Danior knelt, plucked her ankle from under the water, and said, "I'm going to clean your wound."

She had to stop imagining undying love and devotion from Danior. The man was so practical he set her teeth on edge.

Or perhaps it was her cowardice that did that. "No, really, I can clean my wound." She scrunched up her toes trying to protect her fragile arch from his large, clumsy, invasive fingers.

Glancing around, he found a dry flat stone and laid his instruments there. A small, corked bottle, rags, tweezers, scissors, a needle . . . oh, God.

"I can do it," she said.

Turning her sole toward the moonlight, he frowned. "Don't worry. I have battleground experience."

Visions of field amputations floated through her mind, and she sat up again. "I can do it!" She glanced at her injury and wished she hadn't. A slash started at one side of her arch and extended to the other side of her foot, deepening as it went.

Deliberately, Danior placed her foot on his thigh. His big hands approached her face. She backed up tight against the stone, but there was no evading his fingers as they wrapped around her neck and slid into her hair. His thumbs caressed her jaw, slid down the column of her throat, and she didn't know if she was being threatened or pampered.

"Evangeline."

His voice rumbled like a god's. Not Poseidon, she thought crazily, but Vulcan, appearing and disappearing through the vapors of his mighty forge.

"Evangeline, that chemise is almost transparent."

Even in the darkness, his eyes glimmered as he stared into her face, absorbed in her: her reactions, her fears, her desires. She wanted to look away. No one had the right to know her so well . . . yet having this powerful man interested in her was a seduction in itself.

"You look like a water nymph who lives to seduce mortal men."

The sound of his baritone voice sang along her nerves. The drops of water lent an ease to his movement as one of his hands slipped down. She had imagined the waterline as a defense; his hand crossed that boundary with ease, proving once again the flimsiness of her resistance. His palm, callused and practiced, cupped her shoulder and lingered, as if he found pleasure in the stretch of muscle, the density of bone, in the very strength that marked her as a common woman.

That hand traveled down her spine to her waist. His arm wrapped around her and he lifted her from the water, sliding his thigh beneath hers for support, raising her torso toward the stars. Water streamed from her. The chill of the air shocked her. His gaze dropped to the body he had uncovered, and for one moment, as if he couldn't control his reaction, his fingers in her hair clenched.

"I am very mortal, Evangeline." His head dipped toward her breast. "You're cold and excited, and if you don't let me take care of that slash on your foot, I will succumb to your inducements."

She couldn't think of him as a prince, and he insisted he was no god. She spoke, and felt each word transfer itself to the touch of his fingers. "Please, Danior . . ."

"Yes?" He didn't move. He waited on her command.

She should seize this chance. This was a man, healthy, attractive, in his prime. And not just any man. This was Danior, and he wanted her. Not just because he thought she was his princess, but because something in their skins, in their minds, in their hearts mingled and ignited. There wasn't a fire, not yet. But with each word he spoke, each moment he carried her, that something smoldered and she knew it needed only a puff of air to explode into flame.

She had only to ask. "Please . . . please." She *would* ask. "Please would you tend my injury?"

No! No, that wasn't what she meant to say.

"Evangeline." He sounded so disappointed. He still held her exposed to the night, and to him. "You are a faintheart."

"I know." Oh, how she knew! One last try. "Please, Danior . . ." *Make love to me.*

"Say it," he murmured.

She would. She would say it and snatch her one chance, probably her last chance, to explore the mysteries of intimacy.

But what came out was—"Please, Your Highness, would you tend my wound?"

Danior laughed. Damn him, he laughed, and she shut her eyes and curled her fists.

He *didn't* burn with an incorrigible fire. For some secret, incomprehensible, despicable reason, he tended the flames between them, but kept them well under control.

Yet before he lowered her back into the pool, she felt something warm and intimate on her breast. She knew where his hands were—was that his mouth? Her eyes sprang open, but if he had kissed her, he had straightened immediately.

With her hand, she smoothed her chemise over her breast, trying to verify her suspicion, but he'd left no mark. Of course not, how could he? He was only a man, not some human branding iron that labeled her as his own with a simple kiss—if there had been one.

And she thought she must have imagined it, for he let go of her easily, as if her vacillation did not matter to him. "I am delighted you trust me enough to allow me to tend your wound. But first"—he uncorked the small bottle and handed it to her—"drink the brandy. I had hoped I wouldn't have to use it, but as sensitive as you are, I should have known better."

"I'm not sensitive." She took a sip, and it burned all the way down. "I'm as practical as you are."

"That is the last thing you are."

She wanted to fight with him, but he took her foot in his hand. She took another sip of the brandy. Could a man as utilitarian as him really imagine that Evangeline Scoffield was an enticing water nymph? No, it was impossible, or he wouldn't have laughed. She couldn't laugh, and all because of what her imagination had conjured.

Damn imagination.

Then Danior's skilled hands opened the wound, and she forgot her quandary. It had to be cleaned, she knew it did, and she knew it was going to hurt.

Danior plunged her foot into the stream and held the skin apart, letting the current tug at the impurities. As if she'd asked him a question, he said, "He's my brother."

She dragged her mind away from his ministrations, from the impending pain and her fear. "What?"

Catching her gaze with his, he repeated, "Dominic is my brother."

Nineteen

If Danior was trying to distract her, he'd achieved his goal. "I see," she said. Although Evangeline hadn't consciously realized their relationship, still she wasn't surprised. Looking at Dominic had been like seeing the prince through a distorted window. Dominic was slightly shorter. He moved with the whipcord grace of a great cat rather than the stalwart bulk of a bear, and she hadn't seen his face beneath the scarf, but somehow she thought the bone structure similar to Danior's. Most of all, he had impressed her with that stinging intelligence, more cruel and less scrupulous than Danior's, but comparable nonetheless.

Absently, she rubbed at a painful scratch on her shoulder, a momento of her forced march up the mountain. "Not a legitimate brother, I assume?"

"No." Danior lifted her foot and dried it on a rag. "My father's sense of honor was less than a king's should be, and he seduced a young woman—a girl, actually—and when he'd had his fill, he abandoned her. Dominic is the result of that particular mésalliance, and proof positive that there's a price to be paid for every sin."

The brandy was going down easier now, but it didn't make the tale easier to bear—or, she suspected, easier to tell. Danior believed implicitly in honor and duty; to admit such shallow behavior in his own father must gall him. Silently she offered the bottle.

Silently he accepted and sipped, then corked it and placed it on his stone.

"Your father . . . he didn't take care of the girl or . . . the baby?" she asked.

"My father." Like Dominic's, Danior's grin looked feral. "He never concerned himself with the fruit of his liaisons, and as I understand it, when the girl's condition was discovered she was thrown from her home. She and the child lived in the most wretched of circumstances. I believe she prostituted herself to feed her son." With tweezers in hand, Danior began to pluck at Evangeline's wound with small, hurtful results. "She ultimately died from the pox."

Evangeline didn't like Dominic. Hate bubbled from him like hot water bubbled from some underground hell. She had stood in that hate's way, and she'd come away scalded.

But she, too, had been an unwanted child thrust on the world's uncertain charity, and she shared a reluctant kinship with the royal bastard. "No wonder he's savage."

"Yes. And while I don't hate my father with quite the virulence of Dominic, I find that I do not respect his memory as a son should."

It was, she realized, an understatement. Something in his voice, in the way he moved, told her that his contempt for his perfidious father went bone-deep.

And the tale explained his slashing derision for what he considered her lies.

Even though she knew she told the truth, his conviction went so deep that he almost convinced her she was wrong. "No, I suppose not," she mumbled, avoiding his eyes. Then a thought occurred to her. "Is he your only brother?"

Danior pressed his thumb lightly along the seam of her gash.

Almost at once she felt something rolling beneath her skin, and she stiffened.

With the tweezers, he removed the tiny pebble, then continued to work his way along the wound. He had a decidedly light touch, she realized, and slowly relaxed each muscle. He knew what he was doing.

He also wasn't answering the question. "Danior?"

"Dominic is my only brother . . . except for Victor and Rafaello."

"Of course." She sipped the brandy. What better bodyguards for the prince than his brothers who looked so much like him?

She would not have thought brusque Danior capable of conveying irony, but he did so now. "My father thought the country would be greatly improved by sowing his imperial seed far and wide."

She thought of Victor and Rafaello, offering their lives for hers. "Well, for the most part, I would agree. But why aren't they bitter like Dominic?"

"They're older than Dominic, and my mother found out about them and insisted on supporting their mothers and seeing to the boys' care." With his thumbs, he opened the gash wide and pushed her foot back into the water.

The wound stung again, as badly as it had the first

time she submerged it. She twitched, and her eyes filled with tears.

"This pool has healing qualities." He watched as she sank down until the water lapped her bottom lip. "But I wouldn't drink it. It tastes like fire and brimstone."

"I won't," she said in a small voice.

She could see only the gleam of his eyes in the shadows of his face, but he sounded kind as he said, "Before Dominic was born my parents were killed in the rebellion—"

"Then Dominic is young," she said, shocked.

"Twenty," Danior confirmed. "Too young to be so rancorous, but my mother wasn't here to tend another of my father's seedlings."

As the pain began to ease, she laid her head back on her stony pillow.

And stiffened when he said, "Let me assure you that *you* will not have to perform that service for me."

"Well . . . no. I mean . . . yes." Irked at her own stammering, she said, "I'm not the princess, so I won't be wedding you, but I'm sure your queen will be relieved to hear that she won't have to trail after you and pay off the products of your liaisons."

He rumbled on as if she hadn't spoken. "From the moment I realized the anguish my father caused my mother, and the dishonor of a broken marriage vow, I swore to be discreet. I've had few lovers—"

"Really, I don't want to hear about this."

"—And those were mature women who participated in our pleasure without illusion. I took care that every encounter was without issue, for I am determined the only children of my loins will be ours."

Our children.

The phrase resounded in her mind.

He spoke as if their offspring were already conceived, borne, were alive and happy to have two such noble parents. She could almost see them, a tall, thin girl on the cusp of womanhood and a stocky boy with Serephinian eyes. And another girl with raven hair and another boy, and twin toddlers and the baby . . . she brushed her hand over her eyes to dispel the vision. Yes, if she mated with Danior, she had no doubt the union would be fertile. It would be no life for an intelligent woman, a woman better trained to ruling than to parenting. She'd always be with child, or nursing, or running after babies or in bed with Danior making new ones.

"Am I hurting you?"

She stared blankly at Danior. "What?"

"Your toes are curled. Am I hurting you?"

Was he hurting her? He was *killing* her—with temptation. "Yes," she babbled. "Yes, that's it. You're hurting me, but I know it's the right thing to do. You do the right thing, and I'll do the right thing, and somehow this will come out, um, right." She thought he was smiling as if he read her thoughts, saw the children she had created out of a few of his simple words.

He was a simple man. He couldn't have planned to trap her in a dream of her own making. Even if he had, well, she didn't have to let him know he'd succeeded.

Then an extraordinary thought occurred to her. "Wait," she said. "You *know* I'm not Princess Ethelinda!"

"I do?"

"You wouldn't have told her all this. She would have known it."

Leaning forward, he spoke in his stuffy noble prince voice, "I would hope that the good sisters at the school would have the sense not to tell you how my father's callous fornication put you in danger from all sides."

"Oh, you always have an answer." Stupid to pout, but every time she thought she could poke a hole in his insufferable armor, he parried and left her without a weapon. "Anyway," she pointed out logically, "I wouldn't say I'm in danger from all sides. At least Victor and Rafaello are devoted to you."

"Victor and . . ." His voice faltered. "Just when I think I comprehend the complexities of your mind, Evangeline, you confound me again. How did you read my worry?"

She hadn't, of course. If he hid anxiety about Victor and Rafaello, she hadn't known it. Asking about them had been a lucky chance, because she was not, was *not*, tuned in to Danior's thoughts.

"You say they are devoted to me. Yes, I had thought so." His thumbs probed the gash again. "Everything's out of this cut. I'll check it again in the morning."

Wisps of steam and darkness teased her, concealing him from her scrutiny. Frustrated, she said, "Tell me about Victor and Rafaello."

"You know what I think, or you wouldn't have asked. We are not at the village of Chute although I made it appear we were going there." With a groan, he threw out his arms and splashed back into the pool.

Not even the tip of his nose showed above the surface, and she wished she could pummel him for throwing out such an interesting tidbit and then disappearing. Groping under the water, she found his extended leg and curled her fingers around it.

He came up at once. "What?"

"Why aren't we in Chute?"

The muscle in his calf tightened to whipcord constriction beneath her palm. "Because either Victor or Rafaello, or both, are betraying us to Dominic."

Her jaw dropped, but she never thought to argue with him. If Danior thought so, then Danior had reason. "You don't think it was an accident that the rebels found us at Château Fortuné?"

"I did at first. Not any longer. We—Victor, Rafaello, and I—learned to lose trackers in the best school possible—in the war, with Napoleon's huntsmen hot on our trails. We took chances no one else would take, and if we had been unsuccessful, we would have been dead." Leaning on one elbow, he wiped his dripping hair out of his face. "Now, suddenly, we cannot shake Dominic? No."

"But your brothers have been with you all this time! Why would they betray you now?"

"Before we were fighting for our families and our country. Now we're fighting for a way of life many remember as oppressive and barren. The countries haven't been prosperous for the last fifty years. My father ate well for a man whose people were starving. Your mother dressed fashionably for a woman whose people shivered in the cold. No one knows how I'll rule as king, or if you'll be compassionate as queen. I've promised my brothers a just reward for their services, but perhaps one of them sees a chance for more." Sitting up, he scrubbed his face as she had done, and rubbed at his shoulders, arms, and chest. "Perhaps if you and I were out of the way, there would be a place on the throne for a royal bastard."

For years she had lived in a small village, surrounded by people she greeted by name, people who watched her every action, people who immediately recognized a stranger and made it their affair to discover his business. She had thought she liked being away from that constant, gossipy watchfulness.

No man-made surroundings could compare to the grandeur of these mountains, glowing faintly in the moonlight, to those stars, a swathe of silver scattered across a black velvet sky, to these pines, tall, primal, satiated with fragrance.

Yet the sweet hush of silence that enveloped the pond seemed suddenly menacing and oppressive. This place made her aware of her insignificance, of how easily her essence could be extinguished by indifferent nature or by unrelenting enemies. She strained to hear any sound beyond the occasional slight rush of the stream, then very, very quietly, she asked, "Are you sure we're safe?"

"After I left you here, I backtracked. No one has followed us. I took care to leave no sign of our passing. And few know of this place, certainly not Victor or Rafaello." Danior's voice deepened and became warm, enfolding her as surely as the water itself. "We are safe for as long as we wish to stay."

What layers of meaning were wrapped inside his words? "That can't be too long," she said nervously. "You must get to Plaisance in time for Revealing in, what, three days?"

"*We* must get to Plaisance for Revealing, difficult though that may be. No one said the way to the throne would be easy—Your Highness." His hands disappeared under the water.

She realized he was scrubbing everything. All of him. She didn't want to think about what that entailed, and hastily she removed her hand from his calf and looked anywhere but at him.

Yet she could still hear the splash of water and feel the faint current created by his ablutions. She feared enemies of the royal family, known and unknown, it was true. But more than that, she feared Danior. One instinct urged her to flee. Another instinct told her that any movement, however slight, would attract his attention. And in the base of her being she knew that if she stayed, he would inevitably reach for her.

Slowly, taking care to make no noise, she began to stand, to inch away from him, from his too-close proximity and his watchful, beckoning gaze.

But his hand landed on her collarbone. "Wait. I don't want you to put that foot down. Let me get the ointment and the rags to dry and wrap it." His fingers massaged the joint of her shoulder, then slid down to her elbow. "Trust me, Evangeline. I'll take care of you." He didn't sound stuffy or princely or superior.

He sounded seductive.

The air seemed thin, sucked into the vacuum by this man's flagrant sexuality. The way he looked at her in the moonlight, the possession inherent in his touch, the authority in his voice, all made the truth clear to her. He might as well just have said it. This prince who was built like a peasant wanted her.

Her thoughts careened as she stared at the broad hand that held her in place.

All right. He wasn't built so much like a peasant. More like a warrior, with thick forearms that could swing a weapon and broad shoulders that could lift a princess.

He frightened her, yet at the same time some unfamiliar sentiment moved within her. His strength, his
boldness, his maleness brought forth a corresponding
feminine softness in her.

"Do you trust me, Evangeline?" he asked.

"I do," she answered. When he laughed, deep and
overly pleased, she realized how much that had
sounded like a wedding vow. "I mean, of course I do,
or I would have clobbered you by now."

Unoffended and certainly unworried, he relin-
quished his hold on her and stood. Water streamed
off of him, pressing the drawers close to his legs, and
she looked when she should not. He was strong, muscled . . . aroused. Aroused, just as he had been in her
bedchamber at the château, just as he had been in the
storage chamber at the convent. Did the man live in
this erect state day and night?

He stretched, his hands reaching for the stars, and
she realized his condition didn't embarrass him. Sub-
tlety was beyond him.

As was duplicity?

Oh, yes. He thought she was the princess, his to
take and make his own. He wouldn't woo her if he
didn't. Yet if she didn't convince him of her true identity, who was the duplicitous one?

Gathering his tools, he strode toward the shore. He
wrapped them and placed them in the bag, then drew
out several lengths of material. Beckoning to her, he
commanded, "Stay low and keep your foot up, princess. Don't drag it across the bottom."

She couldn't hide in the water all night, so moving
like a crab, on her hands and one foot, she crept toward him. "I'm truly not the princess," she said.

"After tonight, I don't blame you for saying so."

He squatted in the pool and held out his hands, material draped between them.

"I mean it." Cautiously, she held out her injured foot. "I'm Evangeline Scoffield of East Little Teignmouth, Cornwall. What will it take to convince you?"

"You know that very well."

"I do?" She stared at him as he dried her foot with care. Uncorking the bottle, he applied a poultice of mashed leaves. A faint, minty scent teased her nostrils as he wrapped rag strips around her arch.

"Any time you want to show me the proof, I'm more than willing." Leaning over her, he slid his arms around her and warned again, "Keep your foot up." He lifted her out of the water, up against his chest. Her arms went around his neck, grabbing instinctively, desperate not to fall. But her hands found the soft, wet curl of hair at his neck, and the corded muscles that shifted as he walked with her to the shore.

Misgivings deluged her. This was too real. The air was too cold, the water plastered her chemise too closely, his glance was too confident.

How had she come to this moment? What thread of fate had she plucked that wove her into this royal tapestry? She gave a convulsive shiver.

"I have a towel of sorts to dry off with and a rug to wrap up in." He stood her on a flat stone that raised her to his level.

Tentatively, she put her weight on her foot. The wound was better. Much better. "Where did you get all that?"

"When I was a lad we had a hunting lodge not far away where we summered." He spoke carelessly of the kind of wealth she could only imagine. "I found this place. I would bring up supplies and hide them in a hollow tree, wrapped in an oilcloth." He shook out a blanket. "The clothing no longer fits me, the hardtack is no longer hard, and this rug is musty, but I shook it and aired it on the trek back here."

"Very helpful." Her teeth were chattering now, from nerves and from cold.

Handing her a length of cloth, he said, "This is from the bag. I'll hold the rug. You take off your garments and dry yourself."

She remembered the signs of life in his drawers. "I don't think that's a good idea."

"You can't sleep in those wet clothes. You have to take them off so I can hang them to dry. Now do as I tell you." He raised the material between them.

"Why can't you just turn your back?"

"Why can't you do as you're told?" he asked in a muted roar.

Surely his temper was a good sign. She stared at the wool weave and fingered her chemise. Why was she suspicious of him and his intentions? He moved without stealth. He performed every task openly. He'd been in the water with her and managed to keep his hands to himself.

Well, except for that moment when he'd held her face and said he could see her body. Now that the ordeal of purging her wound was over, she conjectured his threat had been nothing more than a ruse to extract bravery from a coward.

If Prince Danior planned to seduce her, she imagined he would inform her before he started, and probably keep her apprised every step of the way.

And tell her she lied if she didn't respond as he expected.

She grinned and lifted the makeshift towel.

"Are you getting out of your clothes?" he demanded.

"I'm drying my hair." Her voice had just as much snap as his did, and she told herself he couldn't be both aroused and irritated.

He sighed like a long-suffering martyr.

She draped the towel around her neck and loosened her chemise. The damp made the fabric stick to her flesh, and her fingers shook, but as quickly as she could, she pulled the garment over her head, tossing everything across a bush. The branches swayed and groaned under the weight of the wet material, and without volition she glanced warily at the blanket. It remained immobile. A warrior stood behind it, but he behaved like a gentleman. As quickly as she could, she rubbed herself down, trying to subdue the goosebumps with briskness, but nothing helped. The ground might be warm, but the air was frigid.

I'm done. A mixture of embarrassment and excitement kept her silent. *Hand me my clothes.* She should have fetched them before she stripped and found herself holding this feeble excuse for a towel. Its thin length wouldn't even cover the important parts, so reluctantly she draped it around her hips and held it with one hand. The other arm she pressed across her breasts, and she cleared her throat. "I'm done?"

She didn't mean for it to come out like that, quavering and unsure, but it didn't matter anyway, because this time when she looked at the blanket, she saw Danior. He still held it out at arms' length, but he had lowered it enough to look at her. At her body.

And he was smiling.

Twenty

Evangeline had never seen the prince smile like that.
As if he were astonished and proud and relieved, a
man facing his fate and finding it wonderful.

"My clothes?" she rasped.

"You won't need them tonight."

The wound in her foot must have weakened her
more than she realized. She heard him, and she didn't
mind. He stared at her, and she liked it. He planned
to debauch her, and she wanted it.

"Danior?" she whispered.

To answer, he enveloped her in the rug, picked her
up, and walked toward the pine bough bed nestled
in the hollow just at the edge of the forest. His face
was close to hers, close enough that the warmth of his
breath touched her cheek, and in the moonlight she
saw the faint, anticipatory glimmer of his eyes.

"Danior?" she whispered again.

He pressed his mouth to hers. A day's growth of
beard scraped her chin. He smelled damp and tasted
clean. Water clung to him and seeped through the
rug, carrying the heat of his determination.

A simple man. She'd seen him as incapable of wily enticement. Nothing had happened to change her mind. There had been nothing wily about his conduct; to a simple man, a bath together in God's most romantic setting must naturally be followed by their coupling.

The worthless little towel fell from her fingers.

Lifting his lips, he murmured, "Evangeline, I want you."

Remembering his earlier laughter, she asked, "Do you really want me?" Madly, truly, uncontrollably, she meant.

"My God, woman, what do you think this is all about?" Taking the last steps to the bed, he laid her down and lay atop her.

He blocked out the sky. He weighed her down, and the woven wool confined her movements. But before the old panic could set in, he freed her from its constraint.

"Stay there," he admonished. "And I mean it this time."

He must not have felt sure of her, for he didn't move far. Just to the foot of the bed, where he stripped off so quickly she scarcely had time to note she lay on the cloak, the pine boughs beneath her were deep and fragrant, the trees surrounding them gave them shelter and shadow, and she was trembling. Trembling from cold, and trembling from nervousness.

Oh, Leona had allowed her to read amazing Oriental texts describing the most outrageous acts men and women could perform together. But much like descending a tower on a rope, knowledge lent little to reality. This adventure, more than all the others, required courage, and her meager store had been depleted.

She clenched her teeth, clutched her fists, locked her knees together. She kept her eyes wide and fixed on the specter that was Danior, and concentrated on maintaining her composure. She couldn't yell, she couldn't run away, so she would endure.

Cold air rushed in as he lifted the cover and slid beneath. Then the goad of flesh against flesh brought a flash of heat. Their bodies pressed together along every inch possible. Above her head was his, outlined against the stars and the silhouette of the branches. Below her feet were his, stretched beyond the reach of her toes. He surrounded her in every way, yet he leaned on one elbow to regulate his weight.

He remembered what she feared, and with the rough glide of his palms up her arms, she realized he also remembered what she desired.

"Evangeline, you are my wife, my only."

She could see nothing of him; the trees protected them from any vagrant beams of moonlight, and his face was a mystery to her. But his voice was deep and inexorable; he bound himself to her, whether she wished it or not. Haltingly, she tried to tell him the truth one last time. "I'm just a woman who sought adventure. I never expected to get this—love at a poolside with a prince. And I know it can't last."

"But it will last." His voice became the murmur of a sweetheart in the darkness of the night. "All my life I've waited for you, and for this."

Did she believe him? She should; he never wavered in his beliefs, he never lost his head. Yet beneath the exceptional control he displayed, she detected signs of volcanic emotion. It was evident in his body, in the way his hips nudged against hers.

And he was big. No matter what the books said, at this moment she didn't believe he would fit inside her. This basic act seemed absurd, a jest played by some deity. Some *male* deity. She'd made Danior lose control once before, and the results had almost swept her, swept both of them, away.

His emotions seemed firmly clamped down, but before a woman dared let a man gain access to her body, she needed to be sure of the man and his passions.

"Danior?" Her voice quavered. "Will this be . . . safe?"

"Safe." One of his hands stroked a lock of her hair back over her ear. The other hand held her waist, pressing her against him. "I live to keep you safe."

"Because I'm the princess?"

He took a breath. She knew he did, because she felt the inhalation against her chest.

"Because you're the princess," he agreed.

Then he held his breath. She felt that, too, and the waiting tension in him. The wretched man wouldn't lie. Probably didn't know how to lie. And she, like a fool, found that more attractive than false and honeyed words.

Her fists had unclenched. Her hands lifted, her fingertips touched his chest. "I'm not the princess. Will you still keep me safe?"

The query was a luxury, bought with bemused certainty. She'd traveled on his back for miles, for hours. She'd touched and been touched by him more than any other human being in her life. She knew him from the words he'd spoken, from his acts of valor, but more important, she knew him with her instincts.

Danior would keep the lowest peasant safe. Even when he discovered the truth—no, when he'd had the truth hammered home to him—he would never abandon her. Somehow, somewhere, he would keep her safe.

And he knew the question required no answer, for his laugh rumbled through him—rumbled through her—and he pressed a kiss on her forehead. "Forever."

She knew his form, but this nakedness was different: shocking and comforting, not enough and yet too much. The muscles that flexed beneath her palms were covered not by cloth, but by skin and hair. He rubbed his legs along hers, and they, too, were rough with hair. She wondered if his whole body was hairy, and why that intrigued her, and if she would discover for herself.

The idea appealed, and in a rush of daring—her hands were already on his chest, after all—she stroked her fingers upward through the mat on his chest.

His muscles clenched, his breath whispered along her face. He grasped her arms and for a brief moment, she thought her simple motion had pushed him from restraint to impetuosity.

She froze, waited. If he grabbed her, forced himself on her in a haste of desire, it would be painful and upsetting, yes. But if he did, she wouldn't have to make this decision, to follow the adventure through, to face the consequences of giving herself.

She was a true coward.

And this prince was a true lover. His grip on her arms loosened. "Touch me," he said, and lifted himself to allow her full access.

She should have known she couldn't take the easy way out. Her questing fingers continued to move, enjoying the texture, the curl, the slight rough sensation as her palm followed the growth of hair toward his shoulder. There she discovered a series of pits, deep marks in his skin, and her fingers lingered. "What's this?"

"When I was little, I fell off my pony into the gravel."

Had he ever been little? But if she asked, he would say she should remember. So she said only, "Ouch."

The patch of skin against his collarbone was too smooth, devoid of hair and slightly rippled. "And this?"

"Boiling tar. We were besieging the French, and they—"

She imagined the agony and flinched.

He, perhaps, remembered her squeamishness and interrupted himself. "It was a long time ago."

A ridge ran along his left ribs, and she explored it gently. "What's this?"

"A bayonet at close quarters." Then, defensively, "But I was only sixteen and unprepared."

Only sixteen. "Napoleon hadn't even crossed the Pyrenees when you were sixteen."

He caught her hand. "It was an assassination attempt. I let a friend get too close."

Horrified, she stammered, "Do you ... trust anyone?"

"You."

If anything, she was more horrified, but before she could speak he kissed her parted lips, then pressed his tongue into her mouth. It was a slow, deliberate invasion, a preparation, an incitement. She had wanted to dispel his illusions, but tonight she would be his greatest illusion.

So she gave him what he wanted and kissed him back. Each sensitive nerve responded to the rasp and slide, and their heads turned and strained as they explored intimacy. He showed her what he wanted, she showed him what she knew, and their two bodies moved in a dance choreographed by nature. His palm rasped across her shoulder and down to her breast, cupping it and pressing it just as he had her lips— firmly, deliberately. He was teaching her, allowing no withdrawal, no second thoughts.

But she had them. With a gasp she pulled back from the kiss. He followed, and his teeth nipped at her earlobe, then his tongue stroked the outer shell.

He was damp and warm and breathy, and she shivered, overwhelmed with sensation and a sense of inevitability. This was the reason she'd run from him when she saw him across that dining chamber. To have her in his arms had been his goal, and all her objections and all the obstacles were nothing but chaff. For Danior, an objection was fated to be overruled, an obstacle meant to be overcome. In his mind, she was his, and through the peril and the struggle he had convinced her of that truth. And one other.

She loved him. Imbecile that she was, Miss Evangeline Scoffield of East Little Teignmouth, a girl from nowhere, an orphan, loved the crown prince of Baminia.

Danior's lips slid to her shoulder, over the rise of her breast to her nipple, catching it in his mouth. She gasped and clutched at him as if he could keep her from this sweet insanity. Keep her from it, when he was the cause. He suckled her, and each nerve stretched and hummed. She writhed, moving against him like a woman with no thought of decorum.

She *had* no thought of decorum. Her knees, so carefully locked together, had somehow separated. He rested between her legs, so close against her his every motion brought her pleasure—and a twinge of fear. So close. He was so close.

When he lifted his head, the dampness his mouth left behind brought her nipple to a tight point, creating a gratification sharper than any she'd ever experienced. A gratification that was almost pain.

Love. Pain. What difference?

Love. Madness. She suffered from a madness carried on the mists and breeze, a madness that swept her to a more primitive time when this man existed alone on earth, and *she* had been created for him.

She had to have this. She had to have him. Like the trip down the rope, she would start with a single, daring breath and trust in luck and God and her own insight to get her through to the end.

"Danior." She slid her hands up over his shoulders, exploring each bulge and ripple. Exalting in each bulge and ripple, as if his strength gave her, the female of his choice, prestige. If Danior were hers, she could smugly prance among the other woman-creatures, secure in the knowledge her man was the best. "You are so beautiful."

"Men aren't beautiful." He sounded distracted, and he arched like a cat being stroked. "I'm not even handsome."

"Who told you that?"

With only the faintest of sarcasm, he replied, "I believe it was a young woman named Evangeline."

Cupping his head, she tugged his mouth to hers.

"She was a fool." A million kinds of a fool.

This time, *she* kissed *him*, touching their lips, then using her tongue as he had, to tease and tempt and imitate. As he arched over her, she felt his control slip.

He caught himself, lurching as if he'd fallen, then held himself still. Whispering, "Evangeline," he made the kiss his.

That kiss became one, then another, each a work of wonder. He embraced her, opening her to him. He stroked her sides, following each contour repeatedly. He touched her breasts lightly, then as she responded, he stroked more firmly. Soon, with every motion, she lifted herself, mindlessly seeking his caress.

She existed in the world he had made for her, nestled in the hollow of the earth, with trails of mist from the pool and the darkness left behind by a setting moon. She caught glimpses of the stars, light torn from shreds of the sky. She breathed in spicy cold air and grappled beneath the rough wool blanket, seeking comfort and desire and satisfaction all from this one man.

At the convent he had said he fought to have her depend on him for everything.

He had won.

His hand stroked over her belly, spanned the width of her hips, then slid lower. The world slowed and stilled as he imitated her earlier quest; he explored the slight triangle of hair that sheltered her femininity, seeming to find delight in each perception. Then he moved lower, and she closed her eyes and tensed. He could bruise her if he touched her roughly. He could excite her if he touched her well. Either way she would reveal her vulnerability. She loved him with a newfound, fragile love; but did she trust him with this?

Feather-light, he smoothed his lips across her forehead, then across her closed eyes. With equal delicacy, he opened her and touched. Softly; oh, he was so gentle, taking care not to give pain and easing her toward . . . ah, that felt good. Heat formed inside her and flowed like the thermal springs. She didn't want him to know, but she couldn't shut him out. Strong as the pines around them, he kept her open with his body. She clutched at his arms, her head moved restlessly, and one of her legs coiled around his leg and one of her feet slid along his thigh.

He kept his hand on her, measured and firm, and when the dampness touched him, he seemed . . . encouraged. Pleased. That questing finger moved lightly, moved closer . . . moved in.

Her fingers dug into his skin, her eyes flew open, and her meandering foot landed on the cloak.

She hadn't said anything, but he shushed her anyway. "I'm not hurting you."

He was telling rather than asking, but as always, he didn't lie. He wasn't hurting, only . . . this was so alien. Odd. Exotic.

Unknown.

He probed deeper, then with that finger inside, he pressed his palm against her. She found herself tightening her thighs around his hips, contracting her muscles inside, trying to force him out, yet . . . she heard him audibly swallow.

"You were built for me," he whispered. "You were meant to give me pleasure."

Love made her daft, for she could scarcely speak

from excitement. "And you? Were you meant to give me pleasure?"

"I am giving you pleasure."

She had thought he was, but response taunted her like a sixth sense, fey and otherworldly, a sensuality too new to be defined. She wanted to explore it, yet caution restrained her. In her fever, what would she say? What would she do?

As if he heard her doubts, he murmured, "I want you so much I can scarcely hold myself back. I want you tossing beneath me, moaning in my ear, scratching at me like a lioness in heat. But I swear to you, no matter how much I enjoy you, I won't forget myself. You're small and delicate and I'm big and stolid, but I have never lost my head with a woman, and I won't now. Not when it's so important you . . . find fulfillment with me."

"So you won't laugh?" Dear heavens, from what pit of insecurity had that question come?

"Not ever. Not even if *you* laugh at *me*."

"I can't laugh at you." Laugh at the prince, who claimed a kingdom and a people and ultimately her heart? Never. And with the faintest tinge of envy, she said, "You have everything."

"Not yet, but I will. I swear I will." Slowly, he removed his finger.

Her vague feeling of disappointment at his withdrawal changed when she realized he no longer held himself apart. His hips nudged her, he prodded the dampness between her legs, but his hands now rested beside her head.

He slid his arm under her head and around her shoulders, embracing her, cocooning them together so they alone existed for the other. With the other hand, he grasped one of her thighs and brought it around his hip. Inevitably, he moved closer. Pressure increased. This wasn't his finger, and he was right about one thing—he was big. As he entered her, she grabbed at him with her hands, her breath coming harshly. This hurt.

And he knew. "Hold on," he said. "Just hold on to me. Even if the world ends, I'm not stopping, but I swear I'll make you happy."

He didn't wait for her assent, he just kept moving inexorably into her. She wanted to fight, but he hugged her too tightly. She tried to warn him. "We don't fit. We can't do this."

He didn't pause. He didn't even give her the courtesy of an answer.

Irate, she dug her nails into the muscles of his back. He grunted, halted, withdrew . . . a little. And came back. He didn't shove. He didn't hurry. He commanded her and the whole situation, and he proceeded accordingly. He met the barrier in her body, he forged forward when she thought there could be no more forward.

The man didn't know when to stop. He wasn't suffering, she was, and fiercely she cursed him for it. Tears trickled down her cheeks as she swore at him in Serephinian and German, Chinese and English, with a vocabulary learned in books and lived at the orphanage. He wiped the tears away with his palm, and continued moving. Thrusting now. He'd reached her deepest depths, but he didn't stop this action. This torture. She didn't know what he was looking for, but she wanted him to stop, because it hurt. It hurt . . . but not so much now.

Contrarily, that made her madder. After all this suffering, now he was going to make her happy? No. Absolutely not.

She erupted in a flurry of movement, shoving at him, pounding him with her fists, trying to buck him off. If he thought she was going to passively accept ecstasy, he was in for a surprise.

Unfortunately, her efforts didn't perceptibly influence him. Holding her as he was, he arched over her. She could gain no momentum, while he seemed to gather strength. His impetus grew as she lifted her hips, trying to push him away . . . gathering him to her.

The binding of pain and pleasure confused and infuriated her. She didn't understand her own reactions, didn't understand how he could force this change of her body. And more than that, of her mind.

Had she gone crazy? She joined him in the motion, opening herself to him, seeking something he offered, wanting to fling it back at him.

And he groaned, the sound torn from him and she, tender idiot that she was, asked, "Did *I* hurt *you*?"

"You're *magnificent*," he muttered with patent sincerity.

Like a bolt from the blue, she realized he liked it when she moved. She had the power to make him groan, and that precarious emotion she called love expanded to fill another empty space in her soul.

She propelled herself against him again.

"That's it. I knew . . ." His motion never ceased, his concentration never wavered, yet he slipped his hand down her thigh and lifted both her legs, he wrapped them around him so he and he alone controlled the speed, the pressure, and the depth. Now each motion brought him in direct contact with newborn nerves.

In the masculine body wrapped around her, she sensed a change, a coiling of intent. It matched the change in her own body. She moved because she had to move, because she couldn't stay still, because she desired something and he, damn him, had better find a way to give it to her.

It overtook her, sent her hurtling in a plunge of heat and scent and sound. Intemperate in her satisfaction, she struggled while he held her hips and made her take him as he chose, and worked the final miracle. She clutched him with her legs, her hands slippery with sweat, her skin burning in a burst of pure, igniting pleasure. Her breath rasped in her throat, her lungs burst with the effort, and low in her belly the undulations took her and carried her—right into his royal possession.

The last words she heard before she passed into sleep were, "I love you, Evangeline. I love you."

Twenty-one

"Wake up, dearling. We have to go now." Danior laid his hand on the shoulder under the blanket and shook it gently.

Evangeline mumbled something in English. Something that sounded like, "Go away."

He answered in Serephinian. "No, dear, I'm sorry, but you have to rise. We need to move on."

This time she blinked and yawned, her lips tucked in like a child waking too soon, and his heart ached at having to rouse her.

Last night when he'd carried her here, she had been exhausted, without sleep for too long, and weary with tension. She'd come awake to bathe and to accept his ministrations—the medicine for her foot and the loving for her body. And he didn't lie to himself about the reason she had come so sweetly into his arms.

Pain, drink, and exhaution most of all had weakened her resistance. He had taken advantage of her.

Now the morning was far progressed, and he needed her to wake. With his mouth close to her ear, he recited, "The sun can't shine. The birds can't chirp.

The whole world is waiting for you." He should have felt stupid, imitating his old nanny, but this unwonted tenderness he felt for Evangeline freed him from his princely dignity.

Unfortunately, she wasn't impressed. She rolled away from him. The blanket slid down. The slender length of her spine was revealed to her waist.

When he had first seen her, all he had thought was how men would envy him with her on his arm, that his marital duty would be easily performed with such an attractive woman. Now he knew she was strongly built, a woman he knew he could romp with, laugh with, live with. She was capable of dealing with the travails of the trip, and therefore capable of dealing with the challenges they would face as new monarchs.

He had had to claim her, and there seemed to be only one thing to do, a surefire way to put down her rebellion.

Make her fall in love with him.

Women loved with their hearts, not their heads. His father had told him that more times than he cared to remember.

"Pick a fresh flower and hand it to her. Smile boyishly into her eyes. Touch her hand, her waist, her back. Tell her you love her. When a woman leans into you, that means she's ready and you've got her." The old man had leaned forward, a sly gleam in his eye. *"You toss up her skirt and give her a romp, and she'll think she's in love, and you can use her until you're bored."*

Danior had never heeded a single word his father uttered, but he'd never been this desperate before.

"I washed out your clothes last night. They're clean and dry." His hand traced the line of Evangeline's spine, down toward the rounding of her bottom. He had held that bottom in his hands last night, lifting her to his thrusts, and he longed to see it now.

But when he would have pushed the blanket all the way down, she flopped back on her back and pulled the blanket around her shoulders.

Of course. She didn't want him to see the mark that proved she was his princess.

Yes, he'd taken advantage of her, and told her the sweet lie he thought she wanted to hear, but he told himself it was for a perfectly good cause. Revealing was now only three days away, and she could *not* refuse to play her part. She had to consent to not only being the princess but also to being his wife, or all was lost.

As they traveled together, he had thought she would resign herself to her fate. Instead, she grew more insistent she was not the princess, and she concocted ever wilder tales about her background. One or both of his bodyguards listened, eager to betray them, and if that false brother spread doubt about Evangeline's identity, it would be the one crisis Danior could not overcome by sheer will and preparation.

He glanced at the frugal fire he had built close to the pond. The thin swirl of smoke mingled with the steam that rose into the still chilly air, and he feared someone might smell the odor of burning pine boughs.

She had to rise. They had to be on their way.

"Evangeline," he said. "I trapped a rabbit. It's roasting. Can you smell it?"

She didn't move, but her stomach growled.

Ah. Perhaps she wasn't fully awake, but she had heard him. "I picked *blueberries*." He drew out the word, savoring its flavor. "Wouldn't you like some *blueberries*?"

She whimpered slightly, and her stomach growled again. She was still sleepy, but the hunger was winning.

Briskly, he added, "Not that I couldn't eat them all myself."

Her slanted eyes snapped open, mahogany brown and sparkling with irritation. "All *right*. I'll get *up*."

Her stomach growled again, and he grinned. She didn't grin back. For all her royal qualities, his dear wife bore hunger poorly.

Her gaze swept him with regal disdain, and his grin faded. How dare she deny her bloodlines? She might not bear a resemblance to the child he remembered, but he'd seen that mien on a dozen portraits in the Palace of the Two Kingdoms, where they would wed.

"If you would turn your back, I would rise," she said haughtily.

He discovered in himself a heretofore undetected desire to tease, to refuse and watch her struggle to maintain her dignity under his vigilant eyes. But uneasiness prickled between his shoulder blades and warned him it was time to move. He needed to get Evangeline to Plaisance, where she would be safe, not loll around like some Oriental pasha indulging in a frolic.

Last night he had laid his claim, and he'd always been a most restrained lover. So such playfulness had no place. Standing, he bowed. "As you command, Your Highness."

He moved to the fire and knelt beside it to turn the spit. The rabbit sizzled as it browned, fat dripping into the flames. All Evangeline had to do was put on that poor, bedraggled gown. Then he would feed her, and they'd be on their way.

Perhaps he should show her the bush where her clothing had dried.

But when he glanced around, he found the clothes were gone. Irresistibly, his gaze slid toward her figure as she picked her way down to the pool. She'd wrapped herself in the rug and held her clothing close to her chest.

She wasn't naked as he imagined, a seductive Aphrodite clad only in golden light. An ugly brown blanket swathed her—and she was just as seductive.

He jerked his gaze back to the crisp, sizzling meat of the rabbit. But he heard her splashing, and glanced again.

Clearly she didn't trust him; she'd hung the blanket on the trees between them.

Damn it. The obvious mistrust the curtain represented infuriated him. Never mind that it was justified; she was his woman, and except for a few formalities, his wife. He'd told her he loved her. He'd guided her into the rites of pleasure. She should trust him implicitly now. So why didn't she?

For that matter, why was he still so . . . so . . . dissatisfied?

He shifted on his haunches. All his life he'd been a man deliberately restrained in his desires. There had never been a woman who could make him forget himself in ecstasy. Such excess was his father's style, and he had taken care not to emulate his father. Even in the most intimate embrace, he held himself back. He gave the lady fulfillment and himself a climax, but he never shared himself. A man who expected too much was greedy, and such greed boded ill.

Yet last night he had almost let go.

He couldn't. He didn't. It was Evangeline's first time, and only an animal would have used her with vigor and unfettered excitement.

But he'd wanted to. Moderation had been almost beyond his control, and even now in the light of day he wanted . . . something more.

At Château Fortuné, she had been disconcerted by the mere act of kissing. Even now he couldn't subdue the smile that kicked up the corner of his mouth. She'd accused him of licking her. If she only knew where he longed to lick, she would have been more than disconcerted—she would have been appalled.

But she had learned rapidly, and last night those first, struggling scraps of desire she'd displayed had blossomed into a splendid passion.

So they would blossom again.

He pulled his knife from the holster in his boot and laid it across the flat rock that would serve as a platter. And listened to her splash as she performed her ablutions in the pool. He imagined going to her, taking her hand, leading her back to the bed and showing her his real self.

Closing his eyes, he fought the urge. It would be so easy. Only a thin blanket served as a barrier . . . a blanket, and years of knowing that if he ever unchained the beast within himself, he would ravenously seek his mate and take her until they both expired in the conflagration.

And Evangeline was his mate.

"Are you ready?"

He opened his eyes and stared at the woman standing across the fire from him. She shivered slightly beneath the blanket she held over her shoulders, but under that she had donned every bit of her clothing—clothing that had disintegrated even more than he had realized. The hem of her gown was shredded. Triangular tears showed the passage of each thorn and branch. A long rip split the front, and her knee poked out, covered only by a sheer petticoat almost as ragged as the skirt. A faint dew covered her skin from her bath, and the gown clung to her legs and her bosom.

For a man poised on the edge of control, she presented an almost overpowering temptation.

And she didn't even realize it, for she had eyes only for the rabbit.

"What?" he said.

"Are you ready?" She squatted opposite him. "Can we eat?"

Silent, shaken by the images his mind conjured, he stared at her open-kneed stance and wondered if she had somehow divined his suffering and tormented him on purpose.

"I've never been this hungry. I think it must be the altitude or the fresh air or the—fresh air." Moving back from the fire, she sat on a log and arranged her skirt so it covered her legs. With a glance at him, she brought the edges of the blanket up, too. "Did you catch the rabbit yourself? I know how to snare a rabbit. I read about it once. You've been up a long time, then. Thank you for letting me sleep, I was exhausted, but I'm feeling much better now. My foot has miraculously closed. Those herbs are very effective."

She wore her old shoes, and through the split in the sole he could see that she'd rebandaged her wound after her bath. He needed to examine it, but . . . he couldn't touch her. Not yet.

"On the other hand, it's not the herbs, is it? I remember what Rafaello said about the royal touch, and I've done enough research to know about the old superstition. A king's touch heals, correct?"

Dragging his gaze away from that one triangle of exposed skin on her bosom, he grunted and opened the bag. Groping among the contents, he brought forth the pieces of hardtack, and laid them on the heated rocks around the fire. Removing the skewered rabbit from the makeshift rotisserie, he laid it on the flat stone, too.

"You're very modest," she said. "Most men would leap to claim such a talent, and certainly this laceration is much improved. It's healed enough that I can walk down the mountain by myself."

He noted she rocked slightly, her hands clasped over her knees, and he realized that the normally reserved lady was babbling. She couldn't look him in the eye, and silence made her uncomfortable. Of course; she was nervous, not knowing the etiquette of a man and a woman who had experienced the greatest intimacy of all.

Maybe she was afraid he would jump her again.

Maybe she was reading his mind.

Resolutely, he pulled himself back from the brink of licentiousness and said, "It's an old wives' tale."

She stared at him, wide-eyed, a doe on the verge of flight.

"The royal touch. It's an old wives' tale." On a plank of bark, he laid out chunks of tender rabbit and a handful of blueberries, concentrating on the task with all his will. "Most of the stories surrounding our monarchy are, of course, but they give us tradition and pageantry, and those are the ties that bind us to our people and our people to us." The urgent need to mate, he noted, diminished as he spoke. Expressing his opinions to the one woman who could truly comprehend them gave him a sense of gratification and, more important, a measure of command.

"You think your sovereignty is maintained by myth?" she asked, sounding incredulous.

Careful not to touch her fingers—restraint could only stretch so far—he handed her the makeshift plate. "*Our* sovereignty, and if I didn't, I would have to believe in magic. Which of course, I do not."

Twenty-two

Evangeline balanced her plate on her knees and took her first bite and her second, her features smooth and serene with enjoyment. Danior thought that in her hunger she hadn't heard him, but she lifted her gaze from her plate and stared at him. "I don't understand. What about Revealing? If that's not magic, what is it?"

She popped a series of blueberries in her mouth, and as he watched her chew, ladylike and starving, stubborn and defiant and everything he wanted in his princess, an idea came to him—an idea so devious he thought his father would be proud.

Elaborately casual, Danior served himself and leaned back against a rock. "The whole tale is, I believe, suspect."

"Suspect?"

"A thousand years ago a king and a queen quarreled so harshly the country was torn in half, forming the two kingdoms."

"What's suspect about that? It's recorded in the histories of all the surrounding principalities." Her voice changed and took on a scholarly tone. "And historically speaking, such a split was not unusual. Peasants owed allegiance to the lord who protected them from marauders. If the king and queen couldn't protect their people together, a split was inevitable and probably in the best interest of the farmers, who form the backbone of any medieval domain."

He stared at her expounding on medieval society, noted that her eyes were alight with interest, and thought she hadn't lied about doing research, at least. Obviously, she loved facts.

And the other girls at the convent must have teased her about her scholarship, for she flashed him a guilty glance and mumbled, "Forgive me."

"Why?"

"Boring."

"Not to a future king."

She muttered something else, but under her breath. He guessed what it was. "I'm pompous?"

"How did you know what I—" Filling her mouth with flatbread, she crunched defiantly.

"Our hearts are one." And if not their hearts, then their minds. He had begun to understand how her mind worked—a useful tool for handling an unpredictable woman such as Evangeline.

Obviously, the thought of having joined hearts with him didn't fill her with the ecstasy he expected or his father had predicted. If anything, she looked dismayed as she finished chewing.

Blast it. Why couldn't the woman just react as other women did? Why did he have to keep thinking about new ways to handle her?

She swallowed, then picked up a berry between two blue-stained fingers and concentrated all her attention on it. "What part of the legend of the Two Kingdoms do you find suspect?"

"That nonsense about Santa Leopolda."

"You don't believe in Santa Leopolda?" Her fingers closed, squashing the berry, and he couldn't tell if her appalled expression was from the waste of food or from his blasphemy.

"Oh, I believe there was someone who put the crowns and the scepters in the crystal case and used a special lock to close it." He took a breath and tested Evangeline. "And stole the rings set with the royal seals while she did the deed."

"Stole them?" She looked up, appalled accusation directed at him. "She didn't steal them. They're under the velvet the scepters are resting on."

Danior took a bite of rabbit. Evangeline was falling into his trap without even a pause. "But there's no way to prove that, since the rings can't be seen."

"Leona told me that Santa Leopolda placed the rings under the scepters, and Leona certainly seemed to know the history of the Two Kingdoms." Evangeline's eyes snapped with indignation, even as she continued to pick meat off the bones. "Why would you think Santa Leopolda stole them? And why do you think there's a special lock that closes the case? The legend says that when she shut the case, fire ignited along the seam and sealed it."

"By *magic*." He made mockery of the word.

"It is impossible to open, you know."

"It's not impossible." *That* he truly believed.

She rapped her knuckles lightly on her plate and almost knocked the food to the ground—a true sign of her agitation. "Seven hundred years ago, the case was stolen by the Leons, by *your* family. Who kept it in *your* family stronghold for two centuries. If the case could have been opened, they would have done so and claimed the kingdom."

"They couldn't claim the kingdom because that would have proven the prophecy wrong."

"The prophecy says that anyone who can open the crystal case has the right to wear the crown within, take the title of king or queen, and reunite the Two Kingdoms."

The trap was closing around her, and he was conscious of an almost imperceptible relaxation within himself. "Is that what the prophecy says?"

"You know it does," she said, magnificently impatient with him. "And you can't tell me no one in your family tried to open that case! I heard that sometime while they had it, it was dropped from a castle tower onto the rocks below."

Finishing his meal, he threw the plate into the fire. "I heard that, too."

"And it never shattered."

The flames blazed higher, reducing the bark and bones to ashes. He stared into the flickering light and pondered Evangeline's arrogant and unconscious self-betrayal. "England is a country notorious for being smug and bumptious. However did you hear such a detail about such an insignificant land so far away?"

"Leona taught me everything I know about Baminia and Serephina."

"The language and the history and the legends."

She heard his skepticism, for she said, "Oh, why won't you believe me? You don't doubt that I learned to descend a tower on a rope, or to kick a man where it hurts, or—"

"How a man and a woman make love?"

Crimson crept into her face, but she met his eyes without flinching. "Yes, I learned that from books, too. So why won't you believe that Leona loved to talk about the Two Kingdoms? She must have been Serephinian or Baminian, and in exile after the revolution, and wanting to talk about her home."

"Anything is possible." He didn't care about her imaginary Leona. He only cared that she had betrayed herself, and he wanted her to admit the truth.

For once, she would tell him the truth.

"Now, about that lovemaking . . ."

"You're distracting me on purpose!" she cried.

She baffled him with the twists and curves of her mind—maybe he didn't understand her as well as he hoped. "Distracting you?"

"Because you don't want to talk about your family stealing the crystal case and dropping it out of the tower in a despicable attempt to rule the Two Kingdoms without the Chartrier family interfering!"

Her very indignation gave her away, and satisfaction rolled over him.

She must have seen the complacency imprinted on his features, for she pointed one slender, greasy finger at him. "And get that expression off your face. I'm not angry because I'm the princess, I'm angry because I'm English, and the English always root for the underdog!"

"Of course," he said smoothly.

"You're maddening." She took a long, indrawn breath. "Any woman who marries you will spend her life fuming."

"I won't allow that." He caught her gaze through the small ripples of heat created by the fire. "The woman who marries me will be gloriously happy. I will demand it."

She challenged him with a lift of her chin. "You don't always get what you want."

"I will this time." They sat still, silently testing each other for character and determination, neither giving way until he nodded and made judgment. "You, dearling, are my princess in waiting."

"I am *not* anybody's princess. Santa Leopolda predicted it would take a thousand years before a prince and princess were born at the right time to marry, fulfill the prophecy, and unite the countries. Now, when you should be out searching for Princess Ethelinda so you can take command of your country, you are sitting here with me." She picked among the remains of her meal for the last blueberries. "I'm not the princess, and I can't open the crystal case."

If she worried about her capability to open the case, if that was the reason she denied her destiny, then he well understood and would soothe her misgivings. "You won't have to. I will."

"How?" She flung out an arm. "We're on our way to Plaisance. Suppose we get to the city without being killed. Suppose we are taken to the Palace of the Two Kingdoms, there to rest and wait for our wedding. Suppose we rise on the morning of Revealing, dress in the garments of the ancestors, and go to the town square. Suppose we climb the steps to the cathedral and stand in front of all of the people of Serephina and Baminia who have gathered to see the miracle. Suppose that together we place our hands on the crystal case—and suppose nothing happens."

Standing, he went to the pool and washed his hands.

Her voice took on a pleading note. "Suppose for one moment I'm right and you're wrong. Suppose I am not the princess. The magic will not work. The people will kill us."

He went to the bed and dismantled it, folding the cloak and the rug, scattering the branches.

"And all because you're a thickheaded swine."

She bristled with exasperation, but he gave her insult the consideration it deserved.

That is to say, none.

"A thickheaded swine?" He placed the blankets into the bag. "On the contrary. I'm being inordinately clever."

Agitated, she pitched her plate into the fire. "We don't dare take this chance."

He took up the container of herbs and walked to her. "It's time for me to examine your foot."

"Really, it's not hurting . . ." Her voice trailed off as she viewed his determination. "I suppose there's no escaping you."

"There never has been." Kneeling before her, he removed her shoe and unwrapped the bandage. The wound had indeed closed. The edges of the thin red slash looked clean, and nowhere beneath the skin were there pockets of purulence. Evangeline was a healthy young woman, the pond's heat and sulfur had worked to cleanse the cut, and the royal maywort had promoted healing.

His own contribution he did not dismiss—he'd done a good job of removing the dirt and grit that would create infection. Not a royal magic touch, as the old ladies prated, but the touch of good sense and battle-won experience.

Yet he lifted Evangeline's foot and pressed a kiss into the arch.

She wrenched back. "Why did you do that?"

"The royal touch will heal you," he told her. Better to tell her that than to have her realize how much he wished to kiss her other, more secret places.

Maybe she sensed his longing, for she said, "Let's go. I can walk today."

"For a while," he conceded. Opening the jar, he stirred the mash and spread the vivid green herb on her wound.

She sniffed the delicate, minty scent. "What is that?"

"Royal maywort," he answered.

"Really?" With her finger, she took a dab from the jar. She smelled it, rolled it between her fingers, and murmured, "Fascinating. It grows only in isolated pockets of these mountains. I'd heard of it but never seen it."

Very isolated pockets, he thought. If she knew how far he'd had to roam to find the rare plant, she would be dismayed at the effort he'd made.

Bless her, even now she didn't realize he would do anything for the woman who would be his bride.

From the bag he removed the boots and socks the good nuns had given him. As he rolled the socks onto Evangeline's feet, he told her, "From the time of the first revolution when I saw my parents . . . blown apart . . . by a bomb—"

Evangeline lightly touched his hair.

"—I have had nightmares about my future wife and me standing in front of an immense, faceless crowd. Only too clearly can I conjure up the image of us placing our hands on the crystal case. And when it does not open, I hear the crowd's derision, picture my helplessness as the woman I love falls beneath a scythe"—the hair on his arms rose as he brought forth his nightmare—"and I am unable to fight my way to her side."

"Well, then, you don't want me." But she sounded troubled.

"I must have a princess, a *true* princess, at my side for that ceremony, not because I believe in magic but because I will marry that princess and the royal integrity of my line must continue. And Princess Ethelinda must be there to fulfill the prophecy as the people know it."

"What do you mean, as the people know it?" she asked suspiciously.

Carefully, he laced the boots over the socks. "Perhaps I could say that your courage marks you as the princess, but you would say nobility is no guarantee of courage nor does common blood prove a lack of it. In that, you're right, for I've met courageous women in all classes. Perhaps I could say your knowledge and abilities characterize you as royal, but you would say those were the consequences of your rebellion against a desolate childhood. And I would never deny that the fire that melts the candle also tempers the steel."

Standing, he took her hand and pulled her erect. "So I have tested you in every way I could."

"Tested me." Awkwardly, she moved her feet in the boots.

Keeping her close with his palm against her waist, he broke the tidings to her as gently as he could. "Your Highness, you know the secrets only the princess knows."

She watched him with fascination and horror. "What secrets? What do you mean?"

"It's public knowledge throughout the Two Kingdoms that the royal seals were lost when the land split in two. In her fury and anguish at the destruction of her beloved country, the people say, Santa Leopolda lost the seals and they will never be found again."

"That's not what Leona told me!"

"Leona, as you call her, was right. The seal rings are impossible to see, hidden under the scepters. But only the chosen of the royal family know that."

"Perhaps it's not as big a secret as you think," she said belligerently.

"But you quoted the prophecy correctly."

"Everybody knows the prophecy."

"Everybody *thinks* they know the prophecy," he corrected. "Yet it is only in the Book of Santa Leopolda that it is written that *anyone* who opens the case has the right to be crowned king or queen and reunite the Two Kingdoms."

Her brow crinkled in a stirring imitation of confusion. "*The Book of Santa Leopolda?* I don't remember hearing about *The Book of Santa Leopolda.*"

"*The Book of Santa Leopolda* is locked in the vault of the Chartrier stronghold, and that vault wasn't even found until twelve years ago."

"Twelve years ago? Isn't that the last time? . . ."

"The last time you and I met, little Ethelinda."

She moaned slightly and touched her forehead.

"I remember that the two of us were left alone to examine the book. I remember peering over your shoulder as you read the prophecy aloud. Not the prophecy as everyone believed it to be, but as it really was, written in Santa Leopolda's own crabbed, spidery handwriting.''

"It's been read since then!"

"The pages disintegrated as we turned them."

"Magic?"

"Age."

She stepped sideways, away from him. "Why should I believe you?"

Relentlessly, he followed. "Shall we discuss the story about the Leons dropping the crystal case from the tower?"

"Surely everyone knows about that."

"For six hundred years, that's been a tale repeated among the Chartrier family—a tale repeated to only a few, because everyone knew someday Revealing would arrive, and for our people's peace of mind, all trace of conflict between our families should be eradicated."

"Leona told me . . ." she faltered.

"Ah, yes. Your benefactor, Leona, whose name is so much like Leopolda's."

"I didn't make her up! I'm Evangeline Scoffield of East Little Teignmouth, Cornwall, and I tell you—"

"Three things." Thrusting three upraised fingers in her face, he said, "Three pieces of information you knew that were secretly passed, generation by generation, through the royal families. After such proof, do you dare imagine you can convince me you aren't Ethelinda Marcellina Felicia Evangeline Desirée, crown princess of Serephina?"

Her Serephinian eyes widened. "Dear heavens, she even has my name?"

Exasperated by this unwarranted, constant, prodigious obstinacy, he wheeled away from her. He kicked dirt on the fire until it smothered and died.

He'd proved she was the princess by her knowledge. He'd made love to her with magnificent restraint. He'd even gone against his own principles and told her he loved her.

What did the woman want?

He nudged the hot stones away with the toe of his boot.

What did it take to convince her she should gladly proclaim her true identity?

He selected one of the branches as a broom. Then enlightenment burst on him.

What did Evangeline *fear*?

She still stood in the same spot, shoulders hunched, lower lip stuck out.

"Did your Leona tell you how to open the case?" he demanded.

Mutely, she shook her head.

"Not with *magic*, I promise you. Do you remember where the case is kept?"

Bristling, she said, "You don't need to be insulting. It's in the cathedral under eternal armed guard."

"I've studied that case from every angle. Once I even laid hands on it. Along the edge, there's a catch in the crystal, so slight as to be invisible to the eye. But that is the lock, I'm sure of it. I had a tool made that fits in the slot, and I will open it."

She didn't look reassured, as he had hoped. She looked anxious.

"If you're worried that we won't be able to open the case, if you think the people will turn on us, if that's why you're denying your identity, let me swear this to you on my mother's grave. Together we will open the case, and together we will be king and queen."

Twenty-three

Hours later, on the banks of a tiny spring set in the midst of a hoary pine forest, Evangeline realized that she had to escape this man, and she had to do it as soon as possible.

"Stand here." Danior took her by the arm and placed her so she stood on one damp, mossy bank. "Now put your other foot here." He pointed at the other side.

"As you wish." She straddled the trickling rivulet.

He stepped in behind her, one giant foot on either side, wrapped his arms around her waist, and brought her close. His big voice rumbled in her ear as he announced, "These are the eternal headwaters of the River Plaisance. Together we stand with one foot in Baminia and one foot in Serephina."

"Oh." She was sinking—into the mud, into the lies, into the fantasy of living the rest of her life as Danior's wife. If she didn't get away from him soon, Evangeline Scoffield of East Little Teignmouth, Cornwall, was going to disappear without a trace, and Queen Evangeline would take her place.

Danior's tattered shirtsleeves were rolled to the elbow, and dark hair grew on his muscled arms and capable hands. "If you follow this brook downstream, it gathers water from a hundred other springs and becomes the river that flows through the city. Our city, Evangeline. Together we can unite this country and make it a place of peace and prosperity."

Now she understood why he dared halt in his race to avoid Dominic. He wanted to make a point, and he thought this place, ancient and significant, would make that point for him.

He was right. "It flows all the way to Plaisance?"

"All the way."

Queen Evangeline. And what was wrong with that, really? If the crystal case wasn't magic, as Danior seemed sure, and he could open it, there would be no pea beneath the mattress; no test for the true princess.

Someone had to fulfill the prophecy to make the people of the newly named Sereminia think destiny had been fulfilled. She'd be doing a good deed, bringing peace to two war-torn countries, for the real princess didn't want the position.

Now, a voice in her mind mocked. The real princess didn't want the position *now*.

"We'll follow the stream to the village of Blanca."

"What if Dominic is waiting to ambush us there?"

His hands slid up her rib cage and rested just below her breasts. "Don't be afraid. We'll be cautious, but peasants are faithful to me there."

"Dominic could cause them trouble."

"These villagers will fight if they have to, but we'll not overstay our welcome. We'll get a boat and make our way to Plaisance the quickest way possible, so don't fear."

"I'm not afraid," she said, not really listening.

Her mind returned to the problem of the missing princess, and she wondered—what about later? What about when the princess had been out in the world and discovered how difficult it was for a woman to survive? Even a woman with money had to worry about propriety and reputation and her own safety. Evangeline had found that out for herself quickly enough.

So what would happen when the princess came back and demanded her position and proved who she was? Then Danior would turn away from Evangeline with disgust.

She couldn't bear his disgust.

"How far is Plaisance?" she asked hoarsely.

Warm and vital, he hugged her closer, holding her with the strength of a hero who treasured his newly conquered territory. "With God's help, we'll be there tomorrow."

"With God's help," she echoed.

Her mind babbled on, relentlessly analyzing her predicament.

What if the real princess had met with foul play? Heaven knew that was possible. With Dominic running loose, it was more than possible, it was probable. If Danior looked for the princess, really looked for her, he might find her and rescue her from some dastardly fate.

Then he'd be grateful to Evangeline.

He pressed his hand to her belly. "Before the year is out, we'll have a child. Perhaps we've already made him."

"Her," she corrected automatically. "I'll bear only daughters."

She was crazy to think that, to have this discussion, to care.

"I'd love daughters." His voice was as sweet and spicy as cream dotted with cinnamon. "At least a dozen of them."

Shocked by his outrageous response, she said, "No more than three."

"Eight."

"Six."

"Done." He chuckled, warm and deep in his chest.

A smile curved her lips. Sternly, she told herself to stop, but the man had a way of driving her crazy with his possessiveness and his way of spinning dreams from nothing more than a fragile web of words.

He'd even said he loved her.

Loved her. What a moment that had been. Velvet night and overwhelming passion and his deep voice whispering raggedly, "I love you, Evangeline."

She'd treasure that moment as long as she lived.

Not that she believed him. No one had ever loved her. Not at the orphanage and not even Leona. Leona . . . Evangeline could barely conceive of it, but Leona had been using her for some purpose of her own. She hadn't told her about the revolution, the one that apparently occurred in 1796 and had killed both Baminia's and Serephina's rulers. Worse, Leona had told her things—secrets, Danior insisted. How had Leona known them? Why had she done it? Did she know the trouble she would bring on her unsuspecting protégée?

Secrets. Danior said the history Evangeline knew was familiar only to the royal families, and although it would have benefited him to lie, she believed him.

Evangeline believed him because he never lied.

Except about loving her. He would do anything for his people and his kingdom, even compromise his honor to lay claim to the woman he thought held the salvation of his country in her hands. She understood that, and accepted the falsehood, and loved him all the more for his dedication.

It didn't matter . . . it *hardly* mattered that her heart was slowly shattering.

The spring of Plaisance trickled eternally down from the mountains. Baminia and Serephina were nothing but mud beneath her feet, yet the lands existed forever. Only she and Danior were temporary, fragile humans placed here for one reason, to fulfill their destinies.

If only she understood which destiny that was.

Danior whispered homage in her ear, the kind of praise normally reserved for the finest of ladies or the most accomplished of courtesans. "You're so lovely, dearling, so perfect. You challenge me, you satisfy me. I dream of touching you, of readying you, of being inside you."

Her whole body tightened with the impact of hearing his hunger expressed so bluntly. She ought to be shocked, not melting as his big hands stroked her from neck to thighs, petting her as if she were a creature who lived for such pleasures. If she weren't careful, she could easily grow accustomed to his touch, purring and stretching like a pampered cat.

Her foot sank into the mud another inch, and her honesty floundered in a morass of greed, longing, and desire.

Rigorously, she thrust herself away from him, and in her haste she stepped right in the middle of the stream and staggered across the moss.

His hand shot out and righted her, and as the water sloshed over the top of her boots, she exclaimed, "It's cold!"

Stupid comment, but somehow she had imagined the heat from the upper springs had worked its way down here. Heaven knew she had been warm enough these last few moments.

"Yes, it's cold." He still held her, his gaze watching her profile while she pretended not to notice. "Did you get wet?"

"Yes." She lifted her foot and shook it.

"You've walked enough today anyway, and you shouldn't walk with wet feet. I shall have to carry you again."

She didn't want him to. She didn't want to touch him; it was like touching temptation incarnate. But she needed to escape him, and she didn't make the mistake of underestimating him. For any plan of hers to succeed, she needed to be rested and he needed to be exhausted. "Yes, you can carry me. But first let me wash my face."

His fingers reluctantly slid away from her as she knelt on the bank. She dipped her hands into the icy water and splashed it on her face, hoping the cold would help slap some sense into her.

He knelt beside her and splashed his face also, and, cupping his hands, he drank.

She imitated him, and when she'd drunk enough, she lifted her head to find him waiting. He caught her chin between his fingers and turned her wet face to his, and kissed her.

This kiss she now recognized as Danior's. He transmitted strength, courage, and passion with the touch of his lips, with the taste of his mouth. He gave so much, yet she sensed the rein he kept on himself, as if he feared to give *too* much. He challenged her with his reserve, and some unreliable part of herself urged her to stay with him, to fight her way past his restraint and experience the full depth of his fire.

Stupid girl.

She tried to pull away again, but this time he held her face inches from his. "It's appropriate," he said, "that the future king and queen of Bamphina—"

"Sereminia," she insisted.

"—*Bamphina* should wash and drink and kiss at the source of the River Plaisance. It's a baptism of our souls."

She whimpered slightly and shoved against his shoulders, but she had as much chance of pushing him as she had of drinking the spring dry.

"Look at me. *Look* at me."

Unwilling, yet unable to deny the command of his voice, she looked. The sapphire of his eyes blazed with possessiveness. The black of his hair called to be combed by her fingers. His hard-hewn features carried a nobility, not of refinement but of duty accepted and fulfilled. This was a man she could depend on to make a vow and keep it for the rest of their lives together.

She couldn't keep it to herself anymore. She had to tell him the greatest secret. The important secret. "I love you."

A slow, satisfied smile curled his lips. "Yes. Yes, that's what I wanted to hear."

Not quite the reaction she had imagined.

He stood up, bringing her with him. "We need to hurry," he said. "We haven't much time, and I still have a—"

Evangeline watched in wonder as color washed up over his cheekbones. "A what?"

"A premonition of trouble." In one efficient operation he transferred the bag to her and her to his back.

"I thought you didn't believe in magic."

"It's not magic." He adjusted her legs. "It's a premonition."

She wanted to tease him, but he started running down from the heights to the valley. By the time he slowed to a walk, he'd knocked both breath and sauce out of her, and deliberately, she was sure. The man was crafty and could be subtle; she should be grateful for the reminder.

The path became dustier and more worn as they descended, a sure sign that they were at last approaching civilization. The stream widened as other waters joined. Danior leapt over it as he sought the easier way, until the stream became the River Plaisance and there was no longer any way to cross. Then they traveled on the Baminian side.

They approached the ridge above a mountain valley, and he paused at the top where the water tumbled off the cliff. She could hear the mighty roar, feel the ground shake beneath his feet, and a rainbow formed where the sunshine met the mist. Trees lined the banks of the river, and Evangeline caught silver glimpses of it as it wound its way past a hamlet, gleaming white in the sunshine, then out of sight.

He indicated the view. "That's Blanca."

Fields surrounded the picturesque community beside the widening river. Mountains rose all around it in a great, protective embrace. Blanca appeared to be as peaceful and pastoral as any hamlet in England.

Pride gusted through her. "I want to walk in."

"I can carry you."

She might love him, but he could still irritate her more than any man on earth. "I don't care whether you can carry me or not. I care that the people of Blanca might think me frail." She aimed a kick at his stomach. "Or worse, lazy."

She had either injected enough authority into her voice or her heel had made contact with a sensitive spot, for Danior grunted and lowered her to the ground. "Is your foot dry?" he asked.

"Dry enough." She took a few steps. "And scarcely sore at all." Amazingly enough, it wasn't.

Perhaps Danior protested too much. Absurd though the idea might be, perhaps the old wives' tale was true, and this prince of the ancient Leons did have the healing touch.

She had been much enlightened by the study of science that had swept Europe in the past century, yet the mystique of magic fascinated her. She didn't believe in it, she supposed. She supposed Danior was right, and that the crystal case would be opened by guile and not enchantment, yet a separate, secret part of her wished for the magic to be true. That same part of her watched for fairies drifting along the sunbeams that shone through the branches and waited for King Arthur to rise from his burial place on Avalon.

A romantic, that's what she was, and she was paying for it with this adventure.

Grimly, she started into the valley. She would do well to remember where her affections had led her.

As they descended, Evangeline saw what distance had concealed. Piles of charred wood were stacked beside a new barn. Thin cattle were penned in pastures already stripped of grass. And she frowned at the drooping fields of barley. Even the grain looked sad, withered and fighting the curling edges of blight.

"What has happened here?" she asked.

"War and revolution," he answered, looking almost weary as he gazed on the blackened stump of what was once a huge oak. He pointed ahead to the village. "But it seems there are no revolutionaries now."

Ahead of them, the single road swarmed with activity. People moved toward the largest hut, carrying baskets and clothing, their pleasure-filled voices echoing up the path. Several half-loaded carts stood on the road, and children ran and shrieked with laughter.

Evangeline sensed a party atmosphere. Sensed, too, the moment the villagers spotted the strangers.

For the laughter was silenced, the women gathered their children behind their skirts, and a forest of pitchforks suddenly aimed for their stomachs.

Twenty-four

Evangeline halted in the middle of the path, but Danior waved and called a greeting as he strode on- ward. The stupid man would walk right onto the prongs. Running after him, she grabbed his tattered sleeve and set her feet.

He slowed, surprising her. She hadn't thought he would pay attention to so small a thing as her objec- tion to his bloody and unnecessary death.

But no. He put his arm around her waist and pulled her along with him, explaining, "They've been raided times without number. The village was burned to the ground during the Revolution of Ninety-six, and again three years ago when deserters from Napo- leon's army found their way here. The people are wary, but don't fear. They've been unswervingly loyal to me."

She looked again to see if he saw something she didn't, but the sun still sparkled on the sharpened tips of the pitchforks. "They don't look loyal now."

"Can you blame them?" He indicated himself. "I don't look royal."

He didn't. His cravat and jacket were gone. His shirt was dirty, torn, and minus the collar and cuffs that had given it style. The fine cloth of his trousers had lost many a battle with brambles, and here and there his white undergarments shone through. And the black shadow of a beard gave him the appearance of the lowest sort of ruffian.

"Don't worry." His voice contained a soothing tone. "I wouldn't bring you any place where you would be in danger."

It was the second time—no, the third time—he'd alluded to her safety in that condescending manner, and she wanted to retort that she wasn't afraid. But she was.

They had almost reached the glowering peasants, and those pitchforks began to dance and sway.

Holding his hand open so they could see he concealed no weapon, Danior said, "My people, don't you recognize me? I'm your prince!"

"You don't look like our prince," one man called out.

Then a child shrieked and dodged around her frantically grasping parents. "Danior, Danior, what did you bring me?"

Danior strode to meet the gap-toothed girl. He lifted her into his arms and spun her around, a big bear of a man giving a child a ride. But when he stopped, the father pushed a pitchfork at Danior while the mother snatched the child away.

The girl screamed in protest.

Evangeline hurried forward.

"Don't cry, Norita," Danior said. "We'll play after your papa and I have talked." He held the mother's gaze as she backed away.

The mother slowed her retreat. "You knew her name."

"I know yours, too, Lupe." He looked at the father. "And yours, Rainger."

"It is him." Lupe set her daughter down. "It's not Dominic, it's the prince!"

Pitchforks lodged into the ground as the villagers surged forward, laughing and talking.

"Forgive us, Your Highness."

"We heard your brother was on the prowl . . ."

"More revolutionaries we don't need . . ."

Danior laughed, a real laugh of charm and grace. "No need to apologize. I would reprimand you if you welcomed me in any other way."

It was a charming scene. Rather too charming, given Evangeline's susceptible state of mind, and she looked away—and into the Serephinian-colored eyes of an inquisitive old woman. Evangeline smiled weakly and looked elsewhere, and found almost every woman observing her with eager interest.

I'm not who you think I am, she wanted to say.

Instead she kept her mouth clamped shut as Norita tugged at Danior's tattered waistcoat. "What did you bring me?" she insisted.

"I brought you a . . . kiss." Leaning down, he placed a kiss on the girl's cheek. "And that's enough for a minx like you."

Heeding her mother's hissed instructions, Norita curtsied and said, "I like it, Your Highness." Then she added, "Do it again."

Lupe covered her eyes in chagrin, but Danior rumbled with merriment and kissed the girl. Then he held out his arms, and children rushed to him. He ruffled the boys' hair and kissed the girls' cheeks, put one of the little ones up on his shoulders and barely winced when he clutched his hair for support. And he coaxed the shy girl, the one who walked with a crutch, out from hiding, and held her in his arms.

He really did like daughters, Evangeline realized. And sons. He probably really did work at the orphanage and wash faces with royal ruthlessness, and that was good because she didn't know what to do around children.

Not that it mattered, because she wasn't going to wed Danior and have half a dozen daughters. No matter how appealing he looked with his hair rumpled and children hanging off him.

"Where are you going, my people?" He indicated the wagons piled high with belongings. "Did you see me and decide to leave?"

The tumult quieted and the old woman answered, "We're going to see you, Your Highness, at Revealing in Plaisance. Why aren't you already there?"

"There's been some difficulties along the road." Parents began to retrieve their children, and Danior gave them each a pat as they left. The crippled child he held the longest, speaking softly to her before placing her on the bench stretched across the sides of the cart.

A young man, short and sturdy, blessed with an air of authority, leaned against the door sill of the hut. "That's what we heard. Rumors are flying, Your Highness, that the rebels have captured you, or Princess Ethelinda, or both."

"Someday there'll be tales written of our adventures," Danior answered, "but I'll be there to pen them."

The men laughed and slapped each other on the

shoulders. The women nodded, and Evangeline heard one say, "I told you so."

"We assumed as much," the old lady said. "That's why we're on our way."

Striding to her side, Danior placed his hands on her skinny shoulders. "I can always depend on you, Memaw."

"Is that Princess Ethelinda?" Norita asked, her high-pitched voice clear over the adults' talk.

Danior ignored Evangeline's squeak of dismay, but answered as she might have wished. "It is the princess, and she wants to be called Evangeline."

Evangeline smiled as graciously as she could. "I'm not really—"

Danior looked at her, scorching her with the threat in his eyes.

"—Really dressed well enough to feel like a princess," she finished lamely. Right now, discretion seemed the better part of valor.

"Your inner beauty shines through the tattered clothing." Danior sounded warm and loving.

But she knew the truth. He would shake her like a rag doll if she disillusioned his people.

Her admission brought a heightened interest. The villagers looked her over, some cynically, some avidly, but all so thoroughly that she knew they would never forget her face. And what would these people think if, two days hence, they saw the real princess take her place at Danior's side?

Danior lifted a straight-backed chair into the back of the cart, then helped the old lady into it. "There's been no sign of revolutionaries here?"

"No." But the man at the door looked warily around at the mountains rimming the valley. "We've kept a watchful eye out, and the dogs you gave us run loose every night. Those bastards aren't going to catch us with our butts bare again."

"Lauri!" One of the women elbowed him and indicated Evangeline.

He scowled and kicked the dirt. "She might as well know what's gone on around here. The rumors say she ran away, and until she settles down and does her duty, we're all in danger."

"A woman with me is a woman under my protection, and is above reproach," Danior rebuked him, and Lauri lowered his head in acceptance.

Then Memaw snapped, "She was a child the first time, and in a far country the second. D'you think she's responsible, fool?"

Lauri's head came up. He glowered at the old woman, ready to fight, but Danior placed his hand on Lauri's shoulder. "Women make fools of us all, eh, Lauri?"

It wasn't an answer, but an awkward attempt to mollify a young man humiliated by tactless castigation, and into the moment of silence that followed, Evangeline's muttered comment was clear. "Easy enough to do."

The men looked astonished, much as they would if a faithful mule kicked.

The women burst into surprised laughter.

Memaw said, "You'll do, young Evangeline, you'll do."

Danior exchanged a look of disgust with Lauri, then glared at the women. They turned away or covered their mouths to stifle their merriment, and stiffly Danior said, "I, too, inherited a position as leader at a young age, and it's difficult earning respect, but Lauri is proving himself."

He looked around, and the women nodded, but their eyes still danced. Danior frowned at Evangeline, and she smiled back feebly. Stupid thing to be caught saying, yet sometimes Danior's conceit begged to be deflated, and there was no one to do it—except her.

His frown grew into a scowl, and without removing his gaze from her, he said, "The village looks good."

Evangeline looked around with trepidation. Twenty tiny, whitewashed and thatched wooden houses each had one window and one door. Smoke trickled out of a hole in the center of each roof. Mud dabbed the cracks. On the ground around the outside of each, sheaves of hay and leaves were stacked and held in place by large stones. These villagers fought cold, revolutionaries, and poverty. Today they were going to Plaisance for the event they'd anticipated for one thousand years.

It didn't matter that she wasn't the princess. The responsibility for these people, and all the people like them, weighed on her, dragging her onward to a fate she both craved and feared. Even if, somehow, the princess could communicate with Evangeline and joyously relinquish her position, Evangeline couldn't change her bloodlines or her past; she couldn't learn to be royal, nor could she produce the child Danior demanded. A child with noble bloodlines.

She looked pleadingly at Danior, almost as if he could rescue her from this dilemma, when he was really the cause of it.

But he and Lauri had half turned away. "Are you leaving a guard?" Evangeline heard him ask.

"A few guards. The dogs." Lauri gripped the handle of his pitchfork and shook it. "If Revealing doesn't occur, it won't matter anyway. There won't be anything left to come home to. We're going to starve here if we don't bring in a good crop, and the blight's on the barley again."

"Follow the old rituals," Memaw said.

Lauri flung his arms out, making windmills in the air. "The old rituals are useless."

"They weren't." Memaw leaned forward, clutching the arms of her chair. "They helped."

The women whispered among themselves.

"Rubbish!" Lauri shouted.

"We never had the blight when I was young!" Memaw shouted back.

"Stupid rituals, they were nothing but superstition and ignorance."

The men muttered to each other.

An old quarrel, oft repeated, it obviously divided the village. It was a quarrel Evangeline had no business interrupting, yet she found herself saying, "Are you talking about the Broadcast?"

"Aye, aye, that's what we're talking about." Lauri's face was ruddy and his voice blustering. "The Broadcast, done time out of mind to bless the fields. Well, we have a priest in to bless the fields every year, and it's done no good, we're all still starving by the time winter's finished."

"Because we don't do the Broadcast," Memaw insisted, her voice clear and strong. "It's magic."

"I'm sorry to say it, Memaw, but I agree with Lauri," Danior interposed. "It's a modern world and sad as it is, no one has time to waste going into the forest to collect herbs and play at rituals."

Lauri smirked, but Evangeline could keep quiet no more. "Actually, *I* think Memaw's right."

The murmuring stopped; Danior, Lauri, and Memaw, as well as every other adult and child from the village turned and looked at her. So much attention, and for what reason? Because they hoped she was a princess with the magic to save them?

No magic, she wanted to tell them, but science. Surreptitiously, she wiped her damp palms on her skirt. "The herb . . . it's royal maywort, isn't it?"

"So the old wives call it," Lauri said, making his opinion of old wives clear by his tone of voice.

Danior only stared at her, his head cocked, an odd wrinkle between his eyebrows.

"The botanical name is *Mentha nobilis*, an herb used by the ancients known to be a curative for flesh and plants." Delving deep into her brain, she recited the text from the *Genera Plantarum*. "Dried and spread over the growing crop of barley, in the past it was held responsible for the plenteous crops grown in this region known for its short summers and difficult winters."

"Doesn't matter what the ancients said," Lauri pointed out in ill-concealed triumph. "Doesn't even matter if it works. It's rare and delicate, and by royal command we're not supposed to cut it."

"What?" She looked at Danior, and he nodded confirmation. "When did that dictum get handed down?"

"I was a young woman," Memaw said.

"About fifty years ago," Danior added. "I don't know why."

Memaw leaned forward, clutching the arms of her chair. "The royal maywort was thin and hard to find that year, and the king commanded that none be cut until the herb had recovered. The next year, it was thinner still, and so it has gone until it has almost disappeared."

"No wonder!" Evangeline said. "It's called may-wort, you know, because it's commonly gathered in May in the shady corners where the snow has just melted. Probably one year was a cold year and everything was late coming up. Actually, royal maywort is a hardy plant which spreads from the root. It's strengthened by cutting the leaves." She warmed to her subject. "A medicinal plant, its characteristics were noted by the great botanist Linnaeus. Danior . . . His Highness used it on my wound." People were staring, she realized, staring as if each word she spoke stunned them like a blow to the brain.

Even Danior clutched the side of the cart with white knuckles.

"The paste of the herb worked remarkably well, proving its effectiveness, and it's well known that Linnaeus speculated that the same properties that make it cure infection in a wound also eliminates pests and disease on the crops." Her voice faded. There was a moment of unrelenting quiet. What was wrong with everyone? Why did they look so eager, and yet so frightened? She must have said something wrong . . . perhaps she shouldn't have contradicted a royal decree. Dropping her gaze to her unwieldy boots, she wished she could sink into the dirt.

Then shouting exploded around her.

"Impossible!" "It's true!" "We have to do something!" "I told you so!" "It's the prophecy!" "She's the princess!" "Wouldn't hurt to try!" "The prince said *no*." "He's not saying *no* now." "Prophecy, I tell you!"

And finally, "She's the princess!"

"She's the princess!"

"She's the princess."

Twenty-five

"*Another prophecy fulfilled.*" Danior rubbed his hands together and thought about the scene just outside the open door, outside of this very hut. The villagers had gone on to Plaisance, celebrating as they went, leaving him and his princess to enjoy the thin hospitality of a hamlet stricken by poverty—and now, overwhelmed with optimism.

"Stop gloating," Evangeline said.

"I can't help it. This couldn't be more perfect."

They sat shoulder to shoulder on a bench, table before them, while she studiously avoided his gaze. In between sips of thin cabbage soup from a tin cup, she said, "I never heard about *this* prophecy."

In his jubilance, he couldn't help mocking her. "Your learned friend Leona didn't tell you about it?"

Magnificently sullen, she glared through the dim and smoky air at the tiny fire that flickered in the firepit, every inch a princess with her regal air and her disdain.

He laid his hand on her elbow. "The people took it as a sign."

"I *know* they took it as a sign." She jerked her arm away. "I heard them."

But while he wanted her to show that hauteur to others, with him he wanted the Evangeline who would be his wife. He wanted her to acknowledge him, and the significance of what had happened. He wanted her to say she loved him again. He wanted her to look at him.

"I couldn't believe it when you started in." He slid his arm around her waist. *"Before the wedding day, the princess shall feed the hungry and return us to the prosperity of the old days.* And there you were, in front of a whole village of people, telling us how to cure the blight that has plagued us for half a century."

"That's a vague prophecy." She tried to shrug him away. "I still don't understand why they were so excited. I didn't recommend anything new."

"No, just the best old medicine there is."

"We don't know if it'll work yet."

"It will. You know it will."

Leaning forward as if she hoped to brush his arm off, she took a bite of the day old bread she'd toasted over the flames. "I know," she said glumly.

"The villagers will spread the word that the princess has fulfilled the prophecy, and hope will spread on its own."

Evangeline slammed her empty cup onto the table and turned to him, face ablaze with fury. "I'm not the princess!"

She was really angry, Danior realized. Angry and dismayed and hostile.

She reminded him of a cat: soft and purring when she was contented, but underneath a fine, nervous strength bolstered by tooth and claw. He had to calm her, to keep her happy.

Her stomach must still be empty.

Taking her cup, he filled it again from the pot steaming on the fire's edge. He cut her another slice of the rank white goat's cheese, and came back to the bench. Sliding in beside her, he placed the food before her. "Eat some more."

She took a bite of cheese.

And because he could not let her deny her birthright, he added, "I can't have my princess go hungry."

She stared into the cup at the thin broth and the floating pieces of cabbage, and in her face he thought he saw desperation.

"I'll go out and get us another rabbit," he promised.

She paid no attention to that—another sign of her perturbation. "Why are all the prophecies about *me*?" she demanded. "Why aren't any of them about *you*?"

"They are. Or rather, one is."

"One. How eye-popping." She almost prickled with animosity. "What is this prophecy?"

"The prince shall embrace his greatest fear and make it his own."

"Another vague prophecy. What does that mean?"

She irritated him with her deliberate obtuseness. "It's not vague at all. I shall have to face the revolutionaries, probably even Dominic himself, and somehow subdue them."

"Why should Dominic and the revolutionaries be your greatest fear?"

"When the revolutionaries lobbed the bomb that killed my parents, my mother didn't die at once. She screamed and screamed. I couldn't get to her, the

Lord Chamberlain dragged me away to safety, and I—''
His heart pounded as he remembered. Thrusting his
hand out, he let her see how it shook. ''I am afraid of
dying in agony. I'm afraid that you could be mortally
wounded. And I can't kill my own brother.''

''Oh.'' Discomfited and too compassionate to let
him suffer alone, she took his hand in hers and held
it. ''So you think that trial is yet to come?''

''Either that, or the prophecies are, as you said,
vague, and no more magic than the crystal case.''

She dropped his hand. ''So you just used the villagers' expectations of the princess to bond me to the
fulfillment of an old, ambiguous prophecy?''

He was heartless, he knew, and not romantic in the
way this tender female desired. He didn't believe in
magic, or in anything he couldn't touch or smell or
reason with. His occasional premonitions he ascribed
to years of clandestine fighting. But his ruthlessness
had its purpose. ''I will use any means to secure our
place on the throne.''

From the way she looked at him, it was obvious
she wasn't liking him right now. ''Will you be gone
long rabbit hunting?''

The woman never gave up. ''Not long enough for
you to escape.''

She kicked the table leg like a recalcitrant child.

''I'll bring in one of the dogs. I trained them, and if
I tell them to stay with you, they will.''

''I'm afraid of dogs.''

''Good.'' Standing, he flung his rucksack over his
shoulder. ''While I'm in the mountains, I'll cut as
much royal maywort as I can find to leave here.'' He
couldn't keep the chagrin out of his voice. ''I should
have known that was what the problem was, but I've

been off fighting and—well, there's no excuse good enough."

"Besides, when the old wives say to gather royal maywort in the dark of the moon in the month of May, it sounds like magic, and you don't believe in magic." She mocked him in her turn. "You only believe it when it's couched in scientific terms."

"No need to be snippy, miss." He rubbed his knuckles at her temple. "I've been a dimwit. Now give me your word that you won't try to leave."

She turned her head away.

"Your word, Evangeline, or I'll tie you while I'm gone *and* set the dogs to watch."

"I won't leave"—she promised—"while you're gone."

"That's good enough." Danior almost got to the door when her voice stopped him.

She stood with her hands on her hips, looking, much to Danior's delight, like a scolding wife. *His* scolding wife. "I still think we should have gone with the villagers."

"Lauri and I considered it. He was willing, I was not."

"But why? There's safety in numbers. We could have mingled with the crowds going to Revealing and got to Plaisance without incident."

"There are only two roads into Plaisance. The revolutionaries must be watching both. I am not easily disguised, and you, dearling, have been scrutinized by Dominic. There's no way we could go with the villagers without putting them in danger."

She pressed her mouth into a firm line that told him she wanted to object more.

Of course she wanted to object more. In a crowd,

she hoped to lose *him*. With giant strides, he reached her and cupped her haughty chin. Looking into her eyes, he rubbed his thumb across her lips. "The trip will be safest by boat. We won't lose each other that way." He almost laughed at her transparent expression of aggravation. "You have to trust me, Evangeline."

"Oh, I do."

She sounded as grumpy as Memaw, and he couldn't resist. He pressed a kiss on her tightly shut mouth . . . and lingered. As cautiously as a bud opening to the sun, she opened to him. She was new, delicate, unsure, yet with an allure so potent it pulled at him as powerfully as the moon pulled the tides. Desire slammed through him, and he dragged her into him in an embrace that gave no quarter.

Then he pulled back. This woman plucked at his ragged control, drawing him to the edge and almost beyond. Almost. But he was a man, mature and disciplined. He would not grant himself leave to behave like a randy boy. To behave like his father.

With one more light kiss—he didn't want her to think she had affected him too much—he let her go and walked back to the door.

"I suppose I shouldn't be surprised that you refuse to travel with them. They are common, after all."

He swung around and glared at her, a solitary figure in rags, yet defiant to the last. "I don't feel that way! There is a great difference between traveling with, visiting with, and being with the peasants, and wanting to mix my blood with them. Why is this so difficult for you to understand?"

"Oh, I understand. You're an aristocrat." She made it sound like an insult.

He squeezed the door sill, using only the grip of his fingers to keep himself from going to her and doing her an injury. "Of course I am. And so are you."

"No, I'm not." She pleated her fingers together. "I'm Evangeline Scoffield of East Little Teignmouth, Cornwall. I don't even have a real surname—Scoffield is the town where I was found orphaned."

"You fulfilled the prophecy!"

"It was an accident!"

"You've had a lot of accidents lately, then!" He took a breath and groped for his lost temper. "I will go and hunt. You will stay here and think about how you could benefit Bamphina—"

"Sereminia."

"—by performing the role of princess to which you were born." Once again he started out.

Once again she called him back. "Danior, wait!"

He paused, but he didn't turn around. "Evangeline, you can't conceive what you are asking for when you try my patience so."

In a rush, she said, "Memaw told me you sent them materials to rebuild Blanca."

"Aristocrats do that," he said dryly, but he faced Evangeline once more. "The revolutionaries burned them out because they were loyal to the Leons. The French burned them out because they helped the resistance. Of course I had to help rebuild."

"Memaw says the royal coffers are none too full."

"They will be when we're married and the prosperity of the country is guaranteed." He held out his hand as if presenting her to the court. "Royal maywort. Who would have thought it?"

That shut her up, he noted with satisfaction. Leaving the door open, he stepped out and took a breath of the fresh air. The shadows were long, reaching across the valley as the sun moved toward the western horizon. The land appeared empty, yet he had met the five men left behind to patrol the paths that descended from the mountains. He would find one and tell him to guard the cottage with his dog, while Danior escaped to hunt a rabbit he didn't really need. The villagers had offered him anything he wished, and it would be better if he stayed close by Evangeline.

But it was only late afternoon. They had two hours before darkness; two hours before he could take her to the simple featherbed fastened in the corner.

He couldn't take her to bed when the few guards Lauri had left might enter the hut at any moment to talk or eat or just gaze at the couple they considered their salvation. Yet he couldn't stay by her and still resist the urge to mate. So he would run like a coward until night had fallen and he could once more hold her in his arms.

And make love to her tethered by the restraint he must use.

Restraint. He'd lived with restraint all these years. Why did it gall him so much now?

From the path behind the hut, he heard a bark, and a man's loud voice.

Who was it? And why?

Stepping back into the shadow of the doorway, Danior listened intently.

"As you can see, we're a poor village. It's been a bad year, and we haven't a lot of food to share, but there's fresh ale." It was Justino, one of the guards, a quiet man now projecting his voice with the virtuosity of an opera singer. "How many are you?"

"A dozen of us," a strange man's voice said. "How many of you live in this pathetic village, and why don't you join our cause?"

Danior grew cold with disdain and repressed fury. The revolutionaries had come to Blanca.

Twenty-six

Danior fought the drive to lie in wait, to catch this stinking rebel and throttle him with his own hands. If not for Evangeline, he probably would, but . . . but he couldn't endanger her. Not when he'd brought her so close to Plaisance, and the throne. Not when he'd made her his woman.

The revolutionaries must have been watching from above, and when the villagers left, they had sent a scout down. The rules of hospitality were strong, so Justino welcomed him, but the two men verbally circled each other, testing for strengths, testing for weaknesses.

"You'll stay in my hut," Justino said.

"Why there? There's a fire in here. In the largest hut." The rebel's voice became accusing. "What are you trying to hide?"

"That's our head man's hut!" Justino managed to sound indignant.

The stranger laughed. "He's gone. He won't care." With fine carelessness, he asked, "Have you had any royal visitors lately?"

Had the revolutionaries seen Danior and Evangeline on their trek across the valley, or were they fishing for information?

The rebel and the guard were coming closer. "How odd you should ask, " Justino said. "The prince and princess were just here today. You'd better hurry or you'll miss them."

Slipping back into the hut, Danior found Evangeline placing the dishes in a pan, picking up his cloak, preparing to flee.

Too late for that.

Through the window, the rebel replied, "We have a band searching the road ahead. We'll get them."

The confidence in his voice raised the hair on Danior's neck. Taking Evangeline's hand, he led her toward one windowless side of the hut. Inside where the walls met the packed dirt floor, sheaves of hay and leaves were stacked to protect against the whistle of the winter blizzard—and to disguise Blanca's hidden cache.

A false wall ran the length of the hut, two feet inside, floor to ceiling. To the careless eye, it appeared to be the inner wall, but behind it were stored bags of grain and casks of salted meat. If marauders burned the hut, all would be lost, but in the lawless times created by the revolution and Napoleon, it had safeguarded the villagers' survival more than once.

One sheaf camouflaged the tiny hatch in the wall, hooked to it with twisted lengths of hay. Searching for it, Danior pulled at several sheaves. Nothing. Wasted minutes.

The guard and the rebel were almost to the hut.

Almost too late, Danior yanked on a sheaf, and the

weight told him he'd found the one connected to the hatch.

Sheaf, hatch, and all came up in his hand. He set the crude assemblage down and propelled Evangeline toward the small, dark hole.

She backed up like a recalcitrant mule.

He remembered that she'd been locked in the closet at her school. He understood. He didn't care.

Taking the top of her head, he pushed her down and shoved her in. She collapsed, from surprise or fear, he couldn't tell. Didn't matter. She just had to get in.

He kept pushing, and she rolled inside. He followed, and pulled the hatch behind him.

Total, absolute darkness. Air, close and warm, dry with the scent of grain. Evangeline's harsh breathing.

Groping, he found her huddled against the back wall burrowed between two sacks of grain, her knees drawn up to her chest, her head down. She shivered, little shudders of primal fear. He gave her head a quick pat, dropped the knapsack, pulled his knife, and faced the hatch.

No sound permeated the walls around them. Had Justino kept the rebel outside? Had they entered the hut? Danior had no way of knowing. His real concern was fire. If the rebels were smart, they wouldn't try to torch the village.

But damn, how he hated cowering here in the darkness.

Leaning his head against the wood of the hatch, he strained to listen, but heard nothing.

Except that Evangeline's breathing became more labored.

Keeping his eyes fixed toward the opening, he scooted toward her and bent close to her ear. "Are you ill?"

Her unsteady voice rose and fell. "I can't... breathe."

"Sh." With the knife in one hand, he pulled her close and wrapped his free arm around her. He pressed her head to his chest and tried to infuse her with courage.

But her courage had vanished, dissolved by the darkness she feared. Her teeth chattered. She clasped at his shirt. If he hadn't experienced this himself, he would have never believed it of his valiant princess.

Then, from inside the main room, he faintly heard male voices.

She heard them, too, for she stilled like a cornered creature.

Danior freed himself from her clutch. He moved toward the hatch and crouched there, knife in hand, ready to ambush anyone who tried to enter.

Nothing happened. The voices got louder and more numerous. Danior couldn't make out the words. He couldn't identify the speakers. But apparently the village guards must have been numerous enough that the revolutionaries dared do nothing but eat and drink. And the hatch's camouflage worked. No one came close.

By the time Danior relaxed enough to ease the cramps in his legs, evening had fallen. He could see the rim of light around the hatch; the fire had been stoked, and from the sound of the ever-increasing merriment, the cask of ale had been tapped.

Danior stood, shaking the kinks out of his knees. His head brushed the ceiling, but he thought Evan-

THE RUNAWAY PRINCESS 269

geline would appreciate the sensation of space.

"Evangeline." He reached down to stroke her, but she was gone. "Evangeline?" For one mad moment, he could only think she had taken flight.

Then reality returned. She had nowhere to go and no way to get there. He searched, calling her name in soothing, hushed whispers. He found the knapsack where he had dropped it. He found the cloak wadded into a ball. Finally, he found her, curled up, her back against a cask, barely breathing, chilled, unmoving.

"Evangeline," he murmured, "there's room in here. You can stand up." He tried to lift her to her feet, but she might have been a stone frozen in a sheet of ice. She reacted not at all. He knelt beside her. "Evangeline, it's Danior. You know that." He wrapped his arms around her, warming her with his heat. "You know I won't allow anything to hurt you."

A crash sounded in the hut, and raised male voices brayed a laugh.

Evangeline flinched, and Danior was relieved. Relieved for any indication she was aware of her surroundings. Rubbing his hands up and down her arms, he kissed her cheek. He kissed her mouth. He hugged her as tightly as he could. "Evangeline, we're safe here. There's even some light. Look toward the hatch. You can see—"

She lunged at it. He caught her and she clawed at him, whimpering. Her struggles grew greater as he tried to contain them, and her distress grew louder. If he didn't stop her somehow, they would be discovered.

He put his hand over her mouth to muffle the sounds. "Dearling. Dearling, please don't do this. I love you, but—"

And she lunged at *him*. Grasping his hair, she slammed him against the stacked bags of grain. They tilted. He tumbled back on them, trying to descend as quietly as possible. She fell on him.

Or leapt on him, he couldn't tell. Dust flew as he seized her, sure she would try to run for the hatch.

Instead she grabbed the edges of his shirt so violently that the stitches popped.

Uncomprehending, he caught her wrists—and she kissed his chest.

"Evangeline?"

"Please," she whispered. "Distract me. Take me away."

She found his male nipple, nestled among the curling hair, licked it, kissed it, and set her teeth to it.

He lurched in pain, amazement, and confusion. "Evangeline, we have to be quiet. We can't . . . there are men out there. Men who want to kill us."

"I'll be quiet, I promise, but listen."

He did listen. The revolutionaries were singing a traditional drinking song, and somewhere in the background, two men were brawling.

"They can't hear us."

"No, but I have to be ready in case—"

"They can't hear us," she repeated. "They don't know we're here. We'll be quiet. And I don't care about them. I only care about the dark." A shudder racked her, a shudder he felt through her frame and into his. "I'm not afraid with you."

Damn. The dark, the danger, the noise of the rebels' celebration . . .

Evangeline's breath on his skin, her desperation, the urgency of her body rocking against his . . .

For some reason, for all the reasons, he wanted her,

and he wanted her now. This minute. Without preliminaries, without touching. He just wanted to place her
below him and enter her and have his way, with no
thought to tenderness.

He took a huge breath. He was a beast.

He had to think of Evangeline.

Gently, he squeezed her wrists, then let go of them.
"Dearling, this isn't wise . . ."

She slipped her hands inside his shirt and tore it
from top to bottom.

The noise of the splitting cloth brought him up on
his elbows. He grabbed at her again. "Evangeline,
please, we shouldn't—"

One of her hands slid inside his trousers. The other
tugged at the buttons. She kissed his stomach, and for
a moment his desire blocked all rational thought.

For a moment. Until he fought his way back to discipline.

Fine. She was determined. So they'd do this. Now.
But he couldn't just take her. He would be like his
father, a slave to his passions.

"This isn't the way." His voice cracked. "Evangeline, I'll give you what you want, but we have to be
civilized."

She breathed heavily, but not from fear now.
"Why?"

"Because." Because I might hurt you. "Because
we're the prince and princess."

"I told you, I am *not* the princess." The buttons
gave way. "And right now, you are not the prince."
She grasped his erection.

Pure pleasure shot through him, and he arched his
back. She stroked him, up from the base, around the
head, down again. She handled his balls as if seeking

something . . . the secret of his strength, the heart of his passion.

She had found it. He swore she had.

He couldn't tell if his eyes were open or closed. Red circles spun in the darkness. His hands tore at the rough sacks below.

When he grasped a handful of barley, he realized what he'd done. He'd ripped the seams. His bestial passion was too much like destruction. He had to remain the master.

Half-desperate, he reached for her shoulders and tried to pull her up to him. "Let me touch you. Let me kiss you."

"No," she said softly, gutturally. "Let *me*."

And her mouth, warm and wet and seeking, closed over him.

Her tongue moved, licking like a cat's. Her teeth scraped him, ever so lightly. She sucked on him and blasted control away.

He caught her under the armpits and dragged her up to him, desolate at losing the touch of her mouth, but desperate to be between her legs. He rolled her beneath him, lifting her skirt as he did so. Her thighs wrapped around him, and he found her center, warm and wet. Without preliminaries, he pressed inside her.

She bit off a cry, but he didn't care. He didn't care if he hurt her, he didn't care if the rebels found them, he didn't care if the world ended. He only cared about his satisfaction, about plunging into her again and again, about trying to get all the way inside her, into her center, into the place where he would be king. King, not of Baminia, but of Evangeline.

Her lover. Her lord.

Her master.

His hips hammered, he strained and groaned. Her hands slipped in the sweat forming on his shoulders until she dug her nails into his flesh, and that was good, too. She should mark him. Mark him with tooth and claw, make him her own.

He spread her legs wider, he lifted himself above her, he strained to be inside her—and his seed spurted from him, against her womb, filling her, marking her as she had marked him.

Forever. He'd marked her forever.

Slowly, he sank back on top of her. Her trembling arms wrapped him closer; echoes from her orgasm still quivered through her to him.

He'd done it. He'd lost his restraint, yet bound her to him. She could never escape him now.

"Evangeline," he commanded. "Tell me. Tell me again."

She knew what he wanted. She slid a languid hand between his shoulder blades, and whispered in his ear. "I love you, Danior. You're the only man I will ever love."

Twenty-seven

"Your Highness?" the guard called from the open hatchway.

Evangeline came out of sleep in a rush, her first thought to flee.

But Danior wrapped his arm over her and whispered, "Don't worry. He's a villager."

In a way, that was even worse. To have a man who had seen her yesterday see her again this morning with her hair in a tangle, her dress even more ragged, and . . . well, after last night, she probably glowed with sensual satisfaction. Danior had lost that temperance that normally marked his every deed, and he'd made love to her with vigor and conviction, holding nothing back.

Making a grab for the cloak that Danior had, at some point in the night, brought to cover her, she pulled the edge over her head, and hoped the guard didn't come all the way into the hiding place.

"Yes, Justino?" Danior's voice was deep and froggy with sleep, and he kept himself between Evangeline and feeble sunlight trickling in from the hut.

"Our visitors. They finally all drank themselves to sleep. I tied them up."

"Where are the other guards?" Danior asked.

"I sent them back out on patrol in case there are rebels lurking in the woods. You should leave as soon as possible."

"Thank you," Danior said gravely. "If you'll give us a minute, we'll be out."

"Of course, Your Highness." Justino leaned the hatch half against the hole in the wall, letting in a little light and a trickle of fresh air, but giving them the illusion of privacy.

Privacy which they did not need, in Evangeline's opinion.

But Danior seemed satisfied with the situation. Raising himself on one elbow, he tugged the cloak down and looked her over. She lay on the tumbled sacks of seed and stared back.

The night had been rough on him, too. His beard had grown out to a black stubble. His hair looked as if rats had nested there. His shirt was torn open, his trousers were unbuttoned, and if his condition were anything to go by, he would never be satisfied no matter what service she performed.

But for the first time since she'd met him, that intent, inflexible expression of dominion had disappeared. With rebels in the next room, Plaisance to reach, and a crystal case to open, still he looked almost . . . relaxed. At ease.

And his contentment gave her an unwanted and perplexing thrill.

With the palm of his hand, he stroked her cheek. "So. What are you thinking this morning?"

That I am yours; that you are mine. That nothing could

ever change that now. "That I can speak seven languages and I can't say no in any of them."

His eyebrows lifted. "Did you want to say no?"

She lifted hers back at him. "No."

A faint smile curved his lips, and he looked almost . . . relieved?

"Did you?" she asked.

"As I recall, I tried. You would have none of it."

The memory of her frantic attack brought heated color to her cheeks. "I was . . . worried."

"You were afraid." His smile disappeared, his face grew austere. "Whoever put you in that closet shall be whipped."

"Whoever put me in that closet is far away and long ago." She would do anything to bring back that smile, even grant him every victory he ever wished for or imagined. "Besides, it doesn't matter anymore. Anytime I have to face the dark, I'll think of you and what we did here, and I'll go willingly."

"Only with me, dearling." Turning her head up to his, he gave her a light kiss. "Only with me." Rising, he shook like a dog, and loose barley flew through the air. "We fit together well. I want you, and you want me. We make good mates. You can't deny that."

"Of course. Because I love you and you . . . love me."

He turned his back to her, but she didn't need to see his face. Just the way he rubbed his hand over the back of his neck told her everything she needed to know. "Of course I do."

She smiled with bittersweet anguish at the tousled head. In a king, it was a good thing not to lie well. In a man, this lack of guile revealed too much.

He waited guiltily for her to say something else, but

when she held her peace, he declared, "We have everything in common—our backgrounds and our breeding. We'll have the assurance of knowing our children have blue blood running in their veins."

"That's important," she agreed gravely.

"Yes." He buttoned his trousers and tucked in his pathetic shred of a shirt. "I'm able to trace my ancestors back over a thousand years, and so can you. Our nobility is without blemish. Our children's right to the throne can never be in question."

"That's important, too," said the orphan from England.

"It's the most important reason that we reach Plaisance for our wedding tomorrow."

"Yes, the prince and princess must marry." The prince and the real princess, wherever she was.

Picking up her socks and boots, he knelt before her and lifted her foot to examine it. "It looks good. How does it feel?"

"It aches," she admitted. "A little."

"You walked too much yesterday. Today you'll stay off it." He laced her into her footwear, then stood and held out his hand.

She let him pull her to her feet.

Putting his hands in her hair, he ruffled it, then combed it with his fingers. "The rebels might be watching the river, but we have a chance of eluding them there." He picked up his rucksack and flung it over his shoulder.

She tugged at the strap on the rucksack. "Let me take that. It's not too heavy."

Danior hesitated.

"You might need your hands clear in case of a fight," she added.

"You think like a warrior." He transferred the bag to her and drew his knife, then crawled through the hole on his hands and knees.

She followed, marveling he'd gotten her through there in the first place last night. How had he done it? She didn't remember much of that moment beyond a return to the bone-chilling fear she'd experienced in the orphanage—the fear of never being let out, of being buried alive.

Now she was reborn, sliding out into the light of morning, knowing what she had to do, no longer dogged by fear of the future, because she'd lived more in three days than most women did in their whole lives.

And that was worth something.

The man called Justino stood grim-faced, speaking to Danior, gesturing to the revolutionaries who lay passed out and drooling about the floor. Ropes bound their wrists and ankles, and Danior turned each one with his foot, looking into their faces.

Evangeline knew who he sought. She allowed the knapsack to slide to the floor as she said, "He's not here."

"Hm?" Danior flipped another rebel, who groaned and stirred.

"Dominic's not here. If he were, we would have been dragged out and hanged last night."

Danior looked at her.

"Dominic's smart and he's ruthless." She hadn't been around him long, but that much she knew. "If Dominic had seen us walk into the valley, he would have torn this place apart until he either found us or there were no hiding places left."

Danior nodded slowly as he flipped the last man. "You're right, but I can't take the chance—"

Evangeline sucked in her breath.

"What?" He followed her gaze to the man on the floor. He was awake, red-eyed and vibrant with hatred. "Who is he?"

She tucked her shaking hands into the folds of her skirt. "I called him 'Shorty.' "

"Pasty-faced bitch," Shorty said. "I remember what you did, and I'm going to get you. You'll squeal like a pig when I—"

Danior flipped him back facedown on the dirt floor. When he tried to curse her again, Danior put his foot on the back of his head and ground it into the floor.

Evangeline flinched. "Don't." Not that she felt sorry for Shorty. He was a vile little man. But memories of a similar helplessness loomed close, and she couldn't bear to watch.

Danior lifted his foot. "As you wish, my princess." And as Shorty began to bray invective again, he said to Justino, "Take care of him." Taking her arm, Danior hustled her out the door while Shorty yelled, then fell abruptly silent.

Evangeline craned around. "He didn't—"

"Just a little blow to the head, I'm sure." Danior led her on the path to the river. "Nothing to be concerned about. Justino wouldn't want to bloody the hut. Now we have to find a boat."

"Will they have one?"

"They live on the river. Of course they have one. Probably more than one, but they'll be hidden."

Hidden. Of course. It would be too easy if they were in plain sight.

She caught glimmers of the river through the trees,

and heard its ever-increasing murmur as the water-course wound through the valley, growing broader as it went. Then they reached the bank, and the river spread out before her. Impossible to think this mighty stream started from the tiniest trickle in the mountains, gathered strength so quickly, and now flowed broad and swift on to the city of Plaisance.

Impossible to think this whole affair had started at an innocent dinner at Château Fortuné, and had swept her along to this moment. To this conclusion.

Danior beheld the river with an upsurge of pride. This was his land, his river, and—he gazed at Evangeline—his woman.

They had not a moment to spare. They had to be in Plaisance tonight. Yet he couldn't resist reaching out to her and pulling her close against his body. She came willingly, and lifted her mouth for his kiss without being told. She kissed him as if she drew strength from his existence, as if her soul would wither without his attentions, and that was how it should be.

She'd made love with him as no other woman had, denying him his restraint and reveling in his strength. She was more than a princess, a means to a kingdom. She was the embodiment of the new, united land, of Bamphina at its shining best. With her at his side, he could do anything.

She drew back from the kiss, and put her hands on his cheeks. She looked at his face as if she wished to memorize every feature, every line. And she said, "We have to hurry. Where are the boats?"

He kissed her again, just enough to muddle that practical mind of hers, then set her away and looked around. "There." He pointed to a mound of underbrush just upstream. "They must be there."

Of course they were, and he dragged out the best one with her getting in his way and chatting, "Are there oars? Do we have to row? Is the river dangerous? How long will it take to get to Plaisance?"

"Here are the oars." He set them into the oarlocks. "The current is swift enough we won't have to row, but we'll use them to steer." Through the rapids, but he didn't need to tell her that. "And we'll be in Plaisance before the sun reaches its zenith."

"Oh!" Clapping her hands across her mouth, she looked at him, appalled. "I forgot the knapsack."

He frowned. He hated to lose it, with its supply of royal maywort, but in a few hours they surely wouldn't need it. Pushing the boat into the river, he tied it loosely to a branch. "We'll be in Plaisance by the end of the day, or we'll be dead. In either case, we won't need those supplies."

"Memaw gave me a hat yesterday, and long gloves. On the river, if I don't have them, I'll burn."

She was already tanned, a light touch of sun that brought color to her cheeks and set the jewels of her eyes in gold.

"I hate to burn. My nose gets red and blotchy, and tomorrow is the ceremony. Everyone will be looking. And it's our wedding day."

The boat bobbed in the current, watertight and ready to go, and he answered with a touch of impatience. "You're always beautiful."

"But it hurts when I sunburn." She stood with her hands clasped before her. "Please, I'll just run and get the knapsack."

He thought about her foot. He thought about how long it would take her. He thought about the probably lifeless body of Shorty she would see. And he said, "I've got longer legs. I'll go get it."

He started off at a trot, hurrying back along the path while a clock ticked in his mind. They had to reach Plaisance by noon. Hopefully someone besides Dominic and his revolutionaries would be watching the docks. If they could get to the palace and reassure their attendants, most of whom had to be hysterical by now, then they could bathe and come out on the balcony and show themselves to the people. That would take care of any rumors about their demise . . .

A hat?

Danior stopped trotting.

Long gloves? Yesterday Evangeline had been worried about a sunburn and how that would look at the ceremony and their wedding?

Yesterday? Evangeline—embarrassed and humiliated by the fulfillment of that prophecy—Evangeline had thought of this *yesterday*?

Wheeling around, Danior started off at a run toward the river. Through a break in the trees, he saw an empty boat float past on the current. The extra boat.

As he skidded to a halt on the bank, he saw their boat, with Evangeline at the oars, pulling for the center of the river.

"Evangeline!" he roared. "You come back here right now."

Turning her head, she looked at him, and lifting one oar, she waved.

"Evangeline!"

She called something across the water, and while he couldn't quite hear her, he was sure she said, "I love you. I will love you forever."

Twenty-eight

The boat's bow tilted straight down as it dove into another cataract, and Evangeline desperately leaned into the oars. To no avail. A whirlpool caught her and spun her one hundred and eighty degrees, and she found herself facing upstream, where a veritable waterfall raced down at her. Then she shot around again, just in time to climb up and out and face another mountain of water.

She didn't know how long this had been going on. Forever. Not long. Her sweaty palms clutched the oars, and a boulder loomed before her. She paddled away and the river snatched her, sweeping her around and onward. The bottom of the boat scraped on another stone, it tilted, and water lapped in from the side. If this ordeal didn't end soon, she wouldn't have to worry about Danior. She'd be singing with the angels in paradise—and she couldn't carry a tune.

As rapidly as she'd entered the rapids, she shot out. The roar and splash fell behind her, the river widened, and the churning smoothed into a slow, comforting glide into a valley that extended as far as her eye could see. Evangeline clutched the oars as a similar rush in her veins slowly diminished. She was safe. She was fine. She had made it.

The boat had not. The impact of rocks had broken the seal of tar. Water seeped in from every seam. She steered toward the Serephinian shore, her arms aching as she tried to navigate the increasingly heavy craft through the current.

The boat sank ten feet from the sandy shore, and she had to swim—a skill she had never learned. She went down three times before her feet struck bottom and she crawled up on the sand.

Gasping, spitting up water, she rolled over and stared at the pure blue sky with its delightful, fluffy clouds, and practiced first her German, then her Baminian, then her good old English curse words.

Danior could have told her about the rapids. Who would have thought the river could drop so fast and contain so many rocks? Thank God she'd read those letters from that American frontiersman. If he hadn't described a similar ordeal, and how he'd survived, she might have crashed on the rocks and perished.

As it was, she was still above Plaisance, when she had planned to float past into Spain. From there she had decided to go on to . . . somewhere. Now she'd have to take her chances on the road. Danior would probably start looking for her in this exact site, knowing full well that if she made it through the cataracts, she'd be forced to stop here. And the revolutionaries, too, were watching.

Yet what did they matter? She wasn't the princess, and Danior had made it clear the princess was who he must have.

His pride and his prattling about their children and

their right to the throne had fired her determination to flee.

Should she go to England, with its dark, cloudy days, everlasting loneliness, and bone-chilling damp? No. For the first time, she faced the truth. If she went back there, someone might recognize her as the one who took Leona's fortune, and she'd read too much about English jails to make that an acceptable prospect. Moreover, she had no money. She'd already experienced an English charitable institution, and she'd barely made it out alive.

So she had to go somewhere else. She knew so many miscellaneous bits of information. There had to be a way for her to make a living.

In France, perhaps. She understood the theory of wine-making. Or in Italy. She could guide the English tourists through the Roman antiquities. Or even in Switzerland, descending a cliff on a rope to rescue the local goats.

But if she didn't get moving, she wouldn't make it, because if she knew Danior he was navigating that river as fast as he could. He didn't have a boat or oars, but she didn't believe that would stop him. The man would make do with a log and twigs.

Dragging herself erect, she looked around. Pine trees marched almost down to the river on either side and extended in dark green patches up into the mountains. Here and there across the river she could see clearings with fields and a village. Most villages looked deserted; one bustled with the same excitement and focus as Blanca the day before. The people were going to Revealing. Not just the annual celebration of when Revealing might take place, but *the* Revealing.

For some inexplicable reason, Evangeline gazed on those tiny figures and felt as guilty as a rebellious princess. She shouldn't, but she did.

Turning away, she walked up the bank, favoring her still aching foot.

What were they going to do if the real princess didn't show up? Danior wouldn't get the chance to open the crystal case, not even with that gadget he'd had made, without his princess at his side.

A deeply rutted road wound its way north and south, following the river. This forest was almost eerie in its solitude, although she fought the uncomfortable sensation of being watched. Yet when she turned and looked, she saw no one. Everyone was already in Plaisance. So she turned south.

Danior would be standing on the steps of the cathedral, alone, trying to explain to people who had waited for this moment a thousand years that his princess preferred obscurity to marriage to him. That she'd rather see the two countries fall into the hands of the revolutionaries, to know that war and mayhem destroyed their way of life just when faith gleamed its brightest.

And they'd kill him. She'd read about mobs, and she knew about blighted hopes. They'd tear Danior from limb to limb, and he wouldn't fight them because all his dreams had been dashed by her defection.

By the *princess's* defection, she corrected herself.

The path curved to avoid the boulders and trees. Sometimes she walked beside the river, sometimes it wandered out of sight, but always she heard its continuous murmur as she strode in the grass beside the road.

This whole adventure had been a mishap, a series of coincidences that marked her as the princess, threw her into proximity with the first real man she'd ever met, and ended this morning when she escaped him for the third and last time.

Of course, she wasn't completely gone from him. He kept her heart, and she ached with the kind of pain that made her want to double over and howl.

Princess-like behavior, indeed.

She wasn't the princess, and yet . . . and yet . . . what would it hurt if she went to Plaisance? She could find a place tonight, surely one of the villages had an empty hut where she could sleep, and tomorrow she could go into Plaisance and join the crowd as they went to the cathedral. If the real princess didn't come, and the people were angry enough at Danior to kill him, then she could . . . well, she could do something.

She picked up her pace.

That was a better plan than just walking away and never finding out what happened, torn between imagining the worst—Danior's death—and hoping for the best: Danior's marriage to the real princess.

"Well, it is the best," she said out loud. "It would be the best for everyone."

The road made one of its bends, and off to the left she saw a hut tucked into a clearing. A man sat on a chair in the yard; its legs were tilted back, his hat was tilted forward. He smiled, displaying a full, white set of teeth, two incongruous dimples, and eyes where kindness never reached.

She recognized him, and her heart began to pound in fast, steady, earth-shaking thumps. Picking up her skirts, she ran.

He laughed, that familiar, cruel laughter.

Dominic.

She heard the chair smack the ground and pounding feet behind her. Blind with fear, she dodged off the track and ran into the forest, but before she'd taken two steps, he slammed into her and sent her flying. Before she could even recover her breath, he had her slung over his shoulder.

He held one of her arms twisted backward. He gripped her wrist so tightly that the bones ground together, and if she did anything to free herself, it would be at the expense of her joints.

So she stayed as still as she could, endured the pain, waited for the moment when he put her down and she could fight him.

"Princess Ethelinda, you save me so much trouble. You came to me—again."

By his tone she knew he was amused, and more so when she flinched. "You have a . . . remarkable tendency . . . to be where I am," she gasped as she jostled on top of his shoulder.

"I have my ways."

"Spies," she sneered.

"Of course. Men will do remarkable things for their chance to share in the treasury."

Men like Victor and Rafaello? she wanted to ask, but the less Dominic knew she knew, the better.

Dominic kicked open the door of the hut, and she blinked at the shadow beneath the thatched roof. Without warning he dropped her—onto a bed and facedown. He landed on top of her, crushing her into the straw tick. Dust flew, and she grappled behind her, trying to reach a piece of him that would give him pain and her leverage, but he caught her wrist and bent it back again.

Speaking into her ear as sweetly as a lover, he said, "The revolutionaries are divided because of you. Did you know that? Some of them don't follow me anymore. They say I should have killed you as soon as I got my hands on you rather than let you live to escape. They said I didn't have the stomach to kill a woman in cold blood."

The straw crackled, the mattress smelled of age and dirty bodies, and in the dim light, she saw something skitter across the blanket. "Now you attempt to prove them wrong," she sneered.

Sheer bravado. It was all very well to think she was resigned to her dying without Danior. Right now, facing the knowledge Dominic could, and would, slit her throat in an instant frightened her so much that she shivered like a drenched rat. Worse, she couldn't hide her fear from Dominic.

"Actually, no. Apparently they were right. I can't kill a helpless woman, not even for the cause." He let go of her wrist just long enough for her to have hope. Then he caught her hair in his fist, stretched her neck backward and climbed up to put his knee on her spine. "But do you know what I can do?"

Gritting her teeth, she bore the pain.

His free hand traveled up her bare leg. "I can rape you."

His savagery made her ill. "No."

"You can't stop me," he taunted. "You're smart, and you're good with a kick, but I have you now, princess. Princess Ethelinda. The beloved savior of our countries."

"I'm not!"

He chuckled, a gust of real amusement. "You said that before, but Danior wouldn't be chasing after anyone else the way he's chased after you. Our princeling badly wants to marry you, and do you really think he will when he finds out who's been tasting your delights?''

She struggled, ignoring the pain in her scalp and the grinding of his knee in her back. ''Bastard.''

''That I am.''

He was going to do this. With the door open, in this filthy bed, in this falling-down hut. Feverishly, she wondered if someone walked along the path now. If someone could hear her. Taking a breath, she screamed as loud and as shrill as she could.

He rammed his knee hard into her back, and she choked and quieted.

''If I do this right, I'll put a bastard in your oven. That way''—air flowed across her buttocks as he lifted her skirt away—''even if the revolution fails and Danior-boy forces himself to the wedding for the good of his country, it'll be *my* son on the throne. The bastard of the biggest bastard of''—his voice faded—''all.''

His palm slid across her nether cheeks, not rudely, not lovingly, but as if he were searching for something. Her stomach roiled, and she thought she was going to retch, but he only muttered, ''Impossible.''

He scooted around so the light fell on her, and he searched again. ''No. I don't believe it.''

She clenched every muscle in her body, rejecting him every way she could. ''Believe what?''

He ran his hand over her one last time. Then he let her go. Let go of her hair, moved off her back and the bed in one smooth movement.

Wrenching her skirt down, she whipped over, expecting a trick, expecting a knife or a blow or something.

He stared at her with a wide, disconcerted gaze, and burst into laughter. Pure, loud, blatant laughter.

He doubled up with it, holding his sides and staggering around the tiny chamber like some demented cur stricken with rabies.

She jumped off the bed. She should have run. Instead she stalked him and when he staggered near, she swung her fist and connected with his eye.

Covering his face, he shouted, "Damn, woman, why did you do that?"

She hit him in the stomach.

He fell over, and she kicked him in the ribs with her boots. The boots Danior had laced on her feet.

Dominic rolled away from her. He stopped laughing. He went limp.

The sudden end to laughter, to movement, to his obnoxious mockery stunned her. She stood over him, her fists clenched, one aching from the impact with his skull. Had she killed him?

She took a step back, and another, and another. He didn't move, a dark, still shadow on the floor.

In a rush she remembered what he'd done, what he'd attempted, and his intentions. She remembered that first time she'd grabbed Danior in a Chinese hold, then failed to follow up immediately, and she remembered all the dire consequences since.

Turning, she ran out into the sunshine.

In the hut, Dominic stirred. Standing, he pushed his hair out of his eyes, strolled to the door, and gazed at Evangeline as she fled down the road toward Plaisance. And when she was out of earshot, he burst into laughter once more.

Twenty-nine

"The princess has run away from the prince."

"No, she hasn't, I saw her with him just yesterday, and she fulfilled the prophecy."

"Then why is Prince Danior tearing the countryside apart looking for her? Hey, watch it, old lady!"

Evangeline backed away from the little clump of people congregating by the bakery. She recognized an impassioned Lauri defending the prince, as well as the enfeebled Memaw hanging on his arm and swinging her cane at the city folk.

Evangeline didn't want them to recognize her. She didn't want anyone to recognize her.

Sidling along like a cutpurse, she rounded the corner onto a broader street, one thronging with merrymakers. A tapped cask had been set up before the Kingsway Inn, and an elderly man as round as the cask stood dispensing mugs of the frothy brew. "First one's free in honor of Revealing," he brayed. "Free from Fair Abbé, the finest innkeeper in Plaisance!"

People were lined up for their free mug, and Evangeline joined the queue. She'd run into the city, glancing over her shoulder all the way, fighting the ache in her barely healed foot. Now she was hot, thirsty, and hungry. And frightened. And awed.

London had been a revelation to the country girl she had been. Big and bustling, smelly, and so dirty that she dared not wear white gloves for fear of the black soot that coated every surface.

Not so Plaisance. Plaisance was beautiful. The mountains cupped it like a mother's loving hand, warming and protecting the city astride the great river. Here a medieval stone bridge of gothic proportions joined Baminia and Serephina; here the people met and mingled. Commerce meant more to them than an ancient feud. Shops lined cobblestone avenues, and Evangeline ogled the gold jewelry and fine clothing lovingly crafted by the Serephinians. When she crossed the river, she strolled along and stared at the Baminian-made pottery and shoes.

If she lived with Danior as queen, she could walk these streets anytime she wished, buy what she liked, converse with people and discover their hopes and dreams and fears. This would be her home. She'd have a family. She could *belong*.

Enough, she chided herself. *Don't dwell on your loneliness. Think about your plans . . . insipid though they might be.*

Shopkeepers lived above their shops, but today the storefronts were closed. The merchants came to the people this day, wandering the streets with carts and calling out to the merrymakers. Evangeline had already flinched away from families hawking momentos of this climatic Revealing and the marriage of Prince Danior and Princess Ethelinda.

No one approached her to buy anything. Most people avoided looking at her, except for the ones who glared at the Cinderella rags she wore. One woman said loudly, "You'd think these peasants would have the good taste not to dirty our streets with their presence. There are so many of them—why don't they go back where they belong?"

How could they? Evangeline wanted to ask. With the poverty engendered by the poor crops, too many people, desperate and hopeful, walked in rags. If the crystal case wasn't opened tomorrow and the people given a sign that times would improve, they would be ripe for Dominic's revolution.

"They say she's drowned in the river," offered one woman in line behind her.

"That's not what I heard," another gossiped. *"I heard she's run off with that handsome Dominic."*

With coarse disdain, a man said, *"A prince who can't even rule his woman sure can't rule a kingdom."*

Evangeline put her hand up to half-cover her face, and accepted the ale from Fair Abbé.

He looked her over and joked, "I won't be expecting money for a second pint out of you."

"No, but thank you." Tilting the mug up, she drained it in one pull.

When she came up for air he was watching her and wiping his hands on his apron. "One street over, Honest Gaylord is giving away buns, first one free. Tell him I sent you. He'll give you a big one."

"Thank you." She smiled at him and handed back the mug.

"You're Serephinian, aren't you?"

"I guess," she said cautiously.

"You look like someone I used to know."

She stepped back.

"I never forget a face." He tapped his forehead. "Let me think."

She stepped back again, then took to her heels and skidded around another corner.

"Hey!" he shouted after her. "I remember now. Come back!"

She raced in a panic, racing up streets and down avenues, until hunger caught her again and she realized how pointless it was to run from a man just because he thought he knew her. She wasn't the princess, so she couldn't look like the princess. Or at least, not much. And if her parents were Serephinian, he might have known them.

The idea brought her up short. If she stayed in Plaisance, maybe she could at last unearth her parents' identity. She'd dreamed of them in all those long, lonely years in the orphanage, a faceless mother and father who gave her comfort and support, who even in death watched and guided her along her way.

But no. What difference would it make to know about her parents? That would accomplish nothing . . . except answer the question of her existence, and maybe, if she found other relatives, fill the gigantic void in her heart.

A void Danior had filled.

The savory odor of baking pies caught her, and she followed her nose to a bakery. People gobbled up the flaky rolls the baker handed out as fast as he could—"First one free!" he proclaimed.

Somehow, after all that running, she'd made her way back to Honest Gaylord's Bake Shop. Since she'd reached Plaisance, it almost seemed that destiny shoved her along, directing her every step.

Well, she would defy destiny and go where she wished . . . after she had one of those yeasty-smelling rolls.

She joined the queue and, as instructed, mentioned Fair Abbé. Honest Gaylord, not quite as plump as the innkeeper but clearly his brother, scowled and handed her the biggest bun. "Don't sit down, the benches are for paying customers."

She thanked him, moved off to the side, and sank her teeth into the most delicious concoction of bread, cinnamon, and dates she'd ever tasted. She almost wept with pleasure as she licked her fingers, and she eyed the line with the thought that Honest Gaylord hadn't even looked at her, so how would he know if she went through twice?

In that she was wrong, for as soon as she finished he put his son in charge of distribution and walked toward her, another bun in his hand. She wanted to run; after all, what could he want? But her stomach rumbled, and she obeyed its command.

The pastry he handed her was substantially different than the first; much heavier, rich with the scent of herbs. Eagerly she sank her teeth into a turnover oozing with meat and carrots, and he watched her swallow with an expression of complacency.

"You're kind," she said.

"It's Revealing. Time to feed the beggars, and sister, you look like a beggar." He observed her shrewdly. "A beggar who has seen better times."

Shabby as it was, the silk dress was still silk, and his merchant's eye had noted the formerly fine apparel.

"Besides, you resemble someone I used to know."

She paused, her suddenly dry mouth suspended over the turnover.

"That Serephinian girl. The one who used to hang around here, oh, twenty-five years ago, mooning over young Renaud the barrel-maker."

That pathetic longing for home and family anchored Evangeline in place, and she shut her mouth, torn between the urge to flee and the need to stay.

"Her daughter, maybe. You've got that moon-eyed appeal, like you're afraid the big, bad Baminians are going to eat you up. Don't know how you Serephinians ever get up the nerve to breed."

"It isn't easy," she mumbled.

He glanced at her sharply. "Breeding, are you?"

"No!"

"Well, sit down before you fall down." He propelled her toward a crowded bench at one of the shaded tables and slapped a man on the back. "Get up, Percival, you're done."

With a grin, Percival stood and offered his seat.

"Eleanor was breeding, too, last time I saw her."

Stiff with resentment, Evangeline insisted, "I'm not breeding, and I'm not Eleanor's daughter." Honest Gaylord's hand landed on her shoulder, and she found herself seated at a table where everyone knew each other, and she was the only stranger.

"Whose daughter are you?" Percival asked with interest.

"I don't know," she admitted.

"There you have it. You don't know if you're Eleanor's daughter." Honest Gaylord spoke to an increasingly interested crowd. "Poor thing, her family didn't approve of Renaud because they were royal and he was dirt common."

"Eleanor from over the river?" Percival squinted at Evangeline. "She has the look of her."

Evangeline sat with her half-eaten turnover forgotten in her hand. "Do I?"

"I say she has the look of all of them. The Chartriers." Honest Gaylord spat on the ground. "I've met a right lot of good Serephinians in my day, but that queen of theirs gave them all a bad name. Brought the rebels down on her and that poor slob of a king, and ignited the whole revolution."

"Oh, come on, man," one of the women down the table said. "I'm Serephinian, and I've known a lot of good Baminians, but I say it was your king who brought on the revolution. Couldn't keep his trousers fastened."

"But you think I look like the royal family?" Evangeline insisted. Her world tilted askew. Could she be half royal? Could she be half worthy of Danior?

"We'd salute you as the princess if you'd show us your mark." Percival poked Honest Gaylord, and they both laughed like two naughty boys.

"Mark?" she said, bewildered by their reference and their embarrassed amusement. "What mark?"

"Pay them no heed." The woman turned to the men and chided, "Y'two shush up. Don't embarrass the girl."

Honest Gaylord sobered and cleared his throat. "Eleanor and Renaud had to leave the city, and I heard they disappeared in the Revolution of Ninety-six. Probably killed, poor things. You an orphan? That revolution made a lot of orphans."

The woman down the table looked at Evangeline with disfavor. "She's one of those snooty Chartriers, for sure. Do y' suppose she's capable of opening that

crystal case? Because they say the princess is a drooling idiot, and our prince is only wedding her for the
good of his people."

A babble broke out, conflicting stories piled one
atop the other. Some were patently absurd; others
came too close to the truth for Evangeline's comfort.
The voices got louder and louder until people came
running to see what caused the commotion.

Evangeline kept trying to bring the conversation
back to the suddenly fascinating subject. "About
Eleanor and Renaud . . ."

Until the moment she looked up and saw two familiar men moving toward her.

Victor and Rafaello. Victor watched her without
ceasing, his blue eyes calm, measuring. Rafaello
charmed the people around them, getting them to
move aside for no more reason than his smile.

Evangeline's head began to pound. One of these
men, or both, were traitors, so Danior had said. If they
took her, she might be returned to Danior—or she
might be held hostage or killed.

Honest Gaylord pounded on the table with his fist.
"If the princess is alive and residing in the Palace of
the Two Kingdoms, then I say the prince will show
her to us tonight in the light of the full moon. Otherwise"—he shook his head sadly—"we're all
doomed, Baminian and Serephinian alike. The poor
are desperate. They'll rise and kill us all."

Rising to her feet, Evangeline pointed at Victor and
shouted, "Do you want to know what's happened to
the princess? Ask the prince. There he is."

As one, the crowd turned to Victor.

Honest Gaylord shook his head. "That's not the
prince."

"He's not," Rafaello agreed.

"Yes, it is. It looks just like him," Percival said.

"You've only seen him from a distance," Honest Gaylord said. "I've shaken his hand. That's not the prince."

Evangeline carefully placed the turnover on the table and declared, "It's the prince. He's out looking for his princess."

"She's right." One of the men standing beside Victor grabbed his hand and dropped to one knee. "Your Highness, I have a goiter. Can you cure it?"

A hubbub broke out, louder than before. Victor tried to disengage his hand while loudly denying his royalty. Evangeline sat back down, then ducked under the table. Crouching low, she ran to the next table, and the next, and the next, until she had reached the next shop, where clothes draped the boards and she could hide.

It was fully a minute before Victor's big voice boomed out, "The princess. What happened to the princess?"

Wrapping her hands around her knees, Evangeline peeked out and saw everyone rise to their feet.

"She's not the princess," Honest Gaylord said in disgust. "She's Eleanor's daughter from across the water."

"Eleanor was the princess's aunt," the woman said tartly. "Don't y' think the princess could resemble her, too?"

Evangeline held herself very still, trembling with the need to get away, yet knowing it was safest to remain. Boots and shoes, gowns and trousers strode past. Voices called, seeking the counterfeit princess. Victor shouted, Rafaello charmed everyone he could, but they couldn't find her. They searched down the street, in the alley, down toward the river.

The original crowd gradually dispersed. A new crowd gathered, intent on getting the first bun free. Congratulating herself on the success of her ploy, Evangeline scooted out from under the table, and cautiously stood.

Honest Gaylord kept serving buns. If he saw her, he didn't say. The people snacked, then bought; all was calm. Elaborately casual, she picked up her half-eaten turnover from the table and moved toward the street she'd first come down. She had a mission. She wanted to get back to the Serephinian side of the river. She wanted to see if anyone there remembered the woman called Eleanor, or knew her ultimate fate.

She'd walked perhaps half the way when Victor rounded the corner toward her. She stopped.

He stopped.

She glanced around. There was nowhere to go except back up the street, or down a narrow, shadowed alley.

She looked back at him, at his eyes lit up with unholy amusement. He smiled—a smile of wicked amusement, looking far too much like Dominic. "Your Highness! Enough games. You've had your fun." He patted his thigh as if she were a dog to be summoned. "Come now, girl, let's go."

She threw the turnover at him as hard as she could. Her feet discovered flight. She tore into the alley and raced along, through garbage and around discarded barrels. Behind her, she heard Victor shouting, and she only ran faster. The alley forked. She took the left passage, and almost immediately it narrowed yet more. The shadows deepened. A blank wall of blush-colored stone rose twelve feet on one side. On the other side, a series of dark doors marched along. She tried two. Both were bolted.

She heard Victor calling. He followed like a rat after its cheese. She ran, but she had to do something, before the stitch in her side overcame her, before the pain in her foot grew unbearable. She dove into a small alcove in the wall, and in the alcove she found a small door. She threw her body at it, but it held true. Pounding with the flat of her hand, she cried, "Open, please open."

A melodic feminine voice spoke on the other side. "As you wish."

Evangeline couldn't believe it. Someone had heard her. "Hurry."

"A moment, my sister, I must find the key."

"He's coming." Evangeline leaned against the door and slapped it again. "He's coming."

The door opened and she fell into a garden, stumbled forward, and collapsed onto a graveled path.

Behind her, she heard a solid thunk, and the rattle of a lock. She turned and looked, and Marie Theresia, the postulant from the convent on the cliff, stood smiling before the closed doorway. "She told us you would come here, and you did. Santa Leopolda be praised!"

Thirty

Victor slammed into the door, bringing Evangeline to her feet, wild and hunted.

"Don't worry." Marie Theresia took her hand and patted it. "He can't get in here. And listen"—she lifted one finger as Victor moved along, pounding on other doors—"he's not sure where you disappeared." The little postulant's black-and-white habit stood out among the tangle of pink climbing roses and blazing yellow coreopsis. No wind ruffled the atmosphere here, and dianthus scented each breath. Tiny apples hung in tight green bunches from mature trees placed to give shade to paths and benches. Bees buzzed, tasting each blossom on their way to the row of hives along the outer wall.

"Yes." Evangeline panted. "Good. Thank heaven."

"Indeed, you should. You are destined from above."

Lately, Evangeline had heard too much about her destiny. She had had the sensation of being swept along by her destiny. And she feared she faced her destiny once again. Rubbing her palm against her sweaty forehead, she asked, "*Who* told you I would come here?"

"Why, Santa Leopolda, of course."

Evangeline's pounding heart slowed and her breath became slow and even, but she was too tired to comprehend the little postulant. "Santa Leopolda is dead."

Marie Theresia only smiled as she drew Evangeline's arm through her own. "You don't mind that I call you 'sister,' do you? I feel that we are sisters."

"No." Evangeline glanced at the top of the twelve-foot wall. She couldn't hear Victor anymore at all. Had he gone on, or did he listen for the murmur of her voice? She drew Marie Theresia away from the wall, moving toward the building of blush-colored stone, which it enclosed. "In God's eyes, I suppose we are sisters."

"Exactly."

Here, the sounds of the city were muffled, lost in the width and depth of a broad enclosure where plants flourished, cherished by their caretakers. Here, serenity slipped like a jewel along the golden chain of days, each blending into the other until peace permeated the earth, the plants, the very air.

"This is a convent," Evangeline guessed. "This is the garden."

Marie Theresia gazed around with pride. "Beautiful, isn't it? It's our sister city convent, the original convent of Santa Leopolda. It was here that she placed the crowns and scepters in the crystal case."

Evangeline tested Marie Theresia. "And you talked to her this morning."

"Yes, this morning. Yesterday morning. She's our mother superior, you know."

Evangeline relaxed. The girl seemed normal enough, bright and without a hint of madness. Surely she meant that each mother superior was given the title of Leopolda—although that still didn't explain how she knew Evangeline would land here when Evangeline hadn't known it herself.

Tugging her along a path toward the tall fountain in the heart of the garden, Marie Theresia said, "We just arrived."

"For Revealing?" Evangeline guessed.

"I *have* to be here for Revealing. Ours was a very uneventful trip. I hope your journey was the same."

Evangeline sagged as she remembered Danior, Dominic, the hot springs, the village, the rebels . . . Danior. "Not exactly."

"How foolish of me," Marie Theresia chirped as cheerfully as one of the birds in the trees. "You're the princess. You must be tested by adversity."

"I've been tested enough to be the princess, but in fact I am not." Evangeline knew she sounded a little touchy, but this princess thing had caused her no end of trouble.

Marie Theresia plucked a dozen long-stemmed coreopsis, and added a few snowy white daisies. She detoured into the rose garden, and with the knife at her belt, she cut two perfect blood-red blossoms. "What is a princess?"

Evangeline looked sharply at the plump, girlish face under the wimple. Marie Theresia wasn't a halfwit; Evangeline knew that from their former conversation. Yet today, Marie Theresia seemed distracted, flighty, and definitely a little odd. "A princess is the daughter of a king and a queen," Evangeline answered without a doubt. After all, she'd given the subject a lot of thought.

"No, you're wrong." Marie Theresia arranged the armful of flowers. "A princess is one who is noble of demeanor, who is kind, modest, willing to put her people's welfare before her own, regardless of the advantage she might gain."

Evangeline couldn't believe it. A postulant who waxed philosophical. "No, *you're* wrong. There are plenty of women like that, rich and poor, and if the king and queen and all their children were killed, they still wouldn't be princesses. To have even the remotest possibility of being a princess, one must be born into a noble family."

"Who decides nobility?" Marie Theresia added a spray of stiff greenery sprinkled with tiny white flowers to serve as a background for her bouquet. "If a family is noble, and believes that their line is noble because of God's sanctity, might not God wish to change his blessing if the occasion demands? Might not God have different fates planned than mere mankind determines?"

Evangeline felt trapped by the question. Leona had been quite clear in her faith, and nothing Evangeline had read about the other religions had contradicted those teachings. There was only one answer to Marie Theresia's question, and although she mumbled, Evangeline knew nothing could change this eternal truth. "God is almighty."

"Exactly! God works in mysterious ways, and even the wisest prophets are wrong sometimes." Hooking her arm with Evangeline's again, Marie Theresia pulled her down the twisting path toward the courtyard around the fountain. "You have fulfilled the prophecies, Evangeline, and I believe God brought you to Baminia to be the princess for our people."

They walked around the corner into the courtyard, and Danior rose from the bench where he'd been sitting. "That's what I believe, too."

Danior. Dear Lord, Danior. Evangeline had braced herself to never see him again. She'd waved good-bye and turned her face resolutely onward. Then he'd sabotaged her, creeping into her mind with admonitions about the two countries, about how the revolutionaries would destroy the land and the people if Revealing didn't occur, and she'd come to Plaisance. To this moment which, if Marie Theresia was to be believed, had been foretold by the mysterious Santa Leopolda.

Danior stood watching her, daring her to take flight and promising, with the tension of his body and the expectation of his eyes, that he would run her down. He *wanted* to run her down, to work off his frustration at her intransigence with a hard chase.

Yet it seemed that every time she ran from him, she instead ran right to him. And how could she run away from the big, rough-looking man when she carried his image with her always?

Marie Theresia pressed the flowers into Evangeline's arms. "White for purity, gold for nobility, and red for the blood you've spent getting to Plaisance. This is for the princess that you are."

Funny to be here again, captured by Danior and carried along toward the fate she'd fought so hard against. Time had run out. Tomorrow was Revealing. And she had to decide soon what she would do. Today. Now.

Danior was not making it easy on her. He sat between her and the door of the royal carriage, his long legs stretched out as a living barrier to freedom. He had bathed, he wore clean clothes with an absolutely magnificent waistcoat of royal purple, and his beard had been shaved to display his stubborn, offended, set-in-granite chin. His arms were crossed over his chest and his mouth was set. He stared straight ahead—not at her, not outside—but straight ahead at the buttoned red satin upholstery.

He was the crown prince of Baminia again, elegant and royal and much, much too arrogant.

Evangeline shuffled the flowers from one arm to the other. The rose thorns poked at her, and the stiff greenery chaffed her, much like the words Marie Theresia had spoken.

Might not God wish to change his blessing if the occasion demands? Might not God have different fates planned than mere mankind determines?

Evangeline was Serephinian, and apparently the daughter of a noble house. Possibly even the cousin of the princess, and if that were all the truth, she would bow to destiny and claim her place at Danior's side.

But if Honest Gaylord and his cohorts were correct, she was also the daughter of a barrel-maker. A respectable man, and well-liked, but a barrel-maker nonetheless. Evangeline had to weigh Danior's pride in his royal line against the consequences of refusing his suit.

And the only way she could do that was to talk to him, and breaking the frigid silence took all her courage. Jiggling her foot against the floor, she said, "Your Highness?" Then, "Danior?"

No response.

"Have I angered you?"

He gave no indication that he heard her.

She took a breath. "Well, of course I have, that's obvious, and I'm sorry."

His shoulders hunched.

She was getting nowhere. Looking out, she saw people lining the streets, staring as the royal coach made its way to the Palace of the Two Kingdoms. When they spotted her peering out at them, they waved with such vigor that she didn't know how they remained on their feet. This was what the citizens of the Two Kingdoms wished, that their prince and their princess be in the city, waiting for tomorrow with as much anticipation as the people experienced.

Our appearance will calm the rumors of a lost princess, Evangeline thought. Especially when it's reported Danior fetched me from the convent. They'll think he stashed me there on purpose.

Danior. She peeked at him. He looked positively grim, but she had to try again. "It hasn't been an easy journey for either one of us, but we've learned a lot about each other and I think perhaps . . . that is, when I ran away this time, I think you were worried."

As if she'd turned a tap, his head snapped around and his eyes flashed. "Worried?"

She flinched from the single word roar.

"Of course I was worried. Revolutionaries scouring the countryside, men who you'd already humiliated seeking you with retribution in their hearts, and you think I might be worried? I was frantic!"

At least he was speaking to her once more. Shouting at her once more.

"Running was stupid," she admitted. "The first

time I ran away without realizing how vengeful they were. This time I ran away because—" *Because I made love to you, and you made love to a princess.*

What she had not said hung in the air like a wisp of smoke rising from a barely kindled fire. She blinked away a sudden onset of inexplicable tears.

Danior's fury visibly died before her eyes. He looked away from her, and a dark color stained his cheeks. He looked like a man whose dream had died, yet when he turned back to her, determination etched his face. He grabbed her hands in his grip, the first time he'd touched her since he'd taken her from the convent, and he squeezed them tightly. "Was it that bad?"

She winced. "What?"

He released her to chafe first one hand, then the other. "I know it wasn't what you dreamed. What woman dreams of making love in a dark hole? And we were dirty and it was rough and uncouth, and I was too hurried, but I thought you—I couldn't see you, of course—but I thought you liked it. At least to a point. At least as far as I was able to tell . . . in the dark . . . and I was excited beyond belief."

He didn't understand. He thought he had frightened her with the demands of his body, when it was her fear of disappointing him that drove her away. "No, that wasn't why I ran. I did like it."

He disregarded her so completely that she might not have spoken. "I'm usually better than that. I promised to romance you—remember, back in your bedchamber at Château Fortuné?—and I know how to do this courtship thing right."

"I wouldn't hold you to that!"

"Women like to be courted." He was back to deciding what she thought, making kingly statements and not listening to a word she said. He rapped on the roof of the coach, and immediately it slowed. Even before it had come to a complete stop, he was out the door and running across the street to an old woman who stood hawking confections before her shop.

Even the wisest prophets are wrong sometimes. So Marie Theresia had asserted. Did she mean that Santa Leopolda had not seen the whole truth? Evangeline was meant to be the princess?

She watched as Danior spoke to the old woman, waving his arms in big circles. He stuck his hand in his pocket and poured coins into her palm. The candy maker looked toward the carriage and grinned a toothless grin as he plucked a gaily decorated tin out of her display. Then she insisted on winding it in a ribbon while Danior shifted his feet impatiently.

Snatching the tin, he ran back to the coach. It tilted under his weight as he climbed in. Sliding off the ribbon, he popped the lid and selected a marzipan made in the shape of a seashell.

"Really, this isn't necessary," Evangeline said.

And he put it in her mouth while she was speaking. It melted in sugary goodness across her tongue.

"See? I know how to romance a woman. Especially you. I'll bring you confections every day. And jewelry. There's a shop."

He repeated the drill, running inside.

As she waited, Marie Theresia's words danced in her head. *You have fulfilled the prophecies, and I believe God brought you to Baminia to be the princess for our people.*

Troubled, Evangeline watched as Danior came out

with a gaily decorated box. He climbed in and shoved it into her hands.

She just held the superfluous present and tried to explain. "Danior, really. It's not what you think."

Impatient with her hesitation, he took the box and unwrapped it. Inside, a necklace of pearls glowed like beads of moonlight set with an emerald clasp. She'd never seen jewelry like this. A week ago she would have been ecstatic just to hold them. Now they made her feel faintly ashamed of herself.

Danior looked at her in expectancy. "Good, huh? See? I know what women like. When we're together, it will never be like it was in that place, ever again."

Something tightened in her chest. She'd struck Danior in the one tender spot where he had no armor, and he was bleeding. The blow had been inadvertent, but the blood was still real. "You are not your father," she said.

"No! That's what I'm trying to tell you. I'm not. I have control of myself, and now that I know the consequences of losing that control, it will never happen again. I swear to you, Evangeline—"

She placed her hand across his mouth before he could finish his oath. Looking into the blue eyes she adored, she said, "I just . . . I want you. I want you the way you were in Blanca, in that dark hole where you held nothing back from me. I want it to always be that way. I didn't run because you loved me honestly. That was the reason I wanted to stay."

He shoved her hands aside, and frustration vibrated in his tone. "Then why did you run away from me?"

Carefully she placed the box top over the pearls so she wouldn't have to look at them again, and took his hands. "Would you love me . . . no." She tried again. "Would you want me if I weren't really a princess?"

"Love you, want you—haven't I proved that I *need* you?"

That was the truth. He did need her, for without a princess he could never be king.

I believe God brought you to Baminia to be the princess for our people. No doubt Evangeline didn't understand the will of God. And perhaps Marie Theresia did.

"Then I will tell you the truth. I am your princess, and I will marry you tomorrow."

Thirty-one

Two fires roared in two fireplaces in the royal bed-
chamber, yet Evangeline shivered in her chemise as
she watched four young and bustling maids pour hot
water into the highbacked copper tub. The palace was
old, drafty, massive, and medieval—just as she'd
imagined it. Candelabras held long beeswax candles
that provided shimmering pools of light and accented
the dark corners. The furniture ranged in age from a
new gleaming banquet table bought and placed in the
dining hall for tomorrow evening's festivities to the
thousand-year-old bed slept in by the very king and
queen who fought so wickedly and divided the country.

That tall, broad bed stood sentinel over this bedchamber, drawing Evangeline's gaze until all she
could think of was Danior and the kiss he had given
her in the coach. It had been sweet and chaste, a
touching of mouths without even a hint of passion.

She'd been astonished until he set her away from
him and looked at her. Then she'd understood. Color
blazed along his cheekbones, his blue eyes flamed like

the hottest part of the fire, and his body gave off heat in waves. "If I touch you," he said, "I will take you in the coach as we drive down the Royal Way in Plaisance with all our subjects waving and cheering."

"That'll give them something to cheer about," Evangeline had quipped.

He didn't seem to see the humor in that, but she suspected he might be in some discomfort.

She, oddly enough, didn't find his ready arousal threatening. Rather, a thrill quivered through her. She'd done it, taken the final, irrevocable step. She'd declared herself the princess and placed herself into Danior's hands forever. She would be a queen. His queen.

Her excitement had lasted until the coach had crossed the River Plaisance and she'd seen the Palace of the Two Kingdoms.

Then reality set in.

She had read about state dinners; she had never participated in one. She had read about how to receive foreign dignitaries; she had never greeted one. She had read about behavior appropriate to a princess; she had never been one.

Now she was, and she dared not fail in any detail.

"Your Highness?"

The littlest maid smiled and bobbed curtsies at Evangeline until Evangeline realized the girl was speaking to her. "Yes?"

"Would you like to test the water?"

Evangeline moved to the side of the tub and wondered briefly if there was a proper princessly way to check the warmth. Then common sense took over, and she dipped in her finger. "It's perfect." She smiled at Tacita, one of five maids assigned to her by the extremely stately housekeeper.

Evangeline had wanted to ask how she was supposed to keep five maids busy. Then she thought perhaps Ethelinda would know, so Evangeline had shut her mouth and smiled, and just kept smiling through meeting the majordomo and the butler and the scullery maid and the old governess who hugged her with tears in her eyes and exclaimed how she'd grown. The whole thing had been an ordeal, she didn't remember half their names, and Danior had whisked away to speak to the prime minister who had to first express his pleasure in meeting the princess again after an absence of so many years.

So she could cross one thing off her list of worries. She *did* resemble the princess.

But how did a princess survive the unending scrutiny? Half the palace had come to watch as she consumed the dinner brought her on a tray. The capon on a bed of some kind of grain had been flavored with rosemary, but she couldn't really savor it while the cook, the butler, and the kitchen staff opened their mouths every time *she* took a bite.

Even now she still had five pairs of eyes watching her every move until she wanted to run back up into the mountains and use the hot springs for a bath.

Especially when Tacita tried to tug away her chemise.

Evangeline tugged back.

"I must bathe you, Your Highness," Tacita said in her soft, melting voice.

"I must bathe myself, thank you," Evangeline answered, firm as any proper English matron.

Tacita's lower lip trembled, her eyes filled with

tears, and she looked around at the other maids as if needing support.

Softening her tone, Evangeline added, "I've been too long without a maid, and I prefer my privacy. But you can lay out my clothing if you like."

"As you wish, Your Highness."

But Tacita's tone left Evangeline in no doubt that she was sorely disappointed. Evangeline didn't care. She wasn't going to show herself naked for anyone.

Or—almost anyone.

"Is there a screen or something we can put—*you* can put here?" She indicated a spot between the tub and the rest of the room.

"Of course, Your Highness." Tacita waved at the other maids, who sighed gustily, and hurried to do Evangeline's bidding.

The screen they brought was Chinese, constructed of hardwood, polished to a high gloss, and inlaid with mother-of-pearl and carved pieces of jade. The jade alone probably cost more than all the money Leona had left her, Evangeline decided, and she wanted to ask for another. One fit for a counterfeit princess.

She restrained herself while they placed the screen to provide a private alcove, complete with a tub and drying cloths, draped across a chair and warming before the fire.

As the last maid reluctantly stepped out of the alcove, Evangeline removed her chemise while watching for Tacita's return. She wouldn't put it past the little girl to try and do her ablutory duty regardless of Evangeline's command.

Cautiously, she spread the chemise over the top edge of the screen—and jumped when it was jerked down from the other side.

"Thank you, Your Highness," Tacita cried. "It has been decreed that your clothes shall be preserved in a museum, so all the people can see how you suffered on your journey to Plaisance."

"The silk gown, too?" Evangeline asked, horrified.

"Especially the gown." Tacita tapped on the screen. "Are you ready for me to wash your hair?"

"I'll do it." Evangeline stepped into the tub too hastily, and the fragrant water sloshed back and forth, right to the edge. Half-panicked, she tried to calm the splashing; in her life she had, after all, spent her time cleaning up after others. She looked guiltily at the edge of the screen, but over by the bed she could hear Tacita and the others exclaiming about the condition of the chemise.

Heat eased her tight muscles and worked into her bones as she lathered a cloth with milled bar soap and washed as rapidly as possible.

She hurried, she told herself, because she fretted that the maids would make up some excuse to peek around the corner.

Actually, she knew better. She hurried because she feared Danior would tromp in, making it clear to one and all they were already lovers, disconcerting her and sending the maids off to spread the word. He was the kind of man who would do such a thing deliberately to make her think she had no choice but to marry him.

As if that would influence her.

She didn't enjoy being so self-conscious, but she could live with that. What she couldn't live with was the anticipation of tomorrow. Right now, Marie Theresia and her silly advice seemed far away and long ago, and all Evangeline could think was—what if Danior is wrong? What if the crystal case was magic? She had dreamed of really being the dearly beloved princess, of having a home, of being part of a family that could trace its roots back into the mists of antiquity.

But in the end, she had given herself not for the country or for a home or to the Chartrier family but to the prince.

The prince. A man to depend on.

A man so driven by the sense of his own infallibility that he could look at her and see a princess. She could fool him forever. He'd never know she was truly Evangeline Scoffield of East Little Teignmouth, Cornwall—unless that damned crystal case wouldn't open.

That nightmare preyed on her nerves.

She lathered her hair.

The other nightmare was almost more vivid. The one where the real princess, a lovely, elegant young woman with the slight glow of a halo around her head, interrupted the ceremony with the announcement that Evangeline was a fraud, and Evangeline was hauled off by a constable and stuck in jail until she rotted. Or was killed. Danior, she imagined, would come by at regular intervals to mock her until the execution. After all, that was what happened to Lady Jane Gray.

She ducked for a rinse. As she came up, she watched with horror as the water sloshed to the edge again—and over. The puddle spread across the shining waxed floor toward the priceless Chinese screen. She wrung out her hair, knowing she should call Tacita or one of the other maids to wipe it up. They were her servants.

But the real princess wouldn't have been so untidy.

A real princess wouldn't have this empathy for those who labored for their living.

She heard giggling from beyond the screen, and that settled the matter. She didn't need five maids squatted around her bathtub wiping up the mess she'd made.

Evangeline got on her knees and stretched long, reaching for a drying cloth—and Danior said, "Lovely."

She sat down so hard the water splashed out again.

He stood beside the screen, one hand gripping the edge as if to shove it out of the way.

Her hand shot out, palm toward him, fingers spread. "Don't!"

"Don't what? Don't be here? Don't come closer? Don't take off my clothes and join you?"

The giggling beyond the screen got more intense. He snapped his fingers at the maids, the giggling stopped, and the door to the bedchamber opened and shut with a weighty thud.

Alone. She and Danior were as alone as they had been in the hot springs, for Danior had decreed it so and no one disobeyed the prince.

The washcloth wasn't big enough to cover her breasts, but Evangeline gave it a valiant try, using the water to plaster the flimsy linen to her chest. "I was going to say, don't move the screen. But yes, to all of those."

The formal jacket and cravat he'd worn earlier had been discarded, his satin waistcoat hung open, his shirtsleeves were rolled up. He looked more like the Danior who had been her traveling companion and less like the crown prince of Baminia.

No wonder the maids had been giggling.

"You shouldn't be here." She tried to sound firm and decorous, a possibly futile exercise while sitting stark naked in a rapidly shrinking tub.

He snorted and slipped out of his waistcoat. "Where you are, my dear, so am I. I could scarcely bear to let you out of my sight long enough to speak to that long-winded old noodle for fear when I got up here, you'd have decamped again."

Stupidly, she was hurt by his distrust. "I said I was going to marry you!"

He hung his waistcoat over the screen. "You've said a lot of things, most of them lies."

"If you feel that way, then why do you want to marry me?" As soon as the words were out of her mouth, she wished them back. Despite the way he mouthed those sweet words of love, she knew he didn't *want* to marry her. He *had* to marry her.

Evangeline clutched the washcloth as he came to kneel at the side of the tub.

"Why do I want to marry you?" He stirred the water with his finger like a warlock brewing a potion. "Because you have seen me at my worst and loved me in spite of it. Or maybe because of it. I don't understand, but I'd be a fool to let you go."

His hand crept toward her leg, and she caught it between her own. "For a man with no neck, you're really rather good with words."

"You don't believe me."

She held his palm flat and turned it up to the light. It was broad and strong, with bright red blisters under each finger as if he'd rowed down that river after her. "I believe that if you found out I was a commoner, all my virtues would be for naught."

"You mean, if you were really Evangeline Scoffield of East Little Teignmouth, Cornwall?"

"That's what I mean."

He grinned, so sure of himself that she wanted to smack him. "Thank God, I'll never have to make that choice. It would be impossible for me to give up the only woman who wants not the prince but the man."

He was right, and she ached with the knowledge that he didn't feel the same intense love for her.

His voice got deeper, rumbling with gratification. "In the coach, you said you wanted me the way I was in Blanca, all crazy for you and holding nothing back."

She touched each of his blisters gently, as if she could cure them, not with a royal touch but with a loving touch. "What kind of woman would want to run mad in your arms while you carefully maintain your control?"

"You little innocent. All of them—except you." He shushed her when she would have argued with him. "I was always afraid that if I lost control, even once, I would be like my father, desperately seeking my manhood in one woman after another."

"Danior, you don't need to worry about that. You have the moral strength of ten men. You are the embodiment of resolution. You have been tempered and tried by fire, and you are everything a prince should be." She got a good grip on his thumb before she added, "Besides, if you seek satisfaction with another woman, I'll cut off your royal jewels."

His thumb jerked in her grasp, and while she congratulated herself on holding him in check, his other hand came up and snatched the washcloth off her chest. She snatched back, but he held it out of reach. "Stand up and get it," he challenged.

She splashed water in his face instead.

His thumb disappeared out of her fist, and he tucked his hands under her armpits to bring her to her feet. "You need to be taught a lesson." He gazed at her body, streaming with water, warm and scented, and added, "I'm going to teach you that lesson."

Funny, the words were threatening, but she didn't feel threatened. She felt wanton and utterly relaxed, as if she'd been waiting for his action in anticipation. She smoothed her damp hand across his dripping face. "You're wet."

"I know." Drops splashed onto his shirt. "There was even water on the floor, and I knelt in it."

She gripped his shoulders. "You'll have to take your trousers off."

"So I will." His hands slid around to her breasts. He cupped them, leaned to them, kissed them. "I've seen you in moonlight, now in candlelight. Tomorrow morning, I'll see you in the clear light of day in our own palace."

He suckled, and she shut her eyes. He didn't believe in magic, but he was wrong. When his tongue touched her, his lips pulling strongly at her nipple, he summoned that magic sensation of melting softness, inside and out.

But now she knew—she was a magician, too. She took him out of himself, out of control, mad with desire.

Together they made magic.

She pulled his shirt loose, unfastened his trousers, and let them drop. She slid her hands into his drawers, but he caught her.

"No, you don't." He put her hands away from him and stepped back.

"Why not?"

"If you do that, it'll be a repeat of Blanca."

"I liked what we did at Blanca."

"So did I." He pulled his shirt over his head and yanked his boots off. "But there are other avenues to explore, other pleasures I can give you, and when you touch me all I can think about is my pleasure."

"When can I touch you?"

"Perhaps in a year or two."

He stepped out of his trousers and peeled off his drawers, and whatever objection she wished to make vanished in a spell of forgetfulness. The first time she'd looked at him across the dining chamber at Château Fortuné she had thought him broad and strong as a peasant, a man who overwhelmed his clothing and made them insignificant.

Now, looking at him naked and in the light, her mouth dried and her skin flushed. Clothing was unworthy of this creature. His brawny shoulders were testaments to the strength that carried her up mountains and through forests. His scars were the badges of a hero. His chest and stomach rippled beneath a fine, dark fur that covered him in the shape of an arrow, directing her gaze downward, as if nature feared she might miss the magnificent sight of his erection if not given guidance. His thighs were a horseman's thighs, powerful, muscled and spare, and his feet were callused, rugged, feet that had tromped half a country and, if they had to, would tomorrow tromp the rest.

He let her look, and when she had surveyed him from top to toe, he said, "You like what you see."

Somehow he knew how the mere sight of him stirred her; perhaps her body gave some clue. But even if it fed his conceit, she was compelled to give him tribute. "If you had been Adam in the garden of Eden, God would never have required that you clothe yourself."

He laughed, his head thrown back. "If I had been Adam in the garden of Eden, the fall would have come at once, for you, Eve, are my temptress."

She smiled too, but the cold pressed in, she was still wet, and gooseflesh swept her. He saw, and turning to the towels, he picked one up.

His back was the match of his chest, muscled and broad, tapering to narrow buttocks so taut that the skin clung and moved like fine silk. He had a small, colorful mark on his left cheek just below his waist; that startled her. When he brought a towel, she turned him toward the light of the fire and ran her finger across it.

She'd never seen one before, but she knew it for what it was; a tattoo of a roaring lion. "It's beautiful," she said.

"It's my emblem." Wrapping her torso in the towel, he helped her out of the tub. "The emblem of the House of Leon. Now stand here," he said, leading her to stand in front of the fire while he fetched the other drying cloths.

Suddenly shy, she held the towel tight against her breasts, wondering why no one sewed bigger towels, ones that would cover a person from more than the tips of her breasts to the tops of her thighs. How she appeared to Danior she couldn't imagine, with her hair wild and damp and her body silhouetted by the flames. It was almost as if she demanded that he notice her—and notice her he did. Even though he had just been looking at her stark naked in the tub, he stopped and stared at her with such pride that she thought herself as esteemed as the mountains and valleys of the Two Kingdoms themselves.

"You make me wild." His voice was hoarse. "You say you want me as I am. If that's true, then you should be prepared, for I mean to have you every day and every night. I want to kiss you down here." He brushed the triangle of hair that peeked beneath the towel. "I want to taste you on my lips when you come. I want to be inside you right now. I'll want to be inside you fifty years from now. And I'll make you want it, too."

She already did want it. Her knees felt weak as he towel-dried her hair. He used another drying cloth to blot her face and neck. He tugged away the towel she held, discarded it and began, with deliberate, leisurely strokes, to wipe the water away from her shoulders and arms.

How could she let him care for her in such an intimate way? She'd cared for herself her whole life, and in the past week she'd been forced to allow Danior to carry her, to rescue her . . . to heal her. Now he waited on her, devoting himself to her as if she were really royal and he were really only a man.

She tried to assume command, but he pushed her hands aside. "No. This is my privilege."

The way he dried her was more like one long, tender caress. Her nipples puckered when he brushed them. The skin on her stomach tingled as he patted it, and she braced herself with her hand on his shoulder when he knelt before her and dried her intimately. He pressed so carefully, with such an expression of beatific innocence on his face that she might have laughed—if she'd had the breath. He rubbed gently at her thighs, her calves. He lifted her feet and found out she was ticklish. Then he turned her and started up the back of her legs, up to her buttocks.

And there he paused. He didn't move, he didn't rub, he just knelt behind her.

Time stretched out, silence grew thick, and she grew first abashed, then embarrassed, then when she remembered Dominic and his extraordinary bout of laughter, confusion and embarrassed anger began to bubble.

"What's wrong?" She tried to squirm around, but he grasped her and held her in place. "What are you looking at?"

He didn't speak, not even when she twisted and writhed.

Finally, when she was just about to reach around and rip his hair out, he kissed her bottom, first one side, then the other, and at last at the very base of her spine. "I'm looking at the most beautiful woman in the Two Kingdoms, and I thank God she is mine."

Standing, he dried her, picked her up, carried her to bed, and made such love to her that she knew he had given himself to her wholly.

And later, before he left her, Danior leaned and murmured into her sleeping ear, "Even if you aren't really a princess."

Thirty-two

Evangeline wasn't eating.

Not the spicy sausage, not sizzling bacon cut so thin it was almost transparent, not the roasted trout swimming in a sour cream sauce, and not beef roast of royal proportions. She hadn't touched the potatoes, even though they had been prepared in ten different ways, nor any of the dozens of breads and cakes laid out on the great sideboard in the dining hall. Even when Danior coaxed her with blushing strawberries placed to her lips by his own hands, she had been able to swallow only a few before pushing him away.

"I'm too frightened," she said.

And she was. She hadn't been this pale when he'd pushed her into that small dark hole in Blanca. He kept trying to reassure her, to tell her everything would be all right, but she wouldn't listen.

Everything *would* be all right. He knew it as well as he knew his lines in the Revealing Ceremony. "Evangeline." He stroked her fingers, trying to infuse them with warmth. "We've faced everything together. Bombs, revolutionaries, injuries—opening the crystal case will be easy as apples."

Courtiers and servants stared at the royal couple ensconced in an alcove, but none dared interrupt their tête-à-tête.

"Have you got your implement?" she asked in a whisper muffled by the tapestries hanging around them.

He patted the pouch that hung from his gold corded belt. "It's right here."

"What if that doesn't open it?"

"Then we'll take it to the Leon family stronghold and drop it from the tower onto the rocks," he joked.

She covered her face.

Taking her wrists, he pulled her hands away and looked into her eyes. "Do you believe it's a magic case?"

"I don't know what I believe anymore," she whispered.

Well, of course she didn't. Her whole life had been put topsy-turvy, and only he could right it.

"Do you believe in me?" he asked.

"Yes," she answered without hesitation.

"Then believe me when I tell you—today everything will be flawless."

And it would.

The prince shall embrace his greatest fear and make it his own.

He chuckled when he remembered the prophecy and how blithely he predicted its import. Prophecies were slippery things clear only to wizards and saints, and the fear Danior embraced had nothing to do with revolutionaries and everything to do with pride, folly, and love.

Looking at his folly and his love, he said, "Your

Royal Highness Princess Evangeline, I swear to you we will open the crystal case together."

She moaned softly. "But then we'll have to get married." She leapt from one anxiety to another, barely considering the successful completion of one event before she moved on to another.

"And what if you spill the wine on your gown?" he quipped.

Her eyes rounded; she plucked at the heavy damask material, and whispered, "What if I do?"

She hadn't thought of that, and he cursed himself for adding to her distress. "It's your gown, and you'll be the queen. No one will dare reprimand the queen."

That clearly offered no comfort, so he said, "The wedding is *our* wedding, and if you spill wine, I promise I will spill wine, too, and we'll start a tradition that will last another thousand years."

"Yes. That sounds like a good idea." She brushed at the medieval veil that covered her hair, and crinkled her forehead beneath the narrow blue band of ribbon that held it in place. "Danior, is a wedding legal if they don't use the right names?"

Sitting back, he examined his guileless bride. She wore the glorious silver wedding dress worn by the original queen over a thousand years ago, the queen's sky-blue gossamer veil, and matching embroidered silk slippers. A patina of age had dulled the materials, the queen had been a smaller woman, yet Evangeline wore the costume as if it had been created for her. Not even her fear could dull the glow his lovemaking had imparted, and he smiled at her until she, too, recalled the night, the exchange of passion, his constant demands, her loving response.

"Stop that." She glanced around at the people who

waited at a discreet distance for her to finish her meal. "They already know we spent the night together. There's no reason to enumerate the fine points."

"I didn't say a word."

"You're obvious."

"Only to you." He adjusted the fur trim around her neckline, which he thought too low. "Every archbishop and priest in the Kingdoms petitioned to officiate at our wedding, and I granted every request. Our union will be thoroughly blessed in the eyes of God, and since He knows everything about us, including our true names, I believe our marriage will be most official." He didn't wait for her reply, but stood and extended his hand. "If you're sure that's all you can eat, then we should go now. Our people are waiting."

She put her hand in his waiting palm. "Danior, I have to tell you—"

Hastily cutting her off, he pulled her to her feet. "Tell me after tonight." He summoned their armed guard. "Have you noticed Rafaello and Victor are not with us?"

So both Victor and Rafaello *were* traitors.

Evangeline could only remember the cocky smile on Victor's face when he'd called her like a dog on the street. She looked at Danior, dressed like a medieval prince in the velvets and furs of a king dead almost one thousand years with a sword at his side, and wished she didn't have to tell him a truth that would so hurt him. "I saw them. Victor and Rafaello, I saw them in the city."

To the unobservant eye, Danior remained untouched by the news. But Evangeline saw him pause for just a moment, saw his eyes half-close as he absorbed the blow.

Then, as calmly as if she had told him the weather, he accepted the heavy cloak with its massive train from the majordomo. As he wrapped it around her shoulders, he asked, "Where? Do you know what street?"

"At Honest Gaylord's bakery. Victor tried to catch me, but I escaped him . . ." *Into the convent garden, where you awaited.*

"So they are lurking in the city. I suspected . . . that is, we had heard it was true." Danior looked grim as he turned away to speak to the four massive bodyguards who surrounded them, none of whom looked anything like Danior.

All of Danior's brothers had betrayed him.

Returning to her, he confessed, "Don't fret. We have these good men to protect us, and Pascale to lead them"—the shortest man bowed to her when he heard his name—"as well as the royal guard and a great many men in plain garb who will mingle with the crowd. You will be safe."

"Victor and Rafaello won't be shooting at me." For they didn't share the same father.

"They might."

Only if they miss you.

So now she had something else to worry about. Victor and Rafaello, Revealing, the wedding, the real princess, Danior discovering the truth . . . if Evangeline could just get through this day without divine retribution for her sins, she swore she would be the best queen the world had ever seen.

If she could just get through this day . . .

Danior fastened his cape with a massive gold

brooch in the same shape and design as his tattoo. It comforted Evangeline; time and use had worn away the fine details of the mane and created a snub nose, but the roaring lion remained fearsome, its ruby eyes sparklingly alive.

Taking her by the hand, Danior led her from the palace, and when they stepped out into the sunlight, the force of the cheering almost blew her off her feet. She waved and tripped when her train wrapped around a corner of the stone balustrade.

Danior used her clumsiness as an excuse to wrap his arm around her waist, and the crowd yelled their approval.

She took no comfort in that. The crowd didn't realize the truth. A real princess wouldn't have tried to fall on her nose. As the people pelted them with flowers, Evangeline sniffled and said, "Danior, I have to tell you something."

He sneezed and assisted her into an open carriage for their ride to the cathedral, then climbed in beside her. "You're allergic to flowers, too."

"No, I—"

The coachman's whip whistled as he snapped it with flare. The high-spirited horses pranced and whinnied, and they started with a lurch. The bodyguards, one at each corner of the carriage, walked as the royal carriage wielded its slow and steady way through Plaisance. People lined the streets, waving and shouting, some so overcome they wept with joy. No one seemed to notice Evangeline was the wrong princess, and although she searched the crowds, she saw no elegant, haloed woman who might be true royalty.

At Cathedral Square, a wooden platform had been

built against the stone wall not far from the doors. An ancient escutcheon uniting the emblems of the Chartrier and Leon families hung above it. Purple velvet drapes provided a colorful backdrop for an oak table, stained with age, that stood center stage. Two chairs of great age and dignity rested on either side of the table, and when Evangeline saw them, she thought, "For the dignitaries." Then she thought, "No, for me."

The carriage stopped at the steps. Danior dismounted, and when he nudged the footman aside and helped Evangeline down himself, the rejoicing reached epidemic proportions. Evangeline tried to tell herself the crowd wouldn't cheer if they knew the truth, but their delight was contagious, and she beamed.

While the footman carefully assisted with her train, Danior murmured, "The last time we were here, my feet had so outgrown my body, I fell up the steps."

"*You* did that?"

"It's a royal prerogative." He kissed her hand so passionately and grinned at her so wickedly that a new round of revelry broke out.

Together they mounted the steps, and waved until Evangeline's arm hurt. The bodyguards took their places at the four sides of the platform. And Evangeline searched again for Princess Ethelinda. Again, she saw people she recognized. The Blanca villagers stood in a clump, waving back at her with Lauri holding Memaw so she could see. Honest Gaylord stood with his thumbs hooked into his embroidered suspenders, talking to his neighbor with a smirk on his broad face.

And a great number of nuns, representatives from

probably every convent in the Two Kingdoms, made their way through the crowd toward the front. Soeur Constanza led the entire group toward the front, speaking to the onlookers in such a manner they immediately moved aside. In the center walked Marie Theresia, who caught Evangeline's eye and smiled at her with grave satisfaction before turning her attention back to assisting an old nun—a very old nun by the look of her stooped shoulders.

Looking at that old nun, for one moment Evangeline was flung back in time, to England, where she saw an old, narrow, bony face, knowing eyes, a veined hand turning a book page—

The trumpets blew the fanfare. Evangeline jerked her attention to the great cathedral doors, where the archbishop stood with the wide, flat crystal case in both hands. The clear, carved stone collected the sun like a giant diamond, scattering light in fragments across the square. The crowd hushed, and Evangeline developed an uncomfortable lump in her throat. She didn't know why, only seeing the crystal case, knowing its long history and having a chance to help the Two Kingdoms filled her with awe.

How could Princess Ethelinda give up her chance to do this? Where was she? Why wasn't she here?

Evangeline looked around, desperately seeking the unknown girl, sure that only foul play could keep her from her destiny. Evangeline almost called out to stop the proceedings; she gripped Danior's arm to demand his attention—and in the crowd, she caught the glint of sun off of gunmetal.

She reacted instinctively, throwing herself at Danior, sending him stumbling aside.

A single shot whizzed past her ear.

Danior took her down, crowded her under the table, used his body as a shield. People screamed. More shots rang out. Evangeline fought him, shouted, "No!" He shoved her further back, pushing her toward the back of the platform to the cathedral wall.

Frantic, she grabbed him by his collar. "Danior, listen. You have to let me protect you. I'm not really the princess."

"I know." He pushed her face down to the floor and held a hand in the middle of her back. He stretched up to knock the table over as a barricade. His hand gripped the edge of the table. But before he could bring it down before them, a barrage of shots rang out. He spun around like a top and fell.

At once he rose again, but he couldn't hold her now. She came up like a tigress protecting her cub. Blood covered his chest; she almost punched his face to knock him flat, when he caught her fist.

"Stop," he said. "Listen!"

She paused, but heard nothing but yelling.

No more shooting.

Glancing swiftly around, she saw empty places in the throng, places where each assassin had stood and where country folk and city people alike had jumped them. In the middle of the crowd where she'd seen the first pistol aimed in their direction, a huge fight was in progress. Whoever had fired that shot refused to concede; whoever fought him demanded abject surrender.

The scent of gunpowder drifted on the breeze, but not one assassin was left standing.

Which was fine with Evangeline. Turning toward Danior, she commanded, "Lie down *now*."

He was trying to crawl from under the table, and

he was shouting, "Catch the assassins. Take them to the—"

He caught his breath as she jerked him back and down by his neckline. "Don't get up." She placed herself between him and the crowd. They were in isolation, if she could ignore the thousands of people still shouting, still fighting, still craning their necks to see beneath their table.

She reached for the broach on his cloak. The lion stared at her reproachfully through one ruby eye. Half of him was blown away.

Danior took her suddenly shaking hands in his. "I'm all right."

She struggled against his grip. "There's blood."

"The broach shattered. I've got nicks all over me, and"—he shrugged in discomfort—"I think the shot must have creased my collarbone. But I need a bandage, not a coffin."

"Let me see." She whispered because her voice had vanished, because her world was in tumult, because he was handsome, royal and healthy, and because she was a nobody once more.

Feet thumped across the platform, and Pascale knelt to look under the table. "Your Highnesses!"

"Keep everyone back," Danior commanded. "And find some linens. The princess wishes to bandage my wound."

Pascale thumped his breast in acquiescence, shouted for assistance, then took up his post to warn off any intruders.

Danior found the gash in the velvet surcoat and ripped the antique costume off his shoulder. The wound was worse than he said; probably the lead ball had chipped his collarbone, and she would wager he suffered a lot of pain. But he didn't seem concerned; he was watching her with the same intent scrutiny he'd shown across the dining chamber at Château Fortuné.

"Evangeline . . ."

"Why didn't you tell me?" A tear dripped off her cheek and splattered his chest. People could see them, yet she didn't care. "All this time you knew I wasn't the princess—"

"I didn't know until last night."

"You let me pretend . . ."

"It wasn't pretense."

"When were you going to announce it? Before Revealing? Before the wedding? Tonight—"

Gently, he wiped the tears off her face. "Evangeline, there's a royal mark on me and one on Ethelinda, the emblems of our houses. You saw mine last night."

She at once knew to what he referred. "The lion."

"On my arse." He was inviting her to smile.

She didn't.

"And last night," he said, "I saw you didn't have one."

Her mind leapt back to the moment when he'd knelt behind her, and that long, profound silence. And again to the moment when Dominic had released her to laugh with crazy glee.

"Your Highnesses, here's your linen." Without really looking at them, Pascale handed her a ball of strips he'd found heaven knows where. He stood again, planting his feet, warning off intruders.

She didn't want to touch Danior; of all the nightmares she had feared, this one she had never imagined. That he would have known she was an impostor and let her masquerade as the princess anyway.

Blood still oozed from his wound, so she made a pad with strips of the linen. "What are you doing? Using me until you find the real princess?" She pressed the wadding hard against his collarbone. "Sit up."

He grunted when he tried, and fell back.

Gritting her teeth, she wrapped her arm around him and helped him up.

Funny, no matter how much she thought she must hate him, he still felt like home to her. When he sat up, she thought she saw an invitation in his gaze. She almost leaned into him for the kiss she thought of as hers. But that was just habit.

She turned her attention to unwrapping more strips.

"We've been making love in the dark, and hurrying through the light." He spoke softly, keeping what was between them private.

"So now you know I'm common." She put his hand to the pad. "Hold this."

"Common is the last thing I would call you."

To hold the bandage in place, she had to slip her hand into his surcoat. She had to make contact with his bare flesh. The flesh that last night had been pressed against hers, sharing her ecstasy and his soul.

Illusion.

To hesitate to touch him would reveal how much he had hurt her, and already the defiant orphan was gathering her defenses.

But he wouldn't let her hide behind them. In a warm, soft voice, he said, "You're brave, you're handsome, you're valiant, you're ingenious, and you know everything a princess needs to know."

She pressed the first band of linen under his fingers and started to wind. "But you don't want to marry me."

"I'm *going* to marry you."

How could the man sound as arrogant and sure of himself as he had on the first night of their meeting? How could he make it sound as if he'd said these words forever? "You will not mix your noble blood with a commoner's." She slid her hand under his armpit, around his back, over his shoulder, and the impact of his skin against her fingers jolted her as much as she feared. "You said too many times for me not to believe that."

"I talk too much."

Yes, and she liked to hear him talk. That was the trouble. She liked everything about him.

"Wrap me as tightly as you can," he instructed. "Don't worry about hurting me. Think of what a jackass I've been."

Surprise brought her gaze to his, and his expression brought blood rushing to her cheeks. If there hadn't been ten thousand eyes watching them, assassins to sentence and heroes to commend, and a Revealing to perform, they would have been in bed. "I like that," she said. "A jackass."

"You're my prophecy come true. Remember? *The prince shall embrace his greatest fear and make it his own.* You're my greatest fear. Evangeline, if I had to, I would give up the kingdom to keep you."

She barely exhaled the word. "Oh."

"But I don't have to."

Troubled, she finished wrapping him and tied the linen in a knot. "So where's the princess?"

"After we had . . . finished last night, I sent one of

my most trusted men out to make discreet inquiries. Obviously"—he touched her chin—"*I* have been chasing after the wrong princess. Evangeline, I'm going to marry you today."

"Why?"

He leaned close to her ear. His breath touched as he whispered, "I love you, Evangeline Scoffield of East Little Teignmouth, Cornwall. I will always love you."

Thirty-three

"*I hate to interrupt this touching spectacle, High-nesses.*"

At the sound of Victor's gruff voice, Danior gripped Evangeline as if he would throw her down and buffer her with his body again.

"This is very poignant." Victor knelt beside the table and peered beneath. "But the throng's getting restless, the archbishop can't be persuaded to come back out of the cathedral, and I'm bleeding all over the stage."

Pascale joined him. "Aye, Your Highnesses, begging your permission, but it's safe to come out now and the rumor that you're dying is swiftly spreading."

Danior relaxed. His clutch on Evangeline loosened as he took in Victor's battered countenance. Offering his hand, he asked, "Where have you been, my brother?"

Victor kissed it reverently, but his tone was anything but. "Chasing your other brother all over Plaisance trying to keep him from killing Her Highness. A thankless endeavor, may I say, what with having to wipe meat turnover off my face."

"If you'd told me you were trying to help—" Evangeline said indignantly as Danior gave her a push toward the sunshine.

"Would you have believed me?" Victor helped her to her feet, bringing a full-bodied cheer from the crowd.

She straightened her gown. "No."

Victor knelt beside Danior. "You've got yourself a smart one, Your Highness."

"That I do." Danior scooted forward to face Victor. "Damn, man, you're not supposed to lead with your face."

Victor hadn't been jesting about the blood. One eye was swollen shut, his nose was broken, his ear looked as if it had been half-ripped off. "Hard to fight Rafaello," he mumbled. "He knows my style."

"Why didn't *you* betray me?"

"If I decided to kill my own damned brother, I'll have a better reason than money." Victor's mouth curled in disdain. "You don't kill a king because you want a new robin's egg blue lining to your cloak."

Evangeline blushed as she remembered her early admiration of Rafaello. She had liked him better than Danior. She had thought he should be the prince because he was more handsome, refined, and benevolent. Her gaze sought him out among the prisoners. He wasn't handsome anymore, with his tooth broken and his lips swollen like two eels. His elegance had been destroyed along with his costume. And his benevolence hid a rotten core.

Big, bold, stubborn, too sure of himself, blunt to a fault, right too often for comfort—Danior was more than a prince. He was a man of integrity. The man she adored.

The man who loved her.

"Did you capture Dominic?" Danior asked.

Pascale shook his head. "No sign of him."

"Free, he'll try to incite a riot, and that brother of mine has a persuasive way about him."

"See if he's been spotted." Victor ruthlessly took charge, and Pascale rushed off to obey.

"Help me up, Victor, my collarbone's broken."

Evangeline started for Danior, but he shook his head. "A broken bone is a small charge for a kingdom—and a queen."

She watched as Victor wrapped his arms around Danior's waist. Danior rose slowly, grimacing. The throng saw the blood on him and quieted. Then, when he stood, they screamed their approval. Victor stepped away. Stepping closer, she saw that Danior's complexion was pasty.

"If you fall down in a faint," she warned, "it will ruin the whole effect."

"Standing after being shot is always the hard part." He waved his arm at his people. "And I'm leaning against the table."

"This is nothing," Victor spoke over the chants of the ecstatic crowd. "You should have seen the time we were hiding in the trees to ambush Nappie's troops. I told Danior he was too big, and sure enough, that French sergeant spotted His Highness and shot him. Danior hit the ground bleeding like a pig—"

"Dear heavens." Evangeline's stomach turned, and she swayed.

Victor surveyed her pale face thoughtfully. "Your

princess has got an awful weak stomach—but then she is Serephinian."

"Mind your manners," Danior warned one more time.

Taking her hand, Victor kissed it, and in a voice that traveled no further than their little group, said, "Still, you're royal to your fingertips and I'll serve you as my queen, Miss Evangeline Scoffield of East Little Teignmouth, Cornwall."

He knew. Victor knew the truth, but Evangeline never doubted him. He'd never betray her secret to anyone.

To Danior, he said, "I'll have the assassins sent to the dungeons."

"Get the names of the heroes." Danior's color had returned, and he gestured toward the cathedral. "I'll honor them at the wedding feast tonight."

As if nothing untoward had happened, the ceremony started again. The throng quieted, the fanfare played, and reassured about his safety, the archbishop started out from the cathedral. Perhaps the crystal case trembled in his hands, but he approached with dignity and grandeur and placed the blessed heirloom on the table.

Evangeline stared at it. She'd heard about it. She'd seen a sketch of it in one of Leona's books. But she never dreamed she would be able to see the scepters and crowns so clearly through the quartz-like stone. She could see no seam, no way to open the case; it appeared that nature, not saint, had placed the jewels inside.

Yet as the archbishop intoned a sermon about this exalted endeavor, Danior slipped his hand into the pouch at his belt and drew out—"A pry bar?" she whispered. "You're going to open the crystal case with that puny pry bar?"

"It should work," he said. "It better work."

Eyeing the glazing on the crystal case, she had to agree. She wasn't the princess, so even if Santa Leopolda had put it under a spell, the magic would fail. This lowly pry bar was their only hope.

The archbishop ended his homily.

Danior solemnly took Evangeline's hand and led her to the table. In a clear voice, he spoke the words written so long ago for this very occasion. "Separate have been our countries, separate have been our lives, yet today with the opening of the crystal case we, Danior of the House of Leon and Evangeline of the House of Chartrier, shall fulfill the prophecy."

A slight murmur rippled through the crowd as they heard the princess's new name.

Danior nudged her. "Your turn."

Leona had drilled her on this ritual, but for one terrifying moment, Evangeline's mind went blank.

The archbishop looked at her anxiously.

Danior murmured, "We shall unite . . ."

And the words came. In a clear, strong voice she didn't recognize as her own, she proclaimed, "We shall unite Baminia and Serephina for all eternity. We shall join in marriage until the ends of our lives, and peace and prosperity shall reign forever."

Danior touched her cheek briefly. "You're good at this. But I knew you would be. Stand here." He placed her in front of the case with her back to the gathering, took his place beside her, and with one hand stuck the pry bar in what looked like a tiny chip on the side.

"That doesn't look like a latch to me," she said apprehensively. "It looks like what happened when the Leons dropped the case out of the towers."

Danior ignored her. "Raise your hand high so everyone can see it," he instructed, wiggling the pry bar. "Now place it on the crystal case, right over here. Now I'll do the same"—his warm hand covered her cold fingers as they rested close to the side—"and the case will pop open."

Nothing happened.

Uneasiness rippled through the onlookers.

"Maybe I'm doing it wrong."

With slowly rising terror, Evangeline said, "Maybe it's really magic."

He twisted the pry bar the other way.

The people stirred and murmured.

Danior pulled the pry bar away as the archbishop craned his neck to see what they were doing. With a queasy smile, the exalted priest suggested, "Your Highnesses, perhaps if you placed your hands on a different spot."

"Absolutely." Danior nodded at him. "Thank you for your guidance, Father. Santa Leopolda no doubt meant for us to put our hands in the center."

"She's not the real princess," a voice yelled.

Dominic. Evangeline recognized his voice and swung around, searching the throng. There he was, close to the stage, off to the left, grinning at her with obnoxious delight.

No one laid hands on him.

If the crystal case had opened, they would have shut him up, but the miracle hadn't happened. He spoke to their fears.

"Why didn't it open?"

"Maybe he's right."

Evangeline heard the muttering, saw heads shaking. "Danior, if this doesn't work . . ."

Danior's mouth set in grim lines. "It'll work."

Evangeline remembered the underfed peasants she'd seen wandering the streets of Plaisance. "But Dominic's inciting them. They'll rip us to shreds."

"I'll get it open."

With gestures, Victor directed his men toward Dominic, but the crowd moved restlessly, blocking them. The Blanca villagers jostled their grumbling neighbors. Honest Gaylord had disappeared, and Fair Abbé had taken his place. The nuns split into two groups. One moved toward the stairs. The other moved toward Dominic as the muttering became louder.

Once again, Evangeline raised her hand, and the muttering died, leaving a silence of awesome proportions. Turning back to the case, she placed her hand on it. Danior placed his hand flat on hers. He inserted the narrow pry bar and turned it—and the metal rod twisted in two.

Voices took up Dominic's chant. "Impostors!" "Seize them!"

Danior dropped the parts and laid his hand on his sword hilt. As coolly as if they did not face a horrible death, he said, "My men have instructions to clear a path to the cathedral. Follow Pascale and I'll hold off the mob."

Tasting her fear, she shook her head. This wasn't supposed to happen. Danior was wounded. He had said he was sure he could open the case, so why had he made plans to save her?

"She's not the real princess," Dominic shouted again, vile laughter in his voice. "She's even got a different name. She's a fraud. This is all a fraud."

Evangeline smelled their sense of betrayal as the crowd answered his rallying call. "He's right." "We're doomed." "They're not royal." "Kill them!"

"Go." Danior pushed her toward the cathedral.

"Wait!" a woman's voice rang out above the rest.

Evangeline turned toward the steps.

"Wait." Marie Theresia could be heard across the square as she assisted the old nun onto the stage. The tumult died in little bits as she announced, "We've forgotten the last and most important of Santa Leopolda's instructions. I will convey God's blessing on this holy moment."

"What a pile," Dominic shouted contemptuously.

But the young postulant commanded attention, and people listened. Leaving the old nun, Marie Theresia approached the table, where the crystal case remained stubbornly closed.

"God's blessing," the archbishop said in tones of surprise. "But I should do that."

"You hold the case." Totally at ease, Marie Theresia handed it to him and pushed him toward the edge of the stage.

"Please." She gestured to Evangeline.

Evangeline, startled and dumbfounded, stepped to the front. The people were watching, faces turned up in mingled suspicion and expectation. They could see everything now, and why not? Evangeline and Danior had nothing to hide, only a desperate hope that God would take pity on them.

The archbishop held out the crystal case. Evangeline placed her hand on it.

"Danior." Danior, Marie Theresia called him. Not Your Highness, but Danior.

He watched Marie Theresia with a curl of a smile about his mouth. He stepped behind Evangeline so that he stood at her back, then for the third time, he laid his hand on top of hers. Taking her place at their right, the little postulant lowered her head in prayer. Then, pulling up her sleeve in a workmanlike manner, she laid her hand on top of theirs.

Fire shot through Evangeline's hand.

With an incandescent flash, the crystal case sprang open.

Evangeline jumped back into Danior's arms. He cradled her as, joyous at their release, the jewels flashed in the sunlight.

When the archbishop would have dropped the case, Marie Theresia reached out and steadied him. "It's all right," she said to the shaking cleric. "Everything's all right now. Take it to the table."

A detonation of gladness shattered the moment of silent awe. The people who in desperation had almost turned against their prince and princess now embraced them. Hats flew into the air, flowers pelted the stage, children clung to their fathers' shoulders as their daddies danced.

In the midst of the celebration, Dominic screamed, "No, that's not right. She's not the princess!"

And Danior clasped the little postulant in his arms. "Ethelinda."

"Marie Theresia," she corrected him, and turning, she extended her hand to the old nun. "Here's someone for you, Evangeline."

As the ancient nun hobbled toward her and fixed her in her gaze, Evangeline again had a flash of remembrance. *An old woman with flame-blue eyes looking down at eleven-year-old Evangeline. Taking her chin and lifting it. Turning it from side to side in austere analysis. Saying to one of the hags in charge, "I'll take her."*

"Leona!" Tears of joy welled in Evangeline's eyes as she embraced her mentor. "I thought you were dead. What happened to you? How did you get here?"

"Not Leona," Marie Theresia said. "Santa Leopolda."

The revelry in the square continued unabated, but Evangeline no longer heard. She'd stepped into a place where reality and fantasy, truth and magic melded. "I don't understand."

Leona took her hand. "Of course you do. You have a superior intelligence, for which I was most grateful."

"You're trying to tell me you're over one thousand years old?"

"That is the legend," Danior said.

Evangeline turned on him. "You don't believe in legends."

"I didn't believe in the magic, either." He grasped the edges of his cape and rocked on his heels. "Now I don't believe in pry bars."

Leona—Evangeline had to call her Leona—reached out to Marie Theresia. Holding real princess and counterfeit princess each by the hand, she explained, "As soon as Ethelinda reached the convent school at Viella, it was obvious the child was destined for God. What could I do? I had little time, the prophecy had to be filled, and I had to find another princess. You, Evangeline, were the only one of the House of Chartrier who was the right age, but you were gone, disappeared in the turmoil of the revolution. I had to go to England, find you and train you in far too short a time, then lure you to adventure and send word to the prince that his princess was at Château Fortuné, then make it appear only you could be the princess." The old woman sighed. "I've been busy."

As Evangeline remembered the trials of the last four days, indignation grew in her. "But why all this subterfuge? Why not just tell me?"

"I taught you to be an analytical thinker, Evangeline, so you know the answer to that, too. I don't make up the prophecies, I just speak them. When Ethelinda was born, I thought she was the one I had foretold. She was not, but I didn't know for sure if you were the princess God required. You had to prove yourself worthy. As for Danior of Baminia"—Leona smiled, and all the wrinkles in her face deepened—"he may have been born to the position, but he, too, was tested, and until last night I thought it unlikely he would show the strength of character needed to be king."

Surprising Evangeline, Danior knelt before the old nun, and reluctantly Evangeline faced the truth. This was the saint. The very saint chosen by God to speak the prophecies, place the jewels in the crystal case, and watch over the Two Kingdoms until they could become one.

"May I have your blessing?" Danior asked.

"Evangeline." Leona sounded just like Evangeline's old instructor. "Kneel with your betrothed."

Still confused, amazed, thunderstruck, Evangeline did as she was told.

Leona—Santa Leopolda—laid her hands on their foreheads. "God's blessing on you both. May you rule together in health and wisdom to the end of your lives."

Danior slipped his arm around Evangeline's waist.

She caught a glimpse of his intention right before he kissed her in front of Santa Leopolda, Marie Theresia, the archbishop, the crowd and, she had no doubt, God Himself. It was no polite pressing of the lips, but a full-body declaration of passion and love, the kind that made Evangeline want to slip out of her clothes and into a warm bed . . . with him.

When at last he had removed the starch from her bones and any lingering sense from her mind, he let her go, and she sank back on her heels.

The sounds of the square came blasting back, startling her with the crowd's extravagant approval.

Santa Leopolda grinned a wicked, old lady grin at Evangeline. "Your adventure has just begun."

And before Marie Theresia turned away to help Santa Leopolda off the stage, she whispered, "I give you my name."

Everything was all right, Evangeline realized. They'd found the real princess, the assassins had been caught, Evangeline had found a home, Danior had found . . .

"I love you," he whispered in her ear, and she hugged him and reveled in his ardor.

"Highnesses, I hate to keep breaking this up," Victor said, "but if we don't get this spectacle going again, you won't be married before dark, and you know how irate Cook gets when she has to set back dinner for a thousand."

Laughing, the prince and his princess stood and waved to their people.

"What's happening there?" Evangeline indicated a scuffle in the midst of the largest group of nuns.

"Dominic's trying to get away," Victor said laconically.

THE RUNAWAY PRINCESS   359

Danior and Evangeline looked at him.

He shrugged. "*They* say he came in their care, that he's crazy, and they'll take him to the convent and lock him away again. *I* say I'm not fighting with a bunch of nuns over another bastard brother we don't know what to do with. Now, you want to get your crowns, scepters and seals so we can have a wedding?"

"If he keeps showing such good sense, you're— *we're* going to have to make Victor our prime minister," Evangeline told Danior.

Victor snorted. "Old soldiers don't prime ministers make."

"We'll see." Danior bowed Evangeline toward the table where the crystal case waited, open and displaying two crowns, two scepters and, Evangeline was sure, two seal rings beneath the velvet.

One crown's wide gold oval would fit Danior. One's smaller oval would fit Evangeline. Both were decorated with polished rubies, emeralds, and diamonds set in the medieval style.

But the scepters—Evangeline reached for the biggest and met Danior's hand there. She wrapped her fingers around the gold near the top. His big fingers grasped the gold near the bottom.

They both tugged.

"It's mine," Danior said. "The largest crown is mine, and this matches."

"It's mine," Evangeline argued. "The largest crown is yours, so the largest scepter is mine."

"Don't make me wrestle you for it."

"You won't beat me easily. I hide a few tricks up my sleeve."

He considered that, the memory of their quest in

his gaze, and he decided on a wiser course. "Evangeline." His voice took on a kindly, exasperated tone. "We can't fight in front of our people today. It would be undignified."

He was right, damn him, but . . .

"*Sereminia*," she said.

He understood immediately. She didn't have to explain the fine art of negotiation. He was the prince; he knew what she was doing. "But Bamphina sounds better, and what we decide today will resound through the ages."

"Scepter?" She pointed to it. "Sereminia."

She watched him struggle with himself. The small scepter had a ring of diamonds, or maybe the same crystal as the crystal case. But the bigger scepter had a jewel she thought must be an opal, for it glowed with flames of red and a blue the same color as Danior's eyes. He deserved to carry it, and truth to tell, she didn't care. But she would force him to compromise now, or suffer his arrogance all her life.

"Evangeline . . ." he groaned. Then rapidly, before he could change his mind, he said, "Sereminia."

She let go of the bigger scepter and watched him take it and cradle it in his arm. He handed her the other scepter and pulled back the velvet. The two seal rings rested there where Santa Leopolda had put them one thousand years before. Lifting the smallest, he slipped it on her finger. The larger fit him perfectly.

"What a disappointment," he said. "Now we have nothing to fight about."

"Don't worry," she assured him. "We'll find something."